Praise for

Furbidden Fatality

"If you like cats, dogs, and entertaining mysteries, you're going to love *Furbidden Fatality*."
   —Donna Andrews, *New York Times* bestselling author of *The Falcon Always Wings Twice* and *The Gift of the Magpie*

"*Furbidden Fatality* has everything a cozy mystery reader is looking for—a clever heroine, a puzzling mystery, and a collection of adorable animals. Deborah Blake writes with passion and charm. She's a new mystery writer to watch."
   —Dorothy St. James, author of *The Broken Spine*

"Clever, engaging, and filled with loveable (and furry) sidekicks, *Furbidden Fatality* is an A+ debut in what is sure to be a must-read series by Deborah Blake."
   —National bestselling author Laura Bradford

"*Furbidden Fatality* has all the cute cat and dog cameos you'd want in a fun pet cozy. Animal sanctuary owner Kari Stuart teams up with a knowing kitty and several pet-loving friends to collar the culprit in this fast read."
   —Jennifer J. Chow,
   author of *Mimi Lee Reads Between the Lines*

Furbidden Fatality

A Catskills Pet Rescue Mystery

DEBORAH BLAKE

BERKLEY PRIME CRIME
New York

BERKLEY PRIME CRIME
Published by Berkley
An imprint of Penguin Random House LLC
penguinrandomhouse.com

Copyright © 2021 by Deborah Blake

ISBN: 9780593201503

First Edition: February 2021

Printed in the United States of America
1   3   5   7   9   10   8   6   4   2

Cover art by Anne Wertheim
Cover design by Vikki Chu
Book design by Gaelyn Galbreath

To Donna, who helped and cheered me on, and Elaine, who believed I could do it. Crazy women, both of them. And a special dedication to Super Heroes in Ripped Jeans, the local rescue that inspired the (entirely fictional) one in this book. It was started out of a small apartment by a woman who had a vision of saving all the animals who fell through the cracks. Terra Sky, you are truly a superhero. Thank you for my cats Harry Dresden and Diana, and for all the animals you have helped. A portion of the profits from every book in this series will be going to the rescue. I hope that the people who love the animals in this book will support their own local shelters, either with money or by volunteering.

One

Kari glanced down at the pet carrier sitting on the passenger seat next to her, then up at the sign on the simple but rustic building in front of them. "It doesn't seem so bad," she said. "I'm sure you'll like it here." The shelter was a short drive from her apartment, right on the outskirts of town. The occupant of the carrier had pouted the entire way there, past the stately buildings on Main Street, the lake dotted with canoes and small rowboats, and the tiny park from which the boats were launched.

She glanced down at the frayed denim shorts and simple blue tank top she was wearing, and decided there probably wasn't a dress code for going to the shelter. A good thing, since she tended toward the casual and comfortable, and rarely put on makeup unless she was going out or to work. As usual, her long, dark, curly hair was simply pulled back into a scrunchie, more to get it out of her way than from any sense of fashion.

Round green eyes stared back up at her out of a furry

black face that looked remarkably unconvinced. It let out a plaintive meow.

"I'm sure you'll get adopted right away," Kari said, well aware that having a conversation with a small stray cat was probably one of the first signs of insanity. She glanced around to be certain there were no witnesses and then added in a pleading tone, "Look, I already have two cats and a dog. I can't keep you. But you're gorgeous. Someone is going to be thrilled to have you."

The kitten, which looked to be about three months old, meowed again, this time more assertively. Kari had seen it wandering around outside her apartment for the last week and had finally been able to catch it so she could take it to the shelter. She'd asked all around the neighborhood and no one knew who it belonged to.

There was a two-year college in the next town over, and the students there sometimes rented places in picturesque Lakeview, with its beautiful lake and rolling hills and the changeable seasons of the Catskills in upstate New York. It was June, so most of the students had headed home after the semester ended. Maybe one of them had abandoned the kitten once it outgrew its tiny and cute stage. Although really, it was still pretty cute.

Kari sighed and forced herself to get out of the car, go around to the other side, and pick up the carrier. The kitten yawned at her, showing a bright pink tongue, then meowed again, loudly.

"Not a chance," Kari muttered as she walked across the rectangular asphalt parking lot. "I do *not* need another pet. Not right now. Life is too crazy already." She walked through the door into a neat if sterile anteroom that smelled faintly of bleach. The sound of barking could be heard from out back, and there were pictures of dogs, puppies, cats, kittens, and even a rabbit up on the walls. A stocky middle-aged woman wearing a powder blue *Lakeview Shelter* tee shirt, a frazzled expression, and a nametag that said *Loretta* stood behind the front desk.

"Hi," Kari said, "I caught this stray cat in my neighborhood and I—"

"Sorry, but no," the woman said. "We can't take it."

Kari felt her jaw drop. "What? It seems perfectly healthy. A little thin, maybe, but I think it has been on its own for a while. It's not feral, though." She held up the cage so Loretta could see the kitten. "See, it's perfectly friendly."

The kitten glared out through the front bars, as if to prove Kari wrong.

"Doesn't matter if it can sing and dance and fetch the morning paper," Loretta said in a beleaguered tone. "We're completely full. Heck, we passed full about twenty cats ago. It's kitten season, honey. There's no room here, or at any of the shelters within driving distance that I know about." She shook her head, fiddling with one earring shaped like a pawprint.

"We got people coming in with mama cats and half a dozen kittens, or dropping kittens off in boxes by the door when we're not open. We got kittens coming out our ears." She heaved a sigh, the frazzled look sliding into one of sheer exhaustion.

Kari opened her mouth to argue that one more couldn't matter, but the woman beat her to it.

"We're mostly all volunteers here, other than a few part-timers and the director, who already works more hours than God made in a day. I'm sorry, honey, but you're just going to have to find someplace else to take that cat." The woman gave Kari a sympathetic smile. "Can't you keep it yourself, or maybe get one of your friends to take it?"

"I already have two large orange cats and a medium-sized mutt dog in a tiny apartment," Kari said, trying not to sound too desperate. "I'll probably be moving soon, and things are chaotic enough without adding another animal. My friends already have as many cats as they can handle too. Didn't there use to be another shelter around here?"

Loretta rolled her eyes. "You mean that rescue place? It wasn't a shelter, honey. Leastwise, not an official one like this. Sweet young woman thought it would be a good idea to save all the animals there wasn't any room for anywhere else, started up a place she called Serenity Sanctuary. Turned out not to be so serene, from what I heard.

"Poor thing tried for a while, but she ran out of money, energy, and volunteers. That nasty county dog warden, Bill Myers, has been trying to get it shut down for all kinds of code violations, even though she begged for more time for grant money to come in. Some of the animals are staying with the people she had doing fostering, some got sent here and to other shelters." Loretta shook her head. From somewhere in the back, a dog howled plaintively.

"Luckily that was around Christmas, when we tend to adopt out a few more animals than usual, so we had the space. Not during kitten season, thank God. The place has been sitting mostly empty since then, with just the few animals they couldn't find a place for hanging on for now. But I hear they're going to get sent to one of the big shelters in the city. Lord knows what will happen to them then."

"But," Kari started to say. "I can give a donation. A big one."

The other woman shook her head. "I'm sorry, honey, but I can't help you. We just don't have any room."

"Can't you think of anything?" Kari asked. "I can't just put this poor baby back where I found it." The kitten meowed in agreement, and Kari had a sudden flashback to her father grabbing the stray kitten she'd found as a child and tossing it into the neighbors' yard, saying, *Someone else will take care of it. I'm sure as heck not going to.*

"Not unless you know someone with more money than sense who you could talk into fixing that sanctuary place," Loretta said, giving her a sympathetic look.

The phone rang as Kari turned to go, and she could hear Loretta saying, "No, ma'am, we don't have room for a litter of kittens. Yes, ma'am, eight *is* a lot for one mama cat to have."

Kari thought about it all the way out to the car, and as she placed the carrier carefully on the front seat and walked around to slide in behind the wheel. She stuck her fingers between the bars and scratched the kitten under its chin.

"You know," she said to the purring cat. "I *do* know someone with more money than sense. This could be a problem."

The kitten purred some more. Kari had the sneaking suspicion she'd just lost an argument to a tiny ball of fur. And an even worse suspicion that it wasn't going to be the last time that happened.

You did *what*?" her best friend asked. A pair of scissors dangled from her fingers as she ignored the partially clipped Yorkie on the raised table in front of her. Suzanne's hair was short and spiky, and at the moment she and the dog looked strangely similar. Although the dog's fur wasn't lavender, thankfully. Kari reached one hand up to touch her own long dark curls, feeling somewhat drab in comparison. This was not a new sensation, with a friend like Suz. Luckily, they had been friends for so long, they tended to balance each other out.

"I bought that run-down animal sanctuary up on Goose Hollow Road," Kari repeated. "Oh, and it looks like I've been adopted by a cat." She held up the carrier. "Can you tell if it is a boy or a girl?" She glanced around the small room to ensure it was safe to let the kitten out. The orderly row of cages in various sizes lined up against the far wall was empty except for one bored-looking standard poodle sporting a snazzy pink bow in its topknot. Suz's grooming shop was located just off the main street on the quaintly named Farmer's Lane, conveniently located between a pet supply store and a narrow dog park maintained by the town.

Suz opened the carrier door and picked up the kitten. "A girl," she said, peering at its fuzzy backside. "I'd say she's about three months old. Is this the one you said you'd seen hanging around your apartment?"

She gazed down at Kari from her almost six-foot height, half a foot taller than her friend. As usual when Suz was working, she wore a brightly colored smock, blue jeans, and sneakers. Today's sneakers were lime green with lights that flashed when she walked. "And what do you mean, you bought the animal sanctuary? Are you kidding?"

"Nope," Kari said. "I might be crazy—the jury is still out on that. But I'm not kidding. I took the kitten to the town shelter, and the woman there said that they were full. That everyone was full, and the only thing that could help would be if someone with too much money and not enough sense bought the rescue and reopened it. So I went to the real estate office that is handling it, made an offer, and bam. Done deal."

She stuck her chin in the air and crossed her arms. She knew it sounded completely impulsive and off the wall, which was totally out of character for her, but she'd known it was the right thing to do the second the thought had occurred to her.

Suz shook her head. "You bought an animal sanctuary so you wouldn't have to keep this kitten? I think the jury can come back in."

The kitten in question wiggled out of her hands and jumped onto Kari's shoulder. Once there, she settled into place and started to purr. Loudly.

"I'm pretty positive I'm keeping the kitten," Kari said, as if that weren't already obvious. "I bought the animal sanctuary so there would be someplace for all the other stray cats to go. And dogs. It's crazy, I know. But it just felt . . . meant to be."

Suz sank onto a stool and looked thoughtful. "A good kind of crazy, maybe. You know, the more I think about it, the more I like the idea. I mean, you won five million dollars in the lottery when you stopped to buy cat litter at the convenience store. It's kind of fitting." Suz was very big on things like karma and destiny.

She petted the Yorkie absently. "Even though you got your payout a month ago, you're still living in that crappy apartment, working at the same crappy waitress job. Maybe this is just what you needed to jolt you out of your rut."

"I was trying to figure out what I wanted to do," Kari explained, not for the first time. "I didn't want to go off half-cocked." Normally, she thought things through rationally. Made lists. Weighed pros and cons. She'd made enough bad decisions in her life that she leaned toward being overly cautious about making any major choices now. Until today, apparently.

Suz chuckled. "Well, I think that ship has sailed. But at least you'll finally move out of that horrid apartment. Lakeview doesn't have a bad side of town, but I swear, that building you live in is trying to change that. The place is a dump and your landlord reminds me of Norman Bates. Now you can move into the house out at the sanctuary and have as many pets as you want."

Kari perked up. "Oh, right. I forgot there was a house out there. I've driven past it a couple of times, but that was a while ago."

"Please tell me you didn't buy the place without even going out to look at it. That's completely not like you," Suz said. She tugged on her short hair until it stood up even more. "Never mind. Don't tell me." They'd been friends since school, so Suz knew Kari better than just about anyone. They'd always stuck together through good and bad.

"Okay," Kari said. "I won't tell you." She turned her head to look at the kitten, who was playing with Kari's silver hoop earring. "This is all your fault." The kitten meowed, looking smug.

"What are you going to call her?" Suz asked. "She is clearly going to be the boss of you. What about Queen Nefertiti?"

The kitten meowed again, jumped from Kari's shoulder to the table, and sneered at the dog before settling down for a nap.

"I think she likes it," Kari said. "Queenie it is. When you get done for the day, how about going out to the sanctuary with me to check it out?"

Suz grinned at her and picked up her scissors. "I

thought you'd never ask. We own an animal sanctuary. How cool is that?"

They took Kari's ancient Toyota, with its seats patched with duct tape, and she reminded herself that now that she could afford it, she should really look into getting a newer car. Despite Suz's teasing, Kari had meant what she'd said about trying to figure out exactly what she wanted to do before she went wild with the lottery win. This was a once-in-a-lifetime opportunity. She'd wanted to make certain she handled it wisely.

She wasn't sure buying a defunct animal sanctuary on a whim qualified. But she was committed now, and hopefully she wouldn't regret it. At least she'd be doing something good that had a purpose, and that had to beat serving eggs over easy at the local diner. At twenty-nine, that kind of job was getting old. She was tired of just surviving—it was time to figure out who she wanted to be when she grew up and then be that woman.

She'd put herself through college with no help from her estranged family and graduated with a dual major in psychology and women's studies, only to discover that those degrees pretty much qualified you to say *Would you like fries with that?* Then she'd compounded the error by getting married right out of school to a guy who had seemed charming at first but then spent the three years of their marriage being critical and controlling.

Thank goodness she'd had the good sense to finally leave him. She shuddered to think of what his reaction to her lottery win would have been. No doubt he would have been convinced he was entitled to half and would have tried to bully her into giving it to him. Coming back to

Lakeview had been the best decision she ever made. Not only did she love the town she'd grown up in, but she had her best friend by her side again. And now, apparently, she had a mission.

A meow from the carrier in the back seat brought her out of her funk. "Don't worry, Queenie," Kari said. "This place is going to be great." At least the road up to the sanctuary had a beautiful view. Although it was a steep climb filled with twists and turns, it was lined with green trees and flowering meadows, with only the occasional house to break up the foliage.

They passed a field full of black-and-white cows, and another with huge bales of hay like round wheels dotting the landscape. One section of the road must have been home to some kind of (hopefully friendly) neighborhood competition, since all the mailboxes were ornate and colorful. One featured an outsized John Deere tractor, while the next had a giant chicken instead of the post one would normally expect.

"Watch out!" Suz said, grabbing the dashboard as a rusting white pickup truck came racing up the middle of the narrow country road, nearly causing them to veer into a weed-filled ditch. "Idiot!"

Kari swerved, avoiding the truck at the last minute by a combination of skilled driving and dumb luck. She could see the dust from the truck in her rearview mirror as she loosened her death grip on the steering wheel. As far as she could tell, the driver never even looked back. Queenie let out a loud complaint. "I agree, Queenie. That guy was driving like a maniac."

They pulled into a gravel parking lot at the top of the hill, past a faded sign that read *Serenity Sanctuary*. The building itself was a peeling, pale yellow, single-story structure that rambled off in several directions as if it had been added on to over time or by someone without any kind of plan. Or both. A slightly ramshackle fenced-in area could be seen behind the building, and a driveway veered off to the left and led to a cute but equally run-down farmhouse. Pine, oak, and gnarled old apple trees dotted the property and a few large brown-and-tan chickens with luxurious feathers on their feet wandered around an overgrown garden near the house. Wildflowers ran rampant in the adjacent meadow.

"Well," Suz said faintly. "I'm sure it will look a lot better after a coat of paint."

Kari chewed on her lower lip, trying to ignore the sinking feeling in her stomach. "It might take two coats," she said. "And a new roof."

Suz perked up. "On the bright side, you can afford to do both." She got out of the car, her usual positive attitude instantly back in place.

Kari followed her a little more slowly, still trying to wrap her brain around the fact that she owned this place. Not to mention that she really could afford to fix it up. After years of being not quite poor, having large sums of money at her disposal was taking some getting used to. After a moment's hesitation, she grabbed the cat carrier and brought it along. It was too warm to leave the kitten in the car, even though they were parked in the shade.

They walked through the front door into a room that bore little resemblance to the cheerfully professional atmosphere at the town shelter. It was smaller, for one thing, and had been painted an unfortunate gray that had probably been depressing even when it was fresh out of the can. Fluorescent lights flickered and hummed overhead. Empty cages lined one wall, and a row of leashes hung limply from hooks by the entrance. It was painstakingly clean, but all the furnishings looked old and beat-up, probably donated or bought used on the cheap.

Bizarrely enough, Kari felt right at home. She'd lived in apartments like this her entire adult life, at least since she'd gotten divorced.

"Uh-oh," Suz said under her breath. "This doesn't look like a happy group."

Across the room next to a large wooden table that had clearly been repurposed as a desk, a too-skinny woman wearing ripped jeans and a worn Greenpeace tee shirt that revealed a wolf tattoo on one arm and a panther on the other was being comforted by an older woman with a bold turquoise streak in her cropped gray hair. A dark-skinned girl in her early twenties stood nearby, a frustrated look on her narrow face.

"I'm sorry," the older woman said. "We're not open." She peered across the room. "Suzanne Holden, is that you?"

Suz grinned. When you were a six-foot-tall Amazon with lavender hair, you tended to stand out in a crowd. "Hi, Mrs. Hanover, what are you doing here?"

Ah, that was why the woman looked familiar. Sara Hanover had taught ninth-grade English for over forty years. Virtually every person who had grown up in Lakeview had passed through her classroom at one point or another. Including Kari. Mrs. Hanover was known for being tough but fair, and for speaking her mind to students, parents, and anyone else who crossed her path. Including the principal and the school superintendent, and once, a visiting vice president.

"We're all adults now, Suzanne," the older woman said. "You can call me Sara. Is that Kari Stuart with you?

Goodness, it has been a long time. As for what I'm doing here, I've been volunteering at the sanctuary for a couple of years, since I finally gave up teaching. Couldn't stand sitting around doing nothing. Bryn here"—she gestured at the tall girl next to her—"and I are the last ones remaining. And this is Daisy, who started the place."

"Sorry," Daisy said, swiping at her eyes and then straightening up. She had long blond hair in a single braid down her back, and would have been pretty if it hadn't been for the lines of stress and exhaustion on her face. "I just had another run-in with that stupid dog warden, Bill Myers."

She waved an official-looking piece of paper in the air. "He served me with a summons for one of the few dogs we've still got here, Buster. Says the dog bit someone after he got out through a hole in the fence last week, but I swear, Buster is the sweetest, most harmless animal on the planet. He's a pit bull, and I know the breed can get a bad rap, but there's no way he bit anyone."

Daisy crumpled the paper up in her hand, looking as though she might burst into tears.

"I think we almost ran into him on our way in," Kari said. "Literally, if he has a rusting white truck and acts like he owns the whole road."

"That's him," Daisy said in a bitter tone. "He's been trying to drive me out of here for ages, and after he gave me the summons, he had the nerve to offer me a pittance for the place." She shook her head, thin shoulders slumping in defeat. "His timing couldn't be worse either. Some crazy lady was actually going to buy the sanctuary and take it over, but once she finds out about the court case, she'll probably back out of the deal."

Sara waved her hand at the carrier Kari was holding. "So as you can see, we aren't taking in any more animals right now. In fact, we're desperately trying to find places for the ones we've still got."

Kari smiled at the despondent trio. "That's okay. I'm keeping the cat, even though this is really all her fault. And I'm the crazy lady who made an offer on the place, and I still intend to go through with it, as long as you are willing."

"Crazy in a good way," Suz added, green eyes twinkling. "I think."

"Huh," Kari muttered under her breath. "At least I'm not the one with three dogs, five cats, a corn snake, and a bunch of mice I didn't have the heart to feed to the snake."

"Bought an animal sanctuary sight unseen," Suz muttered back. "Still crazier than me."

"*You* put in the offer?" Sara said, one gray brow arching up in surprise. Then she tapped her chin with the tip of her finger, a gesture Kari remembered from all those years ago. "That's right, I think I read something in the paper about you winning the lottery. It was the same day that councilman was caught with his mistress and a goat, if I recall, so I didn't pay much attention to your news. Congratulations."

Kari had been incredibly grateful to the disgraced politician for his timing. Almost everyone missed the announcement of her win, which was tucked on a middle page of the local paper instead of the front where it might have landed otherwise. So far she'd only had a few people ask her for money or suddenly become much friendlier than they had been before. The last thing she wanted was to become a local celebrity, so she'd been keeping as low a profile as possible.

"I did," Kari said. "And I've been trying to figure out what to do with it. Like you, I didn't see much appeal in just retiring and sitting around. When the woman at the shelter mentioned this place to me when I took Queenie in this morning, I decided that fixing up the sanctuary was the answer to that question." At her feet, Queenie gave a decisive meow of agreement.

"You are certainly the answer to my prayers if you're serious," Daisy said, a hopeful expression on her face for the first time since they'd come in. "And if you aren't going to let Bill Myers's phony charges chase you off."

Kari looked around the room. It was shabby, but she could see the potential. And the sanctuary was clearly needed. "I'm serious," she said. "I'd like to have you show me around, and to meet the animals that are still in residence, but I'll sign the remaining papers with you tomorrow if you want."

"That would be amazing," Daisy said, standing up straighter as though someone had lifted a fifty-pound weight off her. "I couldn't bear to just walk away and abandon the animals, but I can't do it anymore. We've just been struggling along praying for a miracle."

"So you wouldn't mind if I move into the house after we sign the contract?" Kari glanced down at Queenie's carrier. "I already have one more animal than my current lease allows, and apparently I've just added to that number. I don't mind giving you a couple of weeks to find another place to live, though."

"That's really considerate, but I don't need it," the blonde said with a crooked smile. "I've already shipped most of my stuff to my sister's in Virginia. She's expecting her second child and already has a toddler. I promised to move there and help out as soon as I could get the sanctuary dealt with. I've basically been living out of boxes and a couple of suitcases. I've got a friend with a garage apartment I can stay in until I leave, even with all my animals." She laughed. "I seem to end up adopting all the hopeless cases. Nice to see you've got a head start on that."

"Oh," said Kari, the funny feeling coming back to her stomach. "You're leaving town? I kind of hoped you'd stick around for a while and show me the ropes. I don't have the slightest idea what I'm doing." Not that she couldn't figure it out. She'd figured out how to deal with everything else life had thrown at her so far—she could figure this out too.

"Don't worry," Daisy said. "I'll stay at least until after the court date next week. I don't want to leave with Buster's fate still hanging in the balance, and I was in charge when he got loose. They're going to want me to testify."

"Besides, you'll have us," Sara said with a smile. "I love being here, even though it has been a struggle. Having an influx of cash will really help, although I have to warn you, when the place is full, we can spend over twenty thousand dollars a year on food alone, so you are probably going to want to apply for grants and such too, or you'll run through your winnings faster than you'd think."

"I don't know," Bryn said. She'd been so quiet, Kari had almost forgotten the other girl was there. "I'm studying to be a vet tech at the college, and the sanctuary is a great place to get experience. Not that I'm practicing without a license or anything," she was quick to add.

"But it might be tougher than you think to come in here cold. Running a rescue isn't all cute kittens and roly-poly puppies, you know. It's a lot of hard work and dealing with difficult people, and sometimes we lose one of the animals no matter how hard we try." She stared at

Kari with narrowed eyes. "It isn't going to be easy. Or fun, most of the time. You get to clean up a lot of poop. A *lot* of poop. I'm guessing that most lottery winners don't pick up poop. Don't you have people for that?"

Sara raised one eyebrow. "Way to sell it, Bryn," she said. "You are aware that without Kari, we are closing the doors and we can't help anyone?"

"I'm just being honest," Bryn said. "We're better off closing now with just these few animals depending on us to find them homes in the face of impossible odds than we would be if she comes in full of enthusiasm, fills the place up again, and then leaves in a few months when the going gets tough."

A scowl clouded Sara's brow and she opened her mouth to speak, but Kari held up a hand to stop the older woman.

"I understand," Kari said. "What's more, you're not wrong. At least not about that particular scenario. But it's not going to happen. Tough going is nothing new for me, I promise you. I wasn't born a lottery winner, and I've survived worse than a little poop. Even a lot of poop. I don't expect you to trust me. You don't know me. But I would like to ask you to give me a chance. This is important to me, and I really want to make it work. From what I can tell, that will be a lot more likely to happen with you than without you."

Sara patted Bryn on the arm. "I'll vouch for her," the retired teacher said. "She always turned in her homework completed and on time, and if she said she was going to take on a task, she followed through. I trust her, and we need her."

Bryn looked from one to the other, and then at Daisy. "Okay," Bryn said finally. "I'm in. At least for now." She folded her arms across her chest, looking less than enthusiastic. Pretty in a kind of understated way with her dark hair tucked under a bandana, she was slim and a little taller than average, although her worn jeans and cropped college sweatshirt didn't do anything to emphasize it. Of course, she'd probably been scooping the poop she mentioned, which meant her attire was perfectly suitable.

"Fabulous," Kari said, meaning it. "It would really help me if you were both willing to stay. I'd be happy to pay you."

Sara shook her head. "I don't need the money, dear, but I could contact a few of the folks who used to work here and see if they'd be willing to come back."

"I wouldn't mind a small salary," Bryn admitted reluctantly. "College is expensive. My aunt is helping me out and letting me live with her, but I hate being a burden. I work a part-time job, but I do spend a lot of time here, especially during the summer when school is out."

"That's great," Kari said with a sigh of relief. "It sounds like we've got a plan."

"I'll help too," Suz said. "You know how I love a challenge." She glanced around. "Which this is definitely going to be."

"Let me go check that the dogs are all locked up," Daisy said. "Then I'll be happy to give you the tour." She went out through a door at the back of the room, followed by Bryn.

Once Sara was alone with Kari and Suz, her face took on a stern expression that reminded Kari of her student days. "Bryn isn't wrong, you know. Are you sure you've thought this through, Kari?" Sara asked quietly. "It really would be wonderful, both for Daisy and for the sanctuary itself, but I'm not sure you have any idea what you're getting into. It can be incredibly overwhelming, even without the challenges posed by having the dog warden set on closing you down."

Kari nodded firmly. "I'm sure." For the first time in her life, she really was. This was where she was meant to be. She could make a real difference here. "What does Bill Myers have against this place anyway? You'd think he'd appreciate having another organization that took in animals in need."

"You would, wouldn't you?" Sara said, her lips pressed together. "I don't know what his problem is, but I suspect he was somehow responsible for Daisy never getting the grants she applied for, and he's been hounding her for months—no pun intended."

Suz snorted.

The older woman shook her head. "I'm just giving you fair warning. Watch out for that man. He is dead set against the sanctuary for some reason, and I'm going to bet he won't be happy when he finds out that Daisy has found someone to buy it."

Kari didn't much care if he was happy about it or not. Especially after the guy almost ran them off the road. She'd found the purpose she'd been looking for in her life, and nothing was going to stop her from making it succeed.

Two

Four days later, Kari looked down at the paperwork in front of her and wondered why she hadn't bought a nice villa in Tuscany like any sane lottery winner. From her vantage point at the back of the room, she could hear the cheerful banter as a few volunteers and the couple of part-time workers she'd been able to lure back painted the walls a soothing light blue color. Even though the paint was low odor and nontoxic, and they had fans going in all the windows, the slight aroma of chemicals competed with the smell of bleach and a hint of wet dog.

Install air conditioners and look into better ventilation, she wrote down on her list. It was a really long list, and getting longer by the minute. After day two, she'd decided she'd better divide it into three columns: Need, Want, and Do Yesterday. Sadly, the Do Yesterday column was by far the longest. Reluctantly, she moved *Better ventilation* to the Need section. Replacing the worn floor, whose cracked linoleum threatened to trip the unwary and, worse yet, was impossible to ever get completely clean, was way more important. She had someone coming to start on that tomorrow, as soon as the painting was finished.

A small black paw reached over and nudged the pen, causing it to go skittering across the desk and onto the floor.

"That's not helpful," Kari said, smiling despite herself. Queenie looked typically unimpressed. She'd insisted—loudly—on going with Kari when she went in to the shelter, either perching on Kari's shoulder and surveying their domain or sprawling on the table, usually on top of a piece of paper Kari needed.

Bigger desk, *Organizers with drawers*, and *Cat bed* all got added to the Do Yesterday column. As did, after a few moments' thought, *Buy more pens*. The little black kitten not only tossed them on the floor on a regular basis, she seemed to enjoy hiding them in obscure places.

"We're all done," Bryn said, coming to stand in front of the table. She spun around and looked at the room with a broad smile. "The place is looking better already. I can't wait until we get the new flooring in. And then we get the new cages, and better lighting. It's so cool." Once she'd figured out that Kari was serious about the place, Bryn had accepted her with slightly better grace, although the younger woman had made it clear she still had her doubts.

Kari was pretty excited too. She'd been able to order fancier stacking cat kennels with separate spaces for litter and hiding, and attractive wood-look fronts. They were more comfortable for the cats and still easy to clean. They even came with wheels, so they could be moved around if necessary. Of course, she hadn't gotten around to buying new furniture for the house, but at least the cats would be happy. And right now the sanctuary's needs seemed more urgent than her own.

She'd figured that since this room was essentially the heart of the sanctuary, and the space the public would see first, it was the main priority to tackle. Well, that and the outside, but she had professional painters coming to do that next week—it was too big a job for the volunteers. The roof turned out to be reasonably sound, thank goodness, but the fenced area . . . that was on the top of her list, circled in red, and starred.

Speaking of which. "How is Buster doing this morning?" she asked Bryn. Bryn had a soft spot for the pit bull who'd supposedly bitten someone and tried to make sure she was the one who walked him a couple of times a day. Daisy had patched the hole in the fence he'd gotten out through, after he broke the entirely inadequate lock on the door that led from the back of his kennel to the yard where the dogs had been allowed out for exercise and fresh air. Each dog kennel let out onto a narrow run, and from there through another gate to the larger yard they all shared. Apparently Buster had simply muscled his way through the door, and the gate, and then out through a hole in the fence in the yard at some point one night. They hadn't realized he was missing until Bryn had gone to feed him in the morning.

By then he'd already been caught by the dog warden, who had shown up first thing to announce that he'd gotten a complaint that Buster had attacked a man walking a Pekingese, handed them a series of tickets, and told them to expect a summons to court.

For now, they weren't allowing any of the dogs out unsupervised. Luckily, there were only eight still in residence, so Daisy, Sara, and Bryn had taken turns walking them outside, and they'd been able to move Buster to a different kennel with an intact lock. But now that she had taken over, Kari knew that before they could consider taking in more dogs, they would need stronger locks, better runs, and an entirely new fence. She'd already ordered all the supplies, but she was waiting for a contractor to have time to do the work. Hopefully she'd soon be able to cross that one off her list too.

With pleasure, she drew a line through the item that said *Repaint front room*. One thing down, only ten thousand to go . . .

"Buster is great," Bryn said, but she didn't sound happy. They were all worried about the results of the upcoming court case. Town court was held on Thursday night, and today was Tuesday. Each day Kari could see Daisy and Bryn get more and more tense. Sara was a little harder to read, but she'd actually snapped at one of the workers earlier for dripping paint on the floor, so Kari suspected she was anxious too.

"Let's go see him," Kari said, getting up from her chair. There was only so much time you could spend staring at paperwork without going insane, and she was making an effort to get to know the animals at the shelter better. Daisy was leaving soon and there would be times when no other volunteers were available. Kari needed to be able to handle things herself.

She felt pretty confident with the dozen cats in the feline room, most of whom hadn't been accepted into other shelters because of illness or other disabilities. Tripod, a three-legged yellow male, was something of a mascot around the place, wandering around freely when there wasn't painting going on. Fortunately, he and Queenie seemed content to ignore each other's presence in that special way that cats had. As usual, Queenie jumped up on Kari's shoulder to supervise the visit. She was completely unimpressed by the dogs, although fortunately most of the ones currently at the shelter got along with cats just fine.

As usual, their entrance into the canine area was greeted with a cacophony of barking, woofing, and the occasional howl, made worse by the way the sound echoed off the whitewashed cement walls. Kari had looked into soundproofing and baffles for the area, and apparently such things were available. But those were in the Need column, and it would be a while before they could get to them. In the meanwhile, she still found the noise level overwhelming, although the longtime volunteers didn't seem to notice it at all.

Buster's cage was toward the end of the row, past two other pit bull mixes and a black-and-brown Rottweiler. Kari had learned that "pit bulls" (who weren't really one kind of animal, but were actually made up of a number of dogs from the so-called "bully breeds") and certain other breeds made up a large percentage of the dogs that ended up in shelters, more because of people's perceptions of them than because of the dogs themselves. Daisy had started an education program to change that, something Kari intended to continue once they reopened the sanctuary to the public. Sara had volunteered to be in charge, and Kari had handed it over to her without hesitation. If anyone could change people's minds and attitudes, it was the retired teacher. She was a bit of a pit bull herself, in a politely stubborn, turquoise-streaked way.

Buster greeted them with a gentle woof. Kari found it hard to believe that the dog had bitten anyone. He was such a big sweetie, he actually allowed Queenie to ride around on his back. (Although Kari had just about had a heart attack the first time the little black cat made the leap from her shoulder to his.)

"Hey, buddy," Kari said, kneeling down in front of the wire mesh door. "How's the big boy?"

He gave her the typical pittie grin, panting at them happily. She fed him a treat through the door and he licked her fingers. Gray and white, with a black nose and soft brown eyes, he was a solid dog with a huge head and ears that flopped over, lending him an almost comical air despite his size.

"I can't believe they're trying to say he is a vicious dog," Bryn said in a fierce tone. "Just look at him." Buster raised one white paw and waved it at her, rubbing up against the bars of the cage so she could scratch under his jaw.

"It will be interesting to see who this supposed bite victim turns out to be," Daisy said, coming up behind them. Kari hadn't even heard her enter over the sound of barking. Of course, they probably wouldn't have heard a battalion of Scotsmen with bagpipes, all things considered.

"Are you saying you think Myers made it up?" Kari asked, surprised. She hadn't even considered the possibility. He was the dog warden, after all. He was supposed to enforce the law, keeping both people and dogs safe. "Why would he do that?"

Daisy made a noise that sounded remarkably like a growl. "He's really aggressive about pursuing dangerous-dog complaints. Way more so than the previous dog warden. A bunch of people have had their dogs taken away from them, and most of those dogs end up being euthanized. Humanely, so they say, but it's hard to believe that there are so many animals that can't be rehabbed safely." She blinked rapidly. "I hate to think that having Buster put to death will be the last act that happens during my time at the sanctuary. It would break my heart."

Kari gave Buster another treat, gazing into those trusting brown eyes. It would break her heart too. She'd just have to make sure it didn't happen. Somehow.

Thursday night came all too soon. Kari, Suz, Daisy, Sara, and Bryn all trooped in to sit near the front of the courtroom. Daisy would be the one representing Buster and the sanctuary; the rest of them were just there for moral support. Plus Kari needed to see how things worked, since the next time she'd be the one in charge. Although she really hoped there wouldn't be a next time.

It felt weird being in the small, slightly shabby room in the old town hall, which doubled as the courthouse. It was located near the end of Main Street, past the row of small shops and next to the town square that hosted a farmer's market every weekend during the summer, along with the occasional craft fair.

The town hall building was two stories in the standard brick style that could be seen all around Lakeview, while the courtroom itself, at the back of the first floor, had wood-paneled walls and no windows, which made it seem gloomy and a little depressing.

In contrast, the last time Kari had been in a courtroom, she had been facing her angry soon-to-be ex in a brightly lit modern space with high ceilings and large windows that looked out onto a manicured lawn. On the whole, she rather preferred this.

There were about thirty people scattered throughout the room, seated on the rows of uncomfortable wooden chairs. Most of them looked to be there to deal with their own legal issues, but Kari spotted a few who seemed to have come for the entertainment factor. Across the aisle, a couple of middle-aged women chatted over their knitting, and toward the back a group of elderly men in overalls sat together as if they'd been there every week for the last thirty years. For all she knew, they had.

Eventually the judge worked her way through the speeding tickets, impaired-driving tickets, and a noise ordinance violation, and it was their turn. Kari thought the judge looked forbidding and stern, sitting up on her bench in her black robes, snowy white hair tucked into a neat bun, with wire-rimmed glasses perched on the edge of a pert nose. Judge Simmons had been brisk and matter-of-fact as she'd worked her way quickly and methodically through each case. But Kari felt a glimmer of hope when she saw the judge flinch ever so slightly as the court clerk read out Bill Myers's name.

"Back again, Mr. Myers?" the judge said. She flipped through the paperwork in front of her. "Another dangerous dog, I see. Your complaint says this one supposedly bit someone?"

The dog warden stepped forward and Kari saw her inherited nemesis for the first time. He was in his midfifties, she thought, with the rigid posture and buzz cut of a former military man. She bet he was one of those guys who liked to brag that they could still fit into their uniforms. He might have been attractive if it weren't for the deep grooves of dissatisfaction worn into his forehead and next to his mouth. He was of average height and weight but clearly possessed more than average belligerence to make up for it. Cold gray eyes stared back at the judge.

"It did, Your Honor," Myers said. "The dog is the responsibility of the former Serenity Sanctuary. Their negligence allowed him to escape from both his kennel and then the outside fence on the night noted in the complaint. Early the next morning, the dog, a male pit bull known as Buster, attacked an innocent bystander while he was walking his own dog. As you can see from the pictures I provided, the bite was quite serious and required numerous stitches. I'm told that the victim is considering a civil suit for damages, as well as pain and suffering."

Next to Kari, Daisy winced. But she stood up and said in a clear voice, "Your Honor, may I have permission to speak?"

The judge nodded, motioning Daisy forward. The court clerk said, "Please state your name for the record," and Daisy said, "Daisy Parker, former owner of Serenity Sanctuary."

The judge's faded blue eyes opened wider at "former owner," but she merely said, "Do you have something to add to Mr. Myers's statement? I'm also going to need proof of a rabies vaccination, as you know."

Daisy walked over and handed some papers to the court clerk, a nondescript woman in her mid-to-late fifties with graying blond hair, who was seated at a desk to the side of the courtroom. "I brought copies of his rabies certificate and medical history, all up to date." Kari could tell Daisy had been through the court process before. Something else to look forward to, now that it would all be Kari's responsibility.

"I was in charge at the time of the alleged incident,"

Daisy said. "I've had Buster in my care for over eighteen months, and he has never exhibited any aggressive tendencies, either with my staff, with visitors, or with other animals. Bully breeds have a bad reputation, which is why they're so hard to find homes for, but I assure you, Buster doesn't have a mean bone in his body. He did manage to get out on the date in question, but I don't believe for a minute that he actually bit anyone."

"I'm telling you he did," Myers said, thrusting out his square chin. "There are pictures."

Judge Simmons peered through her bifocals at the folder on the desk in front of her. "I see pictures of a bite wound. There is nothing to indicate that this particular dog was responsible. Where is your attack victim? He should be here to speak for himself. I also don't see any medical records showing dates or where this bite wound was treated, just the photos of the injury. This could be from last year for all I know. Did you witness this attack yourself?"

"No, I did not." The dog warden's face turned beet red. "Are you implying I am lying to you, Your Honor? I'm telling you, that dog is a menace. In fact that whole supposed sanctuary is a menace. They shouldn't be allowed to have any animals, let alone potentially dangerous dogs. The place is falling down around their ears, which is how this particular animal managed to escape in the first place. You should issue a cease-and-desist order today."

There was a loud murmur from the people in the room and the judge banged her gavel for silence.

"I am not accusing you of lying, Mr. Myers," the judge said in a calm tone. "I am merely stating that I cannot rule on this case without actually speaking to the person who was supposedly bitten. A fact of which you are perfectly well aware. As for the state of the sanctuary—"

Kari stood up, doing her best not to appear as nervous as she felt. She had dressed up for the occasion, putting on a black skirt and tailored white blouse she usually saved for job interviews. She'd pulled her hair back into a neat braid and even put on a little eyeliner, some blush, and a subdued rose-colored lipstick. This was her baby now, and she might as well make that clear, so she wanted to make the best possible first impression. "Excuse me, Your Honor."

Judge Simmons looked at Kari, seeming more curious than upset at being interrupted. "Yes, and you are?"

Kari cleared her throat. "Kari Stuart, Your Honor. I am the new owner of the sanctuary. I just bought it from Daisy, and I'm already in the process of making significant improvements and upgrades, including new locks on the kennels and brand-new fencing. There shouldn't be any more problems with escapes, and we plan to reopen as soon as the renovations are done."

There was another, louder murmur at this statement, especially from the older contingent in the back, but the judge let it die down on its own. "Did you, now? Well, that's certainly good news for the county. I know all the local shelters are already operating at maximum capacity. I happen to be on the board of the one in the next town, which is out of my jurisdiction."

Kari cheered inwardly. An animal lover! Hopefully that meant the judge would at least give them a chance.

"You did *what*?" Myers said, sputtering. He sent a venomous glare in Daisy's direction, which she fielded without blinking.

"I bought the sanctuary," Kari repeated. Loudly, as if he were hard of hearing. A few of the nearby spectators tittered. She turned back to the judge. "I admit, I hadn't met Buster at the time of his escape, but I have spent time with him since and he's a really nice dog. He lets my kitten sit on his back. I find it hard to believe that he would attack a person without provocation."

The judge held up her hand as Bill Myers started to sputter. "Clearly the dog is well behaved on his own territory. That doesn't, unfortunately, mean that he is incapable of aggression when he is on unfamiliar turf." She tapped a pen on the paperwork and then made a few notes. "I'm going to need copies of any work orders and materials purchased, as proof that you are actually making these improvements."

"Yes, Your Honor," Kari said. She tried not to fidget, and put her hands together to keep them still.

"Ms. Stuart, can you guarantee that the dog can be safely contained, with no possibility for another escape?" the judge asked.

Kari nodded, hoping she wasn't promising something she couldn't deliver. "Yes, Your Honor. We're keeping all the dogs inside right now and only allowing them out on leashes with supervision. And the new fencing should be installed within a week. I'm just waiting for a contractor to find time in his schedule."

Judge Simmons snorted. "Good luck with that. I'm still waiting for mine to finish patching my roof. All right, that sounds sufficient for the moment. Keep in mind that you will be held responsible for the actions of any animal under your care, and I take such things very seriously."

Kari swallowed hard. "Yes, ma'am. Your Honor." Daisy gave her a grateful look.

"Are you dismissing my case?" Myers asked, his lower jaw thrust out belligerently. He reminded Kari a little of a dog they had at the sanctuary. Myers had less of an overbite, but his eyes bulged out in much the same way.

"No, Mr. Myers," the judge said. "I am not. I am granting the sanctuary a stay on having to surrender the animal, based on a lack of evidence. We will reconvene next week, and if you can produce your bite victim and he can prove the incident happened as you've said, then we'll see."

She turned toward Daisy and Kari. "Keep in mind that you are forbidden to adopt this dog out, even if you can find someone who wants him, pending the outcome of this case. He might still have to be euthanized, if Mr. Myers can prove that he is a danger to others." She banged her gavel on the desk. "I will see everyone back here next week. That's our last case for tonight. Court is dismissed."

Kari and the others made their way out of the building. She didn't know whether to be relieved that Buster was safe for now or terrified of what could happen if the dog warden could actually produce his witness. She couldn't even imagine what Daisy was feeling, after looking after Buster for a year and a half.

"I'm sorry for interrupting," she said to Daisy as they reached the parking lot, which even at this time of night was half full of cars and trucks. "I hope I didn't mess things up."

"Not at all," Daisy said. She seemed tired but hopeful, her shoulders only at half-mast. "You did great. I think it really helped that you mentioned all the repairs and new fences. I guess all we can do now is hope that Myers can't get this so-called bite victim to show up. If the guy even exists."

"Oh, he exists," the dog warden said, stepping out of the shadows. He sneered at Daisy. "Your precious dog had better enjoy this week, because it is his last."

He swiveled around to jab a finger in Kari's direction. "As for you, lady, you have no business running an animal rescue. I know who you are. Just some waitress who got lucky and won the lottery, and let the money go to her head. You are totally unqualified to manage a place like that, even if your friend here hadn't already run it into the ground."

"Oh, shut up," Kari said, actually losing her temper for once. Crabby customers, her drunken mess of a father, even her critical ex-husband couldn't make her lose her cool, but this rotten excuse for a public servant had just gotten on her last nerve. She'd spent her life giving in to bullies and she was never going to let it happen again.

"You should be ashamed of yourself. You're supposed to be looking out for the public *and* the welfare of the animals. As far as I can tell, you don't care about either one. You're just a power-hungry bully. But believe me, I have dealt with your type before, and you can't intimidate me."

"You have no idea what you're talking about, missy," Myers growled. "And no idea what you're doing. You're an amateur in dangerously over your head and you won't last six months at that place. Or six weeks, if I have anything to say about it. You'd be better off giving up now and selling me the property so I can put it to a better use. At least that way you wouldn't end up with nothing."

"Over my dead body," Kari spat back, crossing her arms over her chest. "You are never getting your hands on the sanctuary. Or any of our dogs."

"We'll see about that," Myers said, and stalked off into the night.

Kari took a deep breath, feeling her whole body shaking from the confrontation. In front of her, Daisy's eyes were wide.

"Sorry," Kari said. "I shouldn't have let him get under

my skin. I'm not usually that easily provoked. But I *hate* bullies."

Daisy just jerked her head, and Kari turned around to see that they had an audience. Over a dozen people had apparently witnessed the entire argument, including the judge, now dressed in street clothes and obviously on her way out of the building to go home. Kari felt her face flame.

"Sorry," she muttered. Hopefully by next week the judge would have forgotten the whole thing. And it wouldn't be the talk of the town by breakfast tomorrow. Sure, that could happen.

Three

A loud high-pitched yowl right next to her ear woke Kari out of a deep sleep three nights later. A second later, a small black paw batted her on the nose.

"What?" Kari said, turning on the light to check the time on her phone. "Oh, come *on*," she said to Queenie. "It's one o'clock in the morning. I don't want to play now. Go back to sleep."

The kitten yowled again and Kari felt her heart skip a beat. "What's the matter? Are you sick? Does your tummy hurt?" She peered at the kitten, who looked just fine. But Queenie had never done this before. Maybe one of the other cats had upset her? Kari listened, but the house was quiet. From the distance, she could hear the sound of barking coming from the kennels. *Huh?*

Suddenly, her phone buzzed. She had it on mute for the night, and probably would have slept through it if she hadn't already been awake. Cocking her head at Queenie, she picked up the phone. "Hello?" she said cautiously. If this was some kind of robocall at this time of the night, she was going to be really peeved.

"What the heck is going on over there?" a male voice bellowed in her ear.

Darn, not a robocall. She got out of bed and opened the window wider, turning down the fan she'd had running to quiet its whirring. Even though her second-floor bedroom was high in the eaves on the opposite side of the house from the shelter, she could hear the racket the dogs were making, now that the fan was off and she was awake.

"Mr. Lee, is that you?" The Lees were her closest neighbors, and Daisy told her that they'd complained before about the dogs barking. Apparently the Lees' house was fairly close to the back of the shelter where the dog kennels were. But those complaints had usually been during the day when a number of the dogs were outside. In theory, all the animals should be safely locked up for the night.

Crap. What if Buster had gotten out again? Or one of the other dogs. Or all of them? It certainly sounded like something had gotten them riled up.

"Yes, it is me. Daisy gave me your number," the irate voice said. "Make those dogs shut up or I am calling the police." He hung up.

"Great," Kari said to the cat. "Now we'll be back in court for breaking the noise ordinance." She quickly pulled on some jeans and the tee shirt she'd taken off just a couple of hours ago, and ran down the stairs to the front door. At the last minute, she grabbed a pair of thick gloves from the table and stuck them in her back pocket in case she had to deal with an angry dog, and she took the high-powered flashlight from her "in case of emergency" box inside the closet. She wasn't certain if this counted as an emergency or not, but at least she'd be able to see where she was going.

Not that she really needed it to get from the house to the main shelter building. Kari was still settling in and getting acquainted with her new living arrangements, but there was an easy path between the two buildings, and a bright light on the outside of the sanctuary that went on automatically at dusk. She tried to leave Queenie safely shut inside, but the kitten darted out between her legs as she was closing the door and went racing down the path with Kari following more cautiously behind. As usual, it was clear which one of them was in charge.

As they approached the shelter, the pitch of the dogs' barking took on an even more hysterical tone. Kari debated calling Daisy, or even Suz, who was something of a dog whisperer, but with the Lees poised to call the cops, she didn't dare wait for someone to come hold her hand. Besides, the place was her responsibility now. She was just going to have to suck it up and go inside.

She unlocked the front door and looked around, but nothing seemed out of place. The barking reached a fever pitch when she opened the door to the dog room, but when she counted, everyone seemed to be present and accounted for. As far as she could tell, the dogs were more excited than upset, although something had obviously set them off. Only Buster, at the far end, was clearly agitated, throwing his massive body against the door to the outside in a way that made Kari worry that he would break open that lock if she couldn't figure out what was going on. And soon.

She went back out into the main room, Queenie still prancing around at her feet.

"I don't suppose you want to show me what the problem is?" Kari said, more out of desperation than any expectation that a tiny kitten would know the answer. Queenie meowed at the door they'd come in.

"Fine," Kari muttered. "We'll check around outside. But if there is a bear out there, I'd like to remind you that I tried to get you to stay at the house."

She didn't *think* there had been any bear sightings this summer, although the creatures did occasionally come down from the hills and show up in people's backyards, or root around in their garbage cans.

They crept carefully around the side of the building, with Kari moving the beam of her flashlight from side to side. Nothing moved in the dark night, and there was no sound except the barking of the agitated dogs. The wide arc of the flashlight showed her the fence to the dog yard, a square plot of mostly bare ground adorned with a few abandoned half-chewed bones, and as she followed along the fence, everything seemed normal. Until she spotted something that gleamed dully as the light bounced off it. She peered closer. Was that a shovel? What was a shovel doing next to the fence? Had one of the workmen left it? She couldn't think of any reason a painter would have had a shovel, and the fence guys hadn't started yet.

She shifted the light a little bit farther and had to bite back a scream. Lying next to the shovel, one arm outstretched as though trying to reach for it, was the prone body of Bill Myers. He was very clearly dead, his own snare pole around his neck, eyes bulging and furious, even in death.

Kari scooped up Queenie, more for comfort than to keep her away from the body, and called 911. Something told her that the dogs weren't going to be quieting down any time soon.

Kari heard the patrol car arrive almost ten minutes later, its tires crunching on the gravel parking lot. She could vaguely make out the glimmer of a flashing red light from where she stood. She wasn't that far from town, but she suspected the dispatcher she'd talked to didn't really believe her when she'd said, only slightly hysterically, that she'd found a dead body. At least they hadn't used the sirens—that *really* would have set the Lees off.

She could hear male voices muttering something about a waste of time and shouted, "Back here."

Two police officers in uniform rounded the corner of the building, their own, even more powerful flashlights aiming in her direction and making her squint. One of them was older, probably nearing retirement age, with short gray hair, an aggressive mustache, and a sizable paunch. The other one was so young she might have mistaken him for a college kid if he hadn't been in uniform, and had the kind of physique only gained by hours spent obsessively working out in the gym.

The older officer looked bored and disgruntled, as if he was expecting to find out this was some kind of late-night prank. The younger one was twitchy and nervous, looking back over his shoulder and jumping every time a new chorus of barking broke out.

He was the one who spotted Kari first. She was standing as far away from Myers's corpse as possible while still being able to keep him in sight. Truth be told, she would have liked to go back to her house, but she didn't know if there was some kind of rule about leaving the scene of a murder like there was about leaving the scene of an accident. As it was, she was impressed that her knees only shook slightly.

"Hey," the young cop said, his voice a little high. "Are those dogs?"

Kari blinked. "Um, yes. Of course they're dogs." What did he think? That she'd left the television on really loud? "This is an animal sanctuary. In fact, the dogs barking was what woke me up. Well, the neighbors next door calling to complain about it, anyway." She thought she'd sound saner if she left the cat out of it. Things were bad enough as it was.

"Oh," the young cop said. "They can't get out, can they?"

She hoped not. "No," she said, as confidently as she could. "They're all locked up."

"Pull your panties up, Overton," the older cop said. "Yeesh. I can't believe you're afraid of a few dogs." He flashed a badge at Kari. "I'm Deputy Carter. This is my partner, Deputy Overton. Are you the one who called to report a dead body?" Doubt oozed from every pore. "Ya sure you're not just jumping at shadows? It can get pretty spooky up here for a woman by herself." He glanced around as if to check for anyone else. "You're the new owner, right? Bought the place from Daisy Parker? They were talking about you down at the diner this morning."

Of course they were. Small towns. News traveled fast.

"Yes, Deputy, I'm Kari Stuart. I live in the house on the property now." She pointed back in the direction of her small farmhouse. She'd finally quit her waitress job after she'd bought the shelter, so mercifully she didn't have to listen to them gossip about her in person.

"And I'm pretty certain I know the difference between

a shadow and an actual dead body." She tried not to shudder. "He's over there, by the fence. It looks like he was trying to dig a hole under it and someone came up and surprised him."

Carter sighed. "Lady, why don't you let us figure out what happened. All you people, watching too many cop shows. If it was up to me, they'd outlaw the darned things."

He walked forward, followed by his partner. Kari reluctantly trailed after them, still clutching Queenie, who for the moment miraculously seemed content to stay where she was.

Carter stopped abruptly, almost causing Overton to bump into him. "Damn!" the older man said. "You weren't kiddin'." He leaned over and aimed the flashlight at the body. "Crap. That's Bill Myers. I can't believe it. Somebody killed Bill Myers."

He swung around and turned suspicious eyes on Kari. "You want to explain to me why the dog warden's dead body is on your property?" he asked. "And how you just happened to be the one who found him?"

"I have no idea what he is doing here in the middle of the night, alive or dead," Kari said, slightly acerbically. "And I just told you—I found him because the neighbors complained about the noise from the dogs, and when I came out to investigate, thinking maybe there was a bear prowling around here that set them off, I found Mr. Myers instead."

Overton waved his flashlight around, its beam jumping shakily from side to side. "There are bears here too?"

"Oh, for the love of—" Carter reached out one meaty hand and pushed the light down. "There are no bears. But there is a dead body. You'd better call it in. Have the dispatcher notify the sheriff. He's going to want to know about this. Have them send over the coroner to certify the death." He glanced down at the dog warden. "Like we need someone to do that. But rules are rules."

As the younger deputy contacted headquarters, the older one pulled out a pad and a pen and gave Kari a hard stare.

"So, your story is that the neighbors called you because the dogs were barking, and you came out here and found the body," he said.

"That's right," Kari answered. "I checked inside the sanctuary first, to see if I could figure out what set the dogs off. But when I couldn't find anything, I came out here." She nodded at Myers's corpse. "He was already dead when I got here. So I called 911."

"You touch anything?" Carter asked suspiciously. "I notice you just happen to have a pair of gloves on you. Maybe you were digging that hole and Myers came along and found you, so you killed him."

Kari barely managed to keep from rolling her eyes. "Why would I be digging a hole under my own fence, Deputy? And even if I was, why would I kill someone over that? Plus I'd like to know what the dog warden was doing out here after midnight. Doesn't that seem odd to you?"

"I'm asking the questions here, Miz Stuart," Carter said. "Did you or did you not touch anything at the scene?"

"I did not," Kari said. "And the gloves were in case I had to handle an agitated dog."

"You sure none of those dogs got out again?" he asked. "Maybe that's why Myers was out here. Dog warden is on duty twenty-four seven, you know."

"All the dogs are in their cages. I checked."

"Huh," Carter said. Overton was taking pictures of the scene with a camera he'd fetched from the squad car.

"What the holy heck is going on here?" a deep voice said. A man in his fifties with the look of an ex-jock gone slightly to seed came around the corner of the building, followed by Doc Phelps, the local GP, who doubled as the town coroner.

"Somebody killed Bill Myers, Sheriff," Carter said. "This woman says she found the body when the neighbors complained about the dogs barking." His skepticism was clear in his tone. "You sure got here fast. Did the neighbors call you?"

"I was just down the road dealing with an altercation at the Last Stop." The sheriff walked over to the body. "Yep, that's Bill Myers, all right. You ask me, it's a miracle it took this long for someone to murder the man." He walked over to Kari as the coroner bent over the dog warden to get a closer look.

"You're the new owner of the sanctuary, Kari Stuart," the sheriff said with the certainty of a man who likes to know what is going on in his town. "People have been talking about you buying the place. I'm Sheriff Richardson. Heard you got into a fight with Myers outside the courtroom a couple of nights ago."

Kari flushed. "We might have exchanged a few heated words. I wouldn't call it a fight, exactly. It was no big deal."

"Oh, I don't know," the sheriff said thoughtfully. "He threatened to shut you down, you argued with him, and now he's dead on your property. I'd say that was a pretty big deal."

Four

Kari had never had any personal dealings with the town sheriff, having miraculously managed to stay out of trouble up until this moment, but she'd heard that he was gruff and not inclined to put up with nonsense. Hopefully he was also fair and open-minded, unlike his deputy, who seemed ready to condemn her on the spot.

"Any death is a big deal," she said, as calmly as possible. "Even the death of someone I didn't like, although I have to admit, I barely knew the man. But just because I told him off when he tried to threaten me doesn't mean I killed him. Which, just for the record, I didn't."

She didn't add that if she for some reason decided to murder someone, she wouldn't do it on her own property and then call the cops about it. Pointing that out probably wouldn't help her case.

"Hmph," Richardson said, which could have meant anything from *That makes sense* to *I still think you're as guilty as sin and you're going to rot in jail if I have anything to say about it.*

Behind him, two men who had arrived in an ambulance loaded the body onto a stretcher, and the younger cop was putting up crime scene tape in a wide swath around the edges of the fence. The coroner strode over to where she and the sheriff were standing, a large evidence bag in his hand. The doctor was a short, slightly pudgy man with thinning brown hair and eyebrows that seemed to be trying to make up for the shortage of hair elsewhere.

"What have you got?" Richardson demanded.

"Well, he's definitely dead," Doc Phelps said. The eyebrows waggled up and down.

Richardson rolled his eyes. "Yeah, I kind of figured that part out on my own. How about a cause and time of death?"

"Recent," the doctor said. "Body's still warm. Probably not more than half an hour before Ms. Stuart called us. Maybe less. As for the cause, I won't know for certain until I do an autopsy, but I'm guessing the noose around his neck had something to do with it."

"It's called a snare pole," Kari said. "It's used to capture wild animals, or those you can't be sure are safe. They use them for dogs, cats, even alligators." When the sheriff gave her a dubious look, she added, "Not around here, of course."

"So that thing probably belongs to Myers?" the doctor asked, looking interested. "Something he'd carry to catch an escaped dog, for instance?

Kari nodded. "Yes, although as I told the sheriff, all our dogs are accounted for. The rope is threaded through the pole and is looped over the animal's head. We have one at the shelter, although apparently it isn't used much. Mr. Myers would have had one as part of his job."

"Interesting," Richardson said. "So you're saying he was actually strangled with his own snare pole?"

The coroner nodded. "Well, he definitely shows signs of strangulation, and the thing was pulled tight around his throat, so barring any surprises, I'd say that was the most likely scenario."

Richardson stared pointedly at Kari. "Could a woman have done it, would you say?"

Phelps shrugged. "It looks like he was on his knees, bending down by that hole. Which, by the way, it looks like he was digging, which seems a bit strange to me, but I'm just the coroner, not a detective, so I'll leave you to figure out what the heck he was doing. So yeah, he would have been vulnerable and off balance, and if he was caught by surprise, I see no reason why a strong woman couldn't have pulled the snare tight enough to cut off his oxygen before he could get to his feet to fight back."

Kari didn't know whether to be shocked or furious over the idea that the dog warden had apparently been messing around with her fence in the middle of the night. For the moment, though, she had bigger problems.

"Sheriff, you don't seriously think I did this, do you?"

He looked her in the eyes. "What I think, Ms. Stuart, is that you had the means, the motive, and the opportunity. I'm not a man who jumps to conclusions, and I'm not about to start now. Myers had plenty of people with good cause not to like him, and his reasons for being out here certainly raise some questions. So I will be doing what any good lawman would do, and investigating. But in the meantime, I also think you shouldn't make any plans to leave town. Is that clear?"

What was clear, Kari thought, was that buying this sanctuary had just gotten a *lot* more complicated.

*   *   *

Between waiting for the cops to leave, trying to get the dogs calmed down after they were gone, and not being able to get back to sleep from all the excitement, Kari was late getting to the shelter in the morning. She was grateful she didn't have to walk far, because a dismal drizzle blanketed the landscape and the sky felt soggy and low.

Thankfully, Sara, Bryn, and two of the part-time paid employees were already there and hard at work. The cats had been fed and their litter boxes changed, and Jim and Emma were busy cleaning out the kennels. Kari had left a note at the desk telling everyone that the dogs would have to be walked in the area in front of the shelter—the police had instructed her that the entire fenced-in back area was considered a crime scene until they released it.

Sara and Bryn were in the main room, hanging some new curtains, when Kari finally got there around ten, Queenie sitting on her usual perch on Kari's shoulder.

"Sorry I'm late," she said. "It's a long story."

"Did you really find Bill Myers's body out by our yard?" Bryn asked, her brown eyes wide. She looked adorable in denim overalls and a pink tank top, and Kari suddenly felt self-conscious in the jeans and slightly ragged old concert tee she'd thrown on when she'd finally rolled out of bed.

Okay, maybe it wasn't that long a story. Small towns—at least they saved you the trouble of telling everyone when something went wrong.

"I did," Kari said.

She was glad that Bryn seemed to be getting more comfortable around her. The young woman was better with animals than she was with people, but it had helped when she discovered that Kari was friends with Izzy, Bryn's aunt and the town librarian.

"The dogs started barking in the middle of the night, and Queenie woke me up in time to get a call from Mr. Lee complaining about it. When I went out to investigate, she led me to the body." Kari placed Queenie on the floor and helped herself to a cup of coffee from the machine by the desk. Her coffeemaker was still sitting in a box on the floor of her new kitchen, so even the so-so coffee at the shelter smelled like ambrosia.

"That's one smart kitten," Bryn said in an admiring tone. She produced a treat out of one pocket and the cat in question walked over to accept it.

"Did you stick a stake through his heart to make sure he was really dead?" Sara asked dryly.

"Sara!" Bryn gasped. "You can't say something like that!"

"I think I just did," Sara said, helping herself to a donut from a box someone—probably Sara herself—had brought in for anyone who showed up to help. Powdered sugar feathered down to join the cat fur on her flowered shirt. "I'm not going to pretend to like the man just because he had the bad fortune to get killed on our property. I wouldn't have wished him dead, but I can't say I'm sorry he's going to be out of our hair now." She patted the turquoise streak in hers.

"I don't know that he will be," Kari said. "If anything, his death is just causing us new problems. We can't use the yard for now, and we also can't have the new fence put up, which isn't going to make the judge happy."

"Oh, I hadn't thought of that," Sara said. Her face fell. "Darn."

"Is it true that they found him digging a hole under our

fence?" Bryn asked. She wore her hair in many tiny braids, which she said kept it out of her way while she was working, and had a small jeweled stud in her nose. She fiddled with a braid now.

Kari shrugged. "Well, he was already dead by the time I got there, but there was a shovel right next to him and a pile of dirt to show he'd been working on it. One of the deputies, a guy named Carter, actually tried to suggest that I might have been digging there for some reason and Myers caught me at it, but obviously that's not true. All I can think is that Myers was trying to make it look like one of the dogs had dug his way out, and then he was planning to go through the gate, break into one of the kennels, and use the snare pole to take a dog out and say it escaped. Although why he'd do that, I don't know. It's nuts."

"Not when you think about how he was trying to get Daisy to sell him the property for pennies, it isn't," Sara said with all the cynicism of a woman who had spent forty years seeing kids trying to get away with just about everything. "If he was after Buster, and made it look as though we'd let the dog get out after all our promises to the judge, she might have actually shut the place down. Maybe he figured if that happened, you'd just give up and sell him the place after all."

Kari felt her jaw drop. "Was he really that underhanded?"

Sara shrugged. "I guess we'll never know, now that he's dead. But I can't think of any other reason why he'd have been out there in the middle of the night with a shovel and a snare pole."

"The deputy implied that the dog warden might have been called out because someone reported a loose dog,"

Kari said. "And I should warn you, the sheriff considers me to be the prime suspect."

"What?" Bryn covered her full lips with one hand. "Why would he think that?"

"I found the body," Kari said. "He was killed on my property in the middle of the night, I had gloves in my back pocket, and I'd been seen having a very public argument with him three nights before he died. Apparently that makes me suspect number one."

"At least I'm in good company," Daisy said from over by the front door. Now that the hinges had been oiled, it opened so quietly that none of them had heard her come in. "It looks like I'm suspect number two."

What? You're kidding," Bryn said. "But you don't even own the sanctuary anymore."

"That's true," Sara said in a thoughtful tone. She grabbed a napkin and got Daisy a donut with multicolored sprinkles. "And Bill Myers is part of the reason. Are they saying you killed him for revenge because he ruined your dreams?"

"Something like that," Daisy said, her lip curled in disgust. She walked over and poured herself a cup of coffee and joined them where they were standing around the desk. "Although if you ask me, if I *had* been going to do it, wouldn't it have made more sense for me to kill him before I lost the sanctuary, and not after?"

She sighed and rested one hip on the corner of the desk. "Now I can't leave town until they solve the crime or eliminate me as a suspect. I'm stuck here." Like the others, she was casually dressed in jeans and a well-worn shirt, perfect for cleaning cages and walking dogs. No one dressed up at the shelter, especially since it wasn't even open to the public yet.

"Do you have an alibi?" Bryn asked. "Maybe the friend you're staying with?"

"I was out in the guest room over the garage by myself," Daisy said. "So no, no alibi. Unless you count my cats and dogs, which I don't think they do."

"I have the same problem," Kari said glumly. "I tried using the phone call from Mr. Lee to prove that I was home in bed, but the sheriff said I could have been standing over the dead body talking on my cell phone and Mr. Lee never would have known the difference."

Sara shook her head. "I like Dan Richardson. He's a smart man. But he's also stubborn as all get-out and likes to look at things from every angle. When his son was in my class, parents' night always took twice as long because of all his questions." A smile tugged at her lips. "On the bright side, he does have a soft spot for dogs. He has a golden retriever named Duke—after John Wayne—who goes in to the office with him sometimes."

"Do you think that means he'll cut us a break?" Kari asked, sipping her coffee. "Because he seemed pretty sure that I was guilty. That Deputy Carter all but read me my rights."

"He'll be fair, but if Carter is in charge of the investigation, we might not be so lucky with him. He's a year away from retirement and is going to want to wrap this up as quickly and easily as possible. Carter, from what I know of him, is not a fan of complicated or difficult," Sara said. "Plus, there's still the problem of Buster."

Kari felt her heart skip a beat. "But, now that Myers is dead, won't the case against Buster be dismissed?"

"Oh, no," Sara said. "Not once it has gone before the judge. The town board will appoint a new dog warden and there's no way of telling what he or she will do. Buster is still very much at risk."

"This is crazy," Bryn said, blinking back tears. "The man is dead, and he is still messing with Kari and Daisy and Buster. And all we can do is sit around and wait for the cops to either find the real killer or blame one of you guys. And hope that the new dog warden isn't as nasty as the old one."

Kari put her coffee mug down on the desk with a thump. "No, it isn't."

"Huh?" Daisy said. Bryn looked confused.

Sara raised one gray eyebrow in question. "What exactly are you suggesting?"

"I am not going to just sit here and wait for some over-the-hill cop to decide I killed Bill Myers, or let Daisy be stuck here in town when she deserves to go start her new life. And I'm definitely not going to let poor Buster get put to sleep when it is clear that he didn't do what he was accused of either."

Kari put her hands on her hips. "I have spent my whole life being pushed around by bullies, and I'm not going to sit here and let a dead one ruin our lives. I'm not saying we can do the cops' job for them, but I'll bet we could at least dig up a few more suspects, so they'll have to look further than just the two of us."

"Huh," Daisy said. "You know, that's not the worst idea I ever heard. There are plenty of people in this town who hated Bill Myers. It shouldn't be hard to find out who he upset lately."

"Any tickets or summons he issued would be a matter of public record," Sara said thoughtfully. She pulled a small notebook out of her oversized hand-painted leather purse and started jotting down notes. "As would any court cases in which he was involved. The information might be a bit tricky to find, but one of my former students works in the town hall. I could get her to do a little digging for me."

"That's great," Bryn said, her brow furrowed. "But what about Buster?"

"We're going to have to find that dog bite victim, if there is one," Kari said firmly. "Or any witnesses that saw Buster during the time he was loose." She chewed on her lip absently. "Plus I guess we hope that the new dog warden is more reasonable."

Queenie strolled across the desk and pushed at a folder until it fell on the floor and papers went spilling out everywhere.

"That's not helpful," Kari scolded her, bending down to pick them all up and shove them back together. "Huh."

"Huh?" Daisy said. "Did you think of something?"

Kari narrowed her eyes suspiciously at the little black ball of fur. It had to be a coincidence. "This is the paperwork for the sale of the sanctuary. It just occurred to me that you said Myers had been trying to buy the property. He obviously didn't want it for an animal shelter, so why *did* he want it?"

"Another good question," Sara said. "I guess we've got our work cut out for us."

"It beats sitting around waiting for a stubborn sheriff and a lazy deputy to decide to put me in jail," Kari said. "I wouldn't look good in orange, and my animals need me."

She glanced at her watch, which featured Winnie the Pooh and had a second hand that was a bee that moved around the edges of the watch face. "But my part of the mission is going to have to wait for now. I have an even more important one to accomplish first. I have an appointment for Queenie at the V-E—" Before she could get out the third letter, the kitten had scooted under a cabinet. "T."

Bryn just laughed. "I hate to break it to you, but I think that cat can spell."

It wouldn't have surprised Kari at all.

🐱 Five

"Seriously, you're fine," Kari said to Queenie, who was expressing her displeasure loudly. "I swear, I'm not taking you to another shelter. You're stuck with me. We're just going to the vet so you can get a checkup and your shots. Stop making such a fuss."

The black kitten subsided as if she understood every word, although she still glared at Kari through the front of the carrier. Kari sighed and got out of the car, slinging her purse over one shoulder and grabbing the cat carrier with the other hand. This wasn't exactly a good time to be away from the shelter, but there was no way Kari was going to run the risk of getting called out for having an animal without the proper vaccinations or paperwork.

The veterinary office was on a county highway just outside of town and shared a parking lot with the feed store next door, which conveniently also sold pet food and supplies alongside cattle fencing and tractor parts. It overlooked fields full of hay and orderly rows of young corn plants, but the building itself was thoroughly modern and surrounded by neat landscaping and areas set aside for dogs to be walked before or after going inside.

The building was one story high and had a clean-looking exterior of white siding under a black shingled roof. There were two wings coming off the main section, with exam rooms to the right and a boarding kennel to the left. A narrow walkway led to the entrance, which opened into a wide reception room that smelled like bleach mixed with some kind of lemon cleanser, and only a hint of dog. An older couple with an equally elderly hound sat in one corner, chatting amicably with a young woman with a cat carrier at her feet. The carrier emitted the occasional unhappy-sounding yowl. On a bench across the room, a hyperactive black Labrador puppy strained at the end of its leash, clearly wanting to go make friends, while its owner, a local business owner Kari knew vaguely, scolded him halfheartedly while also slipping him treats.

Normally she would have brought Queenie in sooner, but between the craziness of acquiring the rescue and the fact that her regular vet was out of town, it had taken her a few extra days to get the appointment. As it was, she'd had to settle for seeing Dr. Burnett's new partner, who she'd never met before.

After a brief stint in the waiting room, where she had to answer the usual awkward questions about how it felt to win the lottery and was it true she had really bought the animal sanctuary, one of the techs led them into an exam room where the kitten was placed on a large metal table and weighed. Kari's heart contracted when she saw how tiny Queenie looked. She was already so in love with the bossy little cat, she couldn't bear it if the vet found something wrong with her.

The exam room, identical to the other four in the wing,

was a rectangular box with no windows and simple white-painted walls. The front of the room had a door that opened onto the waiting area, and the back had a matching door that led to the space where the vets and techs worked. Kari had been back there, so she knew there were machines to examine blood and urine samples, cupboards full of medicines and supplies, the actual surgery where they performed more complicated medical procedures, and cages for sick or recovering animals.

The side walls were covered with cupboards filled with supplies for the exam room, as well as posters on animal care, a screen for viewing X-rays, and a whiteboard. An exam table that could be lowered or raised depending on the size of the animal took up most of the space, and a computer with its keyboard sat on a counter so the vet could make notes or check previous ones during the exam.

A couple of minutes later, the rear door to the room opened and a tall man with slightly shaggy red hair and twinkling blue eyes strolled into the room. He looked at the chart in his hand and then back at Kari.

"Hello," he said. "I'm Dr. Angus McCoy. And this must be Queenie." He beamed at the cat. "Aren't you a gorgeous girl?"

Queenie purred, clearly approving of this new admirer.

"Hi, Dr. McCoy, I'm Kari Stuart." Kari held out her hand and then hesitated for a second, hearing her own words.

The vet laughed. He was tall and gangly, like a teenage boy who hadn't quite grown into his body yet, although he was probably about Kari's age or a bit older. He had an easygoing aura about him that probably helped to put his patients—and their owners—at ease, and wore a white lab coat over typical medical scrubs in a pleasant light blue color. A stethoscope was slung around his neck. "Yes, I've heard all the Dr. McCoy jokes. Don't worry, I'm used to it. So, I see here that you usually see Dr. Burnett. You have other cats?

"I do," Kari nodded. "A gigantic orange guy with extra toes named Westley and his brother Robert, who is an orange-striped boy of a more normal size. They're both five. Plus I have a mutt dog of dubious parentage named Fred." Fred looked like a cross between a German shepherd and a border collie and possibly about three other things. He had perked-up ears, a pointy nose, and an unerring ability to sniff out foods he wasn't supposed to eat and then eat them.

Dr. McCoy cocked his head. "Westley and Robert? I don't suppose Robert is short for the Dread Pirate Roberts."

Kari laughed, delighted to meet a fellow *Princess Bride* fan. "It is!"

The vet's returning grin revealed a dangerously attractive dimple. "I don't remember a Fred in *The Princess Bride*, though."

"Ah, no," Kari said. "Fred is named after Fred Rogers. You know, from *Mister Rogers' Neighborhood*."

"Because he's kind and patient?" Dr. McCoy asked.

Kari bit her lip, trying not to smile. "Actually, it was because he kept destroying my sweaters when I first got him. I figured that if he had a thing for sweaters, that was something he had in common with Mr. Rogers."

The vet chuckled. "Well, let's take a look at this little lady," he said. "The chart says she was a stray?" As he talked, he gently examined the kitten, taking her temperature (she was not amused), checking her ears, and looking at her teeth, among other things.

"She'd been hanging around my old apartment for

about a week," Kari said. "I finally managed to catch her and take her to the shelter. But they were full, and besides, well . . ."

"You decided to keep her," he guessed.

"More like she decided to keep me," Kari admitted. "But the outcome is the same. So, how does she look?"

"Pretty darn perfect," Dr. McCoy said, eliciting another purr. From the kitten, not Kari, although she would probably have done it if she could. "We'll test her for FIV and feline leukemia just to be on the safe side, but I suspect all she needs are her shots, a dose of flea medicine, and deworming, since most cats that have lived on the streets for a while pick up parasites of one kind or another. I'm assuming you'll want to make an appointment to get her spayed as well, since the last thing we need is more unwanted kittens."

"Definitely," Kari said with feeling. "I had no idea how bad the problem was until recently. The woman I talked to at the shelter really opened my eyes."

"It's a continuing battle," he agreed. "I used to volunteer my time at the Serenity Sanctuary, doing low-cost spay and neuters. I'd just moved to the area, and it seemed like a good way to start making a contribution to my new home. It's really too bad they had to close."

Kari felt a flush warm her face. "Uh, it's actually reopening, if you'd be interested in coming back. Once we're up and running again, it would be a great service to be able to offer."

Dr. McCoy raised an eyebrow. "We?" he said. "Are you involved somehow?"

"I bought the place recently," she said. "I'm having some work done on it and Daisy is showing me the ropes, but we hope to reopen in a few weeks."

"That would be great," he said. "And I'd be happy to help." He gave her that smile again and Kari felt an unaccustomed flutter in her stomach that for once wasn't nerves. Queenie meowed, voicing her own opinion on the subject.

"Great," Kari repeated. And not just because he seemed really nice and was kind of cute. "Daisy told me that when the place is full, there are always sick kittens and people bringing in injured animals they've rescued. We have a volunteer who is training to be a vet tech, but I suspect there are going to be lots of cases that are beyond her ability or skill level."

"No doubt," the vet said. "Although you'll be surprised how many things you can learn to deal with on your own." He grinned. "Daisy is quite the marvel. She gives shots, administers medicine and subcutaneous fluids, even assists with surgeries if she has to. I suppose that running the place on a shoestring, she had to do everything she could not to have the extra expense of calling in a vet. You'll probably end up being just as capable."

Kari felt another unexpected flutter, this time at the thought of mastering new skills that would make a difference in the lives of the animals that would be under her care. "I can't wait," she said, surprised to find how much she meant it.

The rear door swung open again and a vet tech Kari knew from previous visits came in, carrying a couple of syringes.

"I've prepped the shots for you, Doc," the young woman said, placing the shots on the table next to the kitten. Her dark brown hair was chopped off in a cute pixie cut that was undoubtedly also practical for dealing with animals every day, and her scrubs lent her a professional air. "Oh, hi, Kari. This is a new one, isn't it?" She bent down to scratch Queenie under the chin and was rewarded with a quiet purr.

"Thank you, Padma," Dr. McCoy said, administering the first vaccination so efficiently that Queenie barely had time to look indignant. "Meet Queenie."

"Hi, Queenie," the tech said. "Kari, is it true that you bought that run-down sanctuary place? I heard they found Bill Myers up there last night, dead as a doornail."

Kari wondered how on earth people in larger towns got their news, since they probably didn't have the magical telegraph of the small-town gossip factory. And also, why a doornail was considered dead. But that was a lesser issue. She shuddered, seeing the dog warden's corpse flash before her eyes, with its stunned expression and blue-tinged skin.

"Yes," she said, in answer to the first question. "I did buy it. I'm planning to reopen it as soon as possible. Also yes, Queenie and I found Mr. Myers out by the dog yard." She patted the cat, holding her still while the vet gave her the second shot, at least as much for her own comfort as for the kitten's.

"Is it true that he was murdered?" Padma asked in a hushed tone.

"It seems so," Kari said. "Unfortunately, Deputy Carter seems to think I'm the number one suspect, because I got into an argument with the dog warden outside court last week."

Dr. McCoy snorted, causing one lock of red hair to flip down over his eyes. "I've only been in town for about nine months, but I can already tell you that if that's their criteria for possible murder suspects, the police are going to have a very long list to work from. I've heard complaints about that man from dozens of my clients who own dogs."

Kari gnawed on her lip. "Did any of them have dogs that were accused of being dangerous? Daisy and I were at court because Myers said that one of the shelter dogs, Buster, bit someone when he got loose last month. That was before I got involved, but I've met him and he seems really sweet."

"Any dog can be dangerous under the right circumstances," Dr. McCoy said. "If they are startled or perceive themselves to be under attack, for instance. But most real problem dogs have a history of acting out. I actually met Buster when I was volunteering at the shelter, and he seemed perfectly well behaved."

"I don't suppose you'd be willing to sign a statement for the judge saying so," Kari asked hopefully.

"I'd be happy to," he said. "But I doubt it would do any good. Dr. Burnett had a client whose dog was accused of ravaging the neighboring farmer's sheep. The dog was a very valuable purebred Irish wolfhound, and the client had him outside in the yard, which had a tall, sturdy fence, but the dog kept getting loose somehow." He shook his head ruefully.

"Dr. Burnett told me she went to court and spoke on the dog's behalf, but the neighbor and Bill Myers insisted the wolfhound was an animal killer, and the judge was forced to order the dog surrendered and put to sleep. It was right when I first joined the practice, and I know Dr. Burnett said the client was absolutely furious. Dr. Burnett was relieved that Myers had his own vet to take care of things, and that she didn't have to do it."

He patted Queenie one more time and handed her to Padma. "Take her out back and draw some blood for the usual FIV and feline leukemia tests, please. Unless something shows up, we're all done here. It was very nice to meet you, Queenie. And you too, Ms. Stuart."

"Kari, please," she said as the tech walked out the back door with the kitten, who looked as though she owned the place. "After all, if you're going to be volunteering at the shelter, we're going to be working together from time to time."

"Good point," he said. "Then it's Angus. Let me know when you have the place open again, but feel free to call me if you have any problems with the animals you've still got there." He dug out a business card and wrote down what looked like a personal cell number. "Seriously, call any time. And good luck with Buster. He's a great dog."

"He is," Kari said, thinking about the story he'd told her. If the owner of the Irish wolfhound was as angry as Angus said he was, maybe he had finally snapped and taken his revenge. "I don't suppose you can tell me the name of the man whose dog got taken away."

Angus shook his head. "Confidentiality," he said. "But I can assure you he's not the only one who's lost a dog since Bill Myers took over. I don't know if the man was just overzealous, or if an unusual number of animals happened to become problems during his tenure. Either way, there are a lot of people who won't be sorry he's gone."

Padma came out a few minutes later with a disgruntled-looking Queenie tucked back in her carrier, as well as the paperwork from the visit. "Here she is," the tech said. "All the blood tests are clear, so you just need to make an appointment to get her spayed and you'll be all set." She glanced around, as if to make sure that the vet was out of earshot.

"I heard you talking about Steve Clark," Padma said in a quiet voice. "It was terrible what happened to poor

Ranger. If that dog was a sheep killer, I'm a natural blonde." She snorted. "It's not really a secret. You could have found out by asking anyone in town. Clark spent weeks spouting off about it to anyone who would listen. He was absolutely beside himself when Myers seized the dog. I heard Mr. Clark actually threatened the dog warden. Can't say I blame him either. I know you'd not supposed to speak ill of the dead, but a lot of our clients had problems with the man."

"Was he just too serious about doing his job?" Kari asked, clutching Queenie's carrier a little closer to her chest. It was all too easy to envision someone watching in horror and heartbreak as their beloved pet was driven away to certain doom. The very thought made her shudder in sympathy.

Padma shrugged, bitterness coloring her otherwise pleasant features. "Honestly, I think he was on some kind of power trip. Or maybe he was just a mean, nasty man. I'm only surprised it took this long for someone to murder him." She noticed Kari's wince. "Sorry. I forgot you found the body. That must have been horrible."

"It was," Kari said. "I'm still having nightmares. Of course, being the police's number one suspect isn't much fun either."

Padma gave her a sympathetic look and patted her on the shoulder before turning to leave. "Well, if it is any consolation, I expect you've got lots of company, Steve Clark included. If anyone wanted to kill Bill Myers, it was him." She chewed on her lip thoughtfully. "You know, he only lives over the hill from you, on County Route 12. He could have gotten to the shelter pretty easily. Not that I'm accusing him of anything. I mean, he's a college professor, right?"

* * *

Kari mulled over what Padma had said as she and Queenie drove back home down curving sun-dappled country roads bordered by fields full of cows on one side and young corn on the other. The hills were green and the sunshine seemed to turn everything to gold. Lakeview was beautiful all year round, but Kari thought June was one of the times when it really shone. The tourists clearly agreed, since she kept seeing cars with out-of-state plates and the couple of bed-and-breakfasts she passed both had *No Vacancy* signs out.

Kari wasn't sure she agreed with Padma that someone being a college professor automatically made them above reproach, although you certainly didn't hear about a lot of them turning out to be serial killers. As she neared Goose Hollow Road, she saw the turnoff to County Route 12 and made a sudden impulsive turn.

For a woman who prided herself on having finally reached a point in her life where she thought everything out in advance, she sure was taking a lot of leaps these days. "I don't know if this is a good idea," she said to Queenie. "I'm sure you'd rather go straight home and get out of that carrier."

The black kitten yawned at her, then closed her eyes.

"A lot of help you are," Kari said. As always on these rural roads, the houses were spaced fairly far apart from each other, but it wasn't long before she came to a mailbox that said *CLARK*. The long gravel driveway led up to a neat white clapboard house with a corrugated red metal roof. To the side there was a sturdy wire fence, within which could be seen a large doghouse designed to look like a miniature of the bigger home. An empty water bowl sat forlornly in front of it.

Over the curve of the hill, Kari could just make out some barbed-wire fencing and the distant white dots that signified sheep. An occasional plaintive *baaa* drifted toward her on the wind.

She turned off the car and sat there for a minute, wondering what the heck she thought she was doing. It was the middle of the day, and Clark probably wasn't even home. And if he was, he probably wouldn't want to talk to some stranger about what was clearly a sore subject.

But as she reached out to start the Toyota up again, Queenie suddenly sat up and meowed. A tall man with sandy blond hair came out of the house and walked down the drive. As he got closer, Kari could see that he had blue eyes behind black plastic glasses and wore a short-sleeved tan checked shirt and a pair of chinos. In short, he looked like a professor.

She got out of the car, still wondering exactly what she was doing there. "Hi," she said. "I'm sorry to just drop by, but I was driving past and wondered if you'd be willing to spare a minute to talk to me. My name is Kari Stuart. We don't know each other, but we're sort of neighbors now. I bought the Serenity Sanctuary down the road a ways."

"Oh, sure," Steve said, holding out his hand to shake hers. "I heard someone had taken over the place and was giving it a much-needed facelift. Nice to meet you." His high forehead wrinkled. "Uh, what did you want to talk to me about? Are you looking for donations?"

Kari laughed. "No, not at all. It's kind of awkward, really. I wanted to talk to you about Bill Myers."

The smile dropped away from Clark's face and the

warmth fled his eyes. "That bastard," he said. "I heard he died. I won't pretend I'm sorry."

Yikes. "Er, yes. He was killed at the sanctuary. In fact, I was the one who found his body." She shuddered again, and thought, *I can't keep doing that every time I talk to someone about his death.* "I'm afraid I'm the sheriff's prime suspect, since he was trying to dig under our fence at the time he died."

Steve's shoulders relaxed a bit, although he still looked grim. "So, he was doing it to you too, huh."

"Doing what?"

"Letting a dog out so he could claim he found it roaming loose. I'm sure he did that with Ranger, although I never could prove it." He glanced back over toward the doghouse.

"I loved that damned dog. Saved up for two years to buy him. Irish wolfhounds don't come cheap and professors at tiny upstate New York colleges don't make much money, but I've wanted one since I was a kid." He blinked rapidly a couple of times. "Ranger was a great dog. After the second time he supposedly got loose, I locked the gate when he was outside. He was too big and active a dog to leave stuck in a house all day, although now I wished I'd done it. He might have been miserable, but at least he would still be alive."

"You really think Myers let the dog out on purpose?" Kari asked. She was still having a hard time wrapping her head around the idea that a dog warden would so blatantly break the rules.

"Hey, you said he was digging under your fence. What do you think he was doing?" Steve growled. "Trying to improve your drainage?" He lifted up his glasses so he could wipe at his eyes. "You know, I haven't had the heart to get rid of Ranger's stuff. I still miss that dog every day. I didn't kill Myers, but I'm not going to pretend I'm sorry someone did."

Was he protesting too much? Kari wasn't sure. He certainly wasn't pretending not to hate the former dog warden.

Steve went on, still gazing back at the fenced yard with his hands clenched at his side. "It's just too bad they didn't do it sooner. Maybe I'd still have Ranger, and that poor woman wouldn't have lost her dog too."

"Poor woman?" Kari asked. "Who do you mean?"

"Georgia Travis," he said. "You haven't heard about her yet? You think I hated Bill Myers, you should talk to Georgia. She used to be a state trooper, but she was forced to retire after she got hurt in the line of duty. Fought like heck to adopt the K-9 dog she worked with, and was finally allowed to keep him. A German shepherd, I think. I never met either of them, but I heard through the grapevine that Myers took her dog away too, not long before he died, and she actually confronted him at the Last Stop bar and threatened to shoot him. You want someone who had a reason to hate Myers, go talk to Georgia Travis."

Six

"Georgia Travis," Sara said, tapping a pencil idly on the desk. "Yes, she was one of my students."

Kari and Bryn rolled their eyes at each other, since everyone between the ages of fifteen and fifty who had grown up in Lakeview had probably passed through Sara's classroom at one time or another. Kari thought this made Sara the perfect secret weapon. If she didn't know someone, she knew someone who did.

"Well?" Bryn asked impatiently. "What did you think of her?"

Sara tossed the pencil down. "I didn't think, when she was handing in her paper on the subtext in Shakespeare's sonnets, *Gee, I wonder if she'll grow up and murder a dog warden.* If that's what you were asking." She took a sip of her tea as she pondered the question.

"I will say, she's probably capable of the crime," the older woman finally said reluctantly. "She was the captain of the girls' soccer team, and tough as nails. I remember during her senior year they were in the finals and she played with a broken foot rather than sit out the game. Then, of course, she went on to become a state trooper, until she was attacked during a routine traffic stop.

"Shot, I think, although I don't remember the specifics. We prayed for her at church, and I heard that she recovered, but her injuries were severe enough to force her into retirement. It's a pity. I suspect she was very good at the job." She put the teacup down next to a pile of papers on the desk they all sat around in the front room of the nearly ready shelter. "So she's capable enough to have done it, and probably not at all squeamish. But that doesn't make her a murderer."

"Did you hear anything about what happened between her and Myers, or about the dog he took from her?" Kari asked. "Steve Clark seemed to think she was pretty furious, although if he were the killer, he'd probably say that to point suspicions in another direction."

Sara shook her head, making the turquoise streak in her gray hair swing back and forth. "I don't think so," she said. "But we can go to the town hall and talk to Rachel Kertzmann. She's the former student of mine who works in the main offices. She's usually on top of all the local gossip. I call her my personal information superhighway. While we're there, we can ask her to look into the court cases and tickets Myers was involved in, and maybe find out if she knows of anyone else who might have had a beef with him that was bad enough to warrant murder as a solution."

Kari loved Lakeview's small Main Street. It was really only three blocks long or so; the buildings were old and quaint (although admittedly, in some cases, a bit the worse for wear), and the shops and restaurants were individual and quirky. No big chain stores here. Her favorite was the bookstore, Paging All Readers, but there was also an antiques store aptly named Old Stuff where she planned to get some furniture for the farmhouse as soon as she could find a minute, and a thrift shop called Downtown and Upcycled where she had bought most of her clothes since she'd moved back.

A small bakery sat next to an Indian restaurant, the Good Karma Deli, and if you weren't in the mood for either of those, there was a pizza place that was filled with college students during the school year and tourists the rest of the time. The locals tended to prefer the diner Kari used to work in, but there were enough eateries to satisfy almost anyone's taste.

For those who were looking for entertainment, there was also an arts and crafts store (which Kari rarely went into, since she had no crafty abilities whatsoever), a shop that featured knitting and sewing supplies, and a single-screen movie theater that doubled as a performance space for local concerts and plays. Like most of the other structures, it was built out of red brick, with odd architectural details like the occasional gargoyle face on the side of a second-floor wall where you'd least expect it.

And of course, there was Blue Heron Lake, for which the town was named. It sat at the far edge of the main route, just past the ice cream shop. Not a very large lake, as lakes in upstate New York went, but many of the ones in the Catskills were on the smaller side. The residents of Lakeview liked to say that what their lake lacked in size it made up for in beauty, with rocky shorelines and crystal clear water.

During the summer, the lake was popular with tourists

and locals alike for boating, swimming, and fishing. Although, of course, those who lived there year-round never shared the secrets of the very best spots. As far as Kari was concerned, there was no place prettier in the world, and even when she'd been living in a crappy apartment, she had never questioned her decision to return to the place she considered home.

The town hall looked less intimidating in the daylight, when she wasn't standing in the courtroom. There were two doors in the front of the building. The one on the right led to the court, and the one on the left opened into a hallway that led to a series of offices. Engraved signs on the wall pointed to the offices of the town clerk, city code enforcement, public works, and other various places responsible for keeping the cogs of a small town working.

Rachel's desk was toward the front of a room that housed a variety of basic and sometimes overlapping functions. Three women and one man sat at computers typing furiously, while another woman talked into a phone tucked between her ear and her chin while looking something up in a battered file folder.

Sara walked decisively through the slightly chaotic room and introduced Kari to a thin woman with shoulder-length light brown hair and the pale skin of someone who rarely made it outside during daylight hours. Wire-rimmed half-glasses perched on a snub nose, and she wore a light blue cardigan against the arctic chill of the hyperactive air-conditioning.

"Hi," Rachel said, rising briefly to greet them before gesturing them into the two chairs in front of her desk and resuming her seat. "Nice to meet you, Kari. I really admire what you're doing with the shelter. I've been thinking about getting a cat to keep me company, so let me know when you're open."

Kari and Sara looked at each other. "One-Eyed Jack," they both said, like a slightly demented feline-centric Greek chorus. One-Eyed Jack was one of the cats still left at the shelter. He was only five, and really sweet, but he'd lost an eye to an infection as a kitten, and no one had been interested in adopting him. Bryn called him her pirate kitty. He spent most of his time wandering around looking for a lap to curl up in, and only occasionally walked into the furniture.

"We've got the perfect cat for you," Sara said confidently. "Stop by any time. But in the meanwhile, as I told you on the phone, we could use your help."

"Bill Myers," Rachel said, screwing up her mouth as though she'd eaten something sour. "He made my first couple of years here really uncomfortable. Kept coming around asking me to help him look things up he could have found perfectly well on his own computer. Inviting me to lunch no matter how many times I said no. Would you believe he actually pinched my bottom once at the office Christmas party?" She shook her head. "He was such a jerk."

"That seems to be the general consensus," Kari said in a grim tone. "Obviously at least one person eventually found him to be unbearable."

Rachel grimaced. "I'm sorry. I forgot you were the one who found his body." She fiddled with a couple of pens, moving them around and then finally plunking them into a cup holding a dozen more. "That was insensitive of me."

"Not at all," Kari said. "I was hardly a fan."

"But that's why we're here," Sara said, taking control

of the conversation before it could veer further off track. "Believe it or not, the police seem to think that Kari killed Myers. So we're looking into his professional history, trying to figure out who else might have had a motive. People like Steve Clark and Georgia Travis, whose dogs he seized. We were wondering if you could research some things for us."

Rachel opened her mouth, possibly to argue, but Sara never gave her the chance.

"Just things that are in the public record, of course. We could go digging ourselves, but you would have a much easier time accessing it all." Sara gestured toward the computer on the desk between them. "And I'm guessing you already know quite a bit off the top of your head."

"Well, you're not wrong there," Rachel said, plucking a pen back out of the cup and rolling it back and forth across the surface of her desk. "I guess I could probably pull some information for you about things like court appearances and the judge's decisions. Pretty much everything the dog warden—and most other town employees—does is available to town residents. It's just that no one ever asks."

"We're asking," Sara said decisively, but with a smile.

"Okay," Rachel said. "I guess it won't be a problem." But she hunched her shoulders as another woman walked up to the desk. Kari recognized Marge Farrow, the court clerk who had been in the room when they'd had to appear before the judge.

In the courtroom, Marge had been nearly invisible. She was one of those women who seemed to hover somewhere in middle age, with graying blond hair twisted into a bun, a few extra pounds padding her hips and waist, and neat but drab clothing that might have been designed to discourage one's gaze from lingering in her direction. Closer up, Kari could discern piercing blue eyes and a hint of iron backbone in her walk. Interestingly, Rachel appeared to be intimidated by her, for reasons that weren't immediately obvious. Maybe the court clerk carried more weight in the building's hierarchy than Kari knew about?

Marge's first words were certainly innocuous enough, and her tone was mild and friendly. "Hello, Rachel," she said. "I was just checking to see if you had the records from last week's court recording typed up for me yet." She nodded at Kari and Sara. "I didn't mean to interrupt your meeting."

Rachel's fingers twitched and the pen she was fiddling with rolled across the desktop. Sara reached out and adroitly stopped it before it could fall over the edge.

"I'm almost done, Ms. Farrow," Rachel said. "I should have them to you within the hour."

Marge raised an eyebrow, gazing pointedly at the two visitors.

"Ah, this is Sara Hanover and Kari Stuart. They were just asking me do a public records search." Rachel bit her lip, smearing the light pink lipstick she wore. "That's perfectly legal."

"Of course it is," Marge said. If she recognized Kari from the other night at court, she didn't say so. "As long as you stick to the open records. And don't let it interfere with the rest of your work."

Sara sat up a little straighter in her chair. "It was my understanding that assisting the town's residents with inquiries is actually part of Ms. Kertzmann's duties," she said lightly. "Was I misinformed? We certainly don't want to cause her any problems."

"Not at all," Marge said, some expression Kari couldn't

quite discern flitting over her otherwise placid face, like a ripple in a clear pond. "You're quite right." She turned to Rachel. "Let me know if any of their questions are something I can help with." Nodding at the other two, she added, "Have a nice day," before walking away.

"Is she your boss?" Kari asked Rachel.

The clerk snorted. "No, she's not, although you'd never know it from the way she treats me."

"She seems nice enough," Sara said. "Maybe she thought we were bothering you."

"Ha," Rachel said. "She's just nosy. Marge is one of those people who always seem to know everything that's going on in the whole building. If I didn't know better, I'd think she listens in on phone conversations and eavesdrops in the bathrooms. I swear, it's like she can see into my head to what I'm thinking. It kind of freaks me out."

She took the pen Sara handed back to her. "Marge is okay, I guess. I just always feel like I'm doing something wrong when she's around."

"And she's going to report you to the principal," Sara said, nodding. "There was a teacher like that at the school for a while. People fell all over themselves trying not to get on her bad side, and they were never really sure why."

"Yes, exactly like that," the younger woman said. "She never quite comes out and criticizes you, but still . . ." She looked at Sara curiously. "What happened with the teacher? Did she turn out to be okay after all?"

"Oh goodness, no," Sara said with a laugh. "It turned out she was carrying on a torrid affair with the janitor after hours and they were both fired. Last I heard she was working up at the assisted living facility in Riverton and intimidating a lot of old folks."

"Wow," Rachel said. "I guess you just never know about people, do you?"

"No," Sara said in a thoughtful tone, gazing in the direction Marge had gone. "You never do."

A soft paw tapped Kari's cheek. This was followed by a more insistent meow.

"Oh, no," Kari moaned, hiding her head under her pillow. "Not again."

After their visit to the town hall, she'd worked at the shelter until after nine, helping with the cleaning and then plowing through the paperwork for grant applications that Daisy had handed over with a sigh of relief. Dinner had been a peanut butter and jelly sandwich eaten in front of the television, to the palpable disgust of the orange cats and Fred, who had clearly been hoping for something more appetizing. Queenie, who still got the yummy special food for kittens, didn't seem to care.

Queenie meowed again and Kari shifted the pillow to look at the clock on the bedside table. Two a.m. Great. She'd had a whole three hours of sleep. Once she rolled over, she could hear the faint sound of dogs barking from the direction of the shelter.

"One . . . two . . ." The phone rang, right on cue. "Hello, Mr. Lee. Yes, I hear them. Yes, I'm very sorry. I'm going to go out and check right now." She held the phone farther away from her ear but she could still make out irritated squawking. "It really isn't necessary to call the police, Mr. Lee. I'm sure it's just a bear trying to get into the garbage again. I'm sorry they woke you up." He hung up, after a few choice words.

"Well, that was rude," Kari said to Queenie. "I guess I'd better get dressed and see what has them all riled up." She grabbed her pants off the back of the overstuffed chair she'd thrown them onto when she'd finally crawled into bed, and tried to pull them on without falling over. "It better not be another dead body, that's all I'm saying." Kari shook her head. "You know your life is messed up when you're actively *hoping* for a bear."

She grabbed the big flashlight on her way out the door, feeling an uncomfortable sense of déjà vu. At least this time she was able to close the door behind her before the kitten could get out, although the echo of disgruntled meows followed her up the path to the sanctuary.

The night air was warm and redolent with the sweet scent of the wild roses that grew to one side, sprawling in thorny splendor and occasionally reaching out to snag an unsuspecting passerby. Kari was wise to their tricks, though, and dodged them without thinking, her attention focused on the barking dogs and whatever it was that had set them off this time.

It occurred to her that wandering around in the dark in a place where a man had been murdered might not be the smartest move ever, but it wasn't as though she could just ignore the barking, and she wasn't about to call the police to come hold her hand. Sheriff Richardson would just love that. And if she called one of the other volunteers and waited for them to show up, Mr. Lee would probably have filed a complaint before they could even get there.

She flinched as something—an owl or a bat, probably—flew over her head, close enough for her to feel the passage of its wings. She came to a halt right in front of the shelter entrance as silence fell, shattered only by a few lingering halfhearted woofs. Then it was just her, stand-ing alone in the middle of the night, listening to nothing.

"Seriously?" she muttered to herself. Since she was out there anyway, she played the flashlight over the door, which looked untouched, and walked around to the side. Gingerly, she poked her head around to where she'd found the dog warden's body, but all she saw was a ribbon of crime scene tape shining dully in the flashlight's bright beam. A yawn nearly split her face in half and she shrugged. Must have been a bear after all. Or maybe a raccoon. She made a mental note to check the garbage cans in the morning, and maybe look into getting a small shed built to house them. It would be worth it if it saved her more nights like this.

In the distance, she could see the lights in the Lees' house blink out. No doubt they were headed back to bed. That sounded like a darned good plan to her. Morning would come way too soon as it was.

Seven

Kari was sitting bleary-eyed over a cup of coffee the next morning, Westley perched on her knee and Fred sitting at her feet under the rickety card table at the edge of the kitchen that served as her dining area, eagerly awaiting any toast crumbs that might happen to fall in his direction. An unexpected knock on the door made her drop the entire slice, butter, jam, and all, although it didn't stay on the floor long enough to leave a mark.

"Darn," she said as she glanced at the cat clock on the wall. "It's not even seven o'clock yet." Surely the volunteers who came in to feed and clean could manage without her until she finished breakfast. Although it would appear that Fred had taken care of that for her. The kitten trotted next to her and sat down on her haunches, gazing at the door like a tiny black greeting committee. Easy for her to be cheerful—she'd already had her food.

Kari swung the door open in time to see Bryn, her fist poised to knock again. The two of them had arrived at an uneasy truce. The younger woman clearly still didn't trust

Kari's motives or commitment to sticking around when things got tough, but she couldn't help but be appreciative of the improvements Kari had been making. Kari was simply grateful the girl had decided to stay and help. Mostly they maintained a polite distance. Certainly Bryn had never come to the house before. Kari was pretty sure this first time wasn't for a social call.

"I'm sorry to bother you so early," Bryn said. Concern wrinkled her brow and there was a pinched look around her full lips that suggested bad news was coming. "But I think you'd better come to the shelter. There's something you need to see."

"Okay." Kari didn't even bother to ask questions as she slipped her feet into her sneakers. She knew Bryn of all people wouldn't have disturbed her for nothing.

Queenie hopped onto Kari's shoulder as she bent down, and stayed in her favorite spot effortlessly as they walked in the direction of the shelter. But even the determined kitten wobbled a little as Kari came to a sudden stop, stunned by the sight in front of her.

Sara's car was parked at a slight angle, probably because she'd been caught off guard by the same display that had Kari standing there with her mouth open. The older woman was attired in her usual work garb of jeans and a flowered shirt, glaring at the shelter wall with her arms crossed in front of her chest and a scowl on her face that would have curdled milk.

Scrawled across the formerly pristine building was the word MURDERER on one side of the door and HORE on the other. The red paint had dripped wetly across the newly spread gravel underneath. It looked uncannily like blood.

"'Hore'?" Kari asked, her voice only shaking slightly. The other word was fairly self-explanatory.

"I believe whoever wrote that probably meant *whore*," Sara said in a dry tone. "With a *W*. I'd get my red pen, but that seems somewhat superfluous, all things considered." Mrs. Hanover's red pen had struck fear into the hearts of many ninth-grade English students who had found it used prolifically on their papers.

"What I don't understand is how someone could have done this without setting the dogs off," Bryn said. Her expression was calmer than Sara's, but Kari noticed that Bryn's hands were curled into fists at her sides.

Kari sighed. She didn't know how she'd missed the writing, except that it was dark and she had only been focused on checking the lock on the door, not the walls next to it.

"They did bark," she said. "Mr. Lee called me at around two a.m., and I came down with a flashlight to check. But they stopped, and I didn't see anything wrong with the door, so I just went back to bed. I thought it was a bear."

Queenie meowed, as if to say that if she'd been allowed to come, she would have discovered the mess right away. Which wouldn't have surprised Kari at all. She reached up to pet the kitten in silent apology.

"Well, at least we know when it happened," Sara said, sounding resigned. "You'd better call the police and report it, and then take pictures for the insurance company."

Kari winced at the thought of dealing with either one. "I don't suppose it will just rinse off?" she asked hopefully.

Bryn reached out one finger and touched the red paint. "Nope. It's completely dry. You might be able to scrub it off, but that red will leave a stain behind." She shrugged. "There was a lot of graffiti where we used to live when I was a kid."

"Bad neighborhood?' Kari asked.

Bryn rolled her big brown eyes. "It was a perfectly nice neighborhood. Just too close to the college. The students are very big on graffiti, especially anything to do with fraternities or sports teams."

Ouch. Kari winced. That was what she got for making assumptions. "Sorry," she said. "It's early, I haven't had breakfast, and also, I'm an idiot."

Sara patted her on the shoulder. "I'm sure you're slightly less idiotic when you've had more sleep and fewer shocks. I'm afraid you're going to have to call the painters and ask them to come back, though."

Kari winced again, this time at the thought of paying the painters twice for the same job. It would probably take at least two coats to cover that red. "Who would do such a thing? And why would anyone do it?"

"That's a good question," Sara said in the tone that meant she was thinking. It was usually accompanied by a slightly absent look that told the careful observer her mind was elsewhere, hard at work. "You have been asking a lot of questions of a lot of people. Apparently one of them didn't like it." One finger twiddled with the turquoise streak in her hair, although she probably wasn't aware she was doing it.

"Or maybe someone was afraid they were next on the list," Bryn put in. "And wanted to discourage you from asking more questions."

"Darn," Kari said. "Does that mean we should stop looking into Myers's death?"

"Heck no," Sara said with a gleam in her eyes. "We're obviously getting somewhere. It means we push harder."

Kari stared from MURDERER to HORE. "Great," she said. "Maybe it would be easier to just have them repaint the entire front of the building red. Save us some trouble the next time." She was pretty sure if she followed Sara's advice, there would definitely be a next time. She only hoped whoever it was stuck to paint.

To Kari's not very great surprise, Suz found the mis-spelled accusations more humorous than alarming. She'd come over and pitched in with the crew who had washed the worst of the mess off before the painters got there, and commiserated with Kari over both the expense and the police department's exasperating but not unexpected lack of interest in the crime. She had also made Kari pose in front of the door, between the two words, so she could take a picture. Oddly, Suz's reaction made Kari feel less freaked out by the whole thing.

So it was more than a little worrisome when Suz texted her early on Saturday morning a couple of days later and said, Meet me at the diner for breakfast. You have a problem.

Kari pulled her hair back into a scrunchie, hurriedly threw on a pair of reasonably clean jeans and a black tee shirt that said *Everything looks better with cat hair*, and rushed down to the not very imaginatively named Lakeview Diner. Built out of brick like most of the downtown buildings, it had a bright yellow awning and a few cast-iron tables outside that only the tourists used.

Inside, red vinyl booths lined two walls, with a long counter running the length of the third. There were matching red backless stools in front of it for customers to perch on, and no matter what time of day you came in, there were sure to be at least three or four customers sitting there with anything from a cup of coffee to the full three eggs, stack of pancakes, bacon, and sausage breakfast special (which also included home fries, in case there weren't enough carbs and fat on the plate for you already).

The diner was open from five in the morning until eight at night, seven days a week, and featured exactly the kind of food you would expect from a small-town diner. Plus pies, cherry and apple and lemon meringue, home-made and delivered every morning by Mrs. Reynolds, who had been baking for the diner for as long as anyone could remember. The aroma of fresh burgers sizzling on the grill and the hand-cut onion rings in the deep fryer would hit you when you walked in the door and make you want to swoon and instantly reconsider that healthy diet you'd just started.

When Kari had been a kid, one of her favorite things to do had been to spin around on the stools until she was dizzy. She and Suz had had competitions to see who could spin the longest, with the loser treating the winner to a hot fudge sundae. The tiny old-fashioned soda fountain at the end of the counter was popular with kids and adults alike, and in the summer there was often a line that wound half-way through the diner of people waiting for a double-scoop cone of ice cream produced at a local dairy. No fancy flavors—just vanilla, chocolate, strawberry, or chocolate chip, but every bite was creamy, decadent heaven.

Suz was sitting at their favorite booth. There was a pot of coffee in front of her, and two white porcelain mugs on the table, along with a copy of the local paper.

"What's up?" Kari asked, pouring herself some coffee and adding cream and sugar. "Should I order breakfast, or am I going to be too upset to eat?"

Suz ran one hand through her lavender hair so that it stood on end even more than usual and shoved the paper across the table. "You tell me."

Kari flipped open the newspaper and decided to go with the second choice. "You have *got* to be kidding me," she said. She considered banging her head against the Formica surface in front of her, but she decided that the article on the front page already made her head hurt enough without any help. The front page. Crap on toast.

"Crap on toast," she said, deciding the comment was worth repeating outside her own head.

"Yeah. I'm sorry," Suz said. She wasn't very demonstrative, so in lieu of a hug, she called over the waitress and ordered two breakfast specials. With extra bacon. Suz was a firm believer that bacon could solve almost any problem life might send your way. Of course, that was before the newspaper had plastered Kari's face above the fold.

LOTTERY WINNER VICTIM OF VANDALISM! The article went on to tell the story of how Kari had won the lottery and then bought the Serenity Sanctuary. Of course, it used more flowery language, like *luckiest woman in town* and *savior of unwanted animals*.

Kari changed her mind and thumped her head a couple of times on the table anyway. It didn't help. And now she had maple syrup in her hair.

"It must have been a slow news day," Suz said sympathetically. "I guess they ran out of goats and politicians." She nudged Kari upright to make room for their food.

Cookie, one of the waitresses who worked the morning shift, unloaded the steaming plates from her tray and slid them into place as if performing a one-woman ballet. For a large woman with flat feet, she was surprisingly graceful. Her blond bouffant hairdo, which she insisted was the only appropriate style for anyone who worked in a diner, didn't even quiver.

"Here ya go, honey. I had them give you extra, extra bacon." She grimaced. "I saw the paper. Jeez, it's like no one in this town ever won any money before. It's a little late to make a fuss about it, if you ask me." She patted her hair. "Mind you, no one ever asks me. I can't believe we worked together for two years and they didn't even interview me for that article. Not that I would have told them anything anyway."

Kari opened her mouth to say thank you, but a man at a nearby table made the mistake of waving his menu in the air to try to get Cookie's attention.

"Aw, keep your shorts on," Cookie hollered. "I'm coming." She snagged a piece of bacon off Kari's plate, folded it in half, and stuffed it into her mouth. "Mind you, now that you're rich, I guess you can leave me a bigger tip, huh?" She winked and then hustled off, chewing rapidly.

"And so it begins," Suz intoned grimly. She pointed one unvarnished nail at the paper. Suz liked to keep her decorative impulses to her hair and the various tiny studs that ran up the edge of her left ear. Today's theme was rainbow hues. For the earrings. The hair was still lavender. This week. She always said that getting your nails done was for people who didn't spend all their time with their hands in sudsy water. Kari tended to agree, although Cookie's nails were long and brilliant green.

"What do you mean?" Kari asked, but she was afraid she already knew.

"Are you kidding?" Suz said around a mouthful of crispy home fries. "The *Daily Slur* just put a target on your back." The newspaper's actual name was the *Daily Standard*, but nobody local called it that. It was mostly known for putting pictures of cute kids and puppies on the front page instead of actual news, and posting incorrect information for any important event's time, date, or location. "Everybody and his brother will show up asking you for money now."

"It's not like it was a secret that I won the lottery," Kari said, trying not to sound desperate. She gave up on the rest of her breakfast and just nibbled on a piece of bacon. Even its salty, fatty goodness couldn't seem to work its usual magic today. "Hardly anyone has bothered me so far."

"Yeah, that was before the *Daily Slur* put you on the front page and spelled out exactly how much money you won, and where you can be found most days." Suz shook her head. "They'll all forget again soon enough, but in the meanwhile, things might get a little hairy." She snorted. "Get it? Hairy. Dog groomer joke."

Kari ate another piece of bacon despondently. She got it, all right. Although she wished she hadn't. She flipped the page and read the rest of the article. "Oh, for the love of . . . they also mention the run-down state of the rescue when I bought it and how I found Bill Myers's body. They managed to make me sound like an idiot and a murderer, practically in the same paragraph."

"I know," Suz said, reaching out with her fork to snag some of the potatoes Kari wasn't eating. Kari, who tended to run toward plumpness if she wasn't careful, had long envied her friend's seeming ability to eat anything and everything, and still stay as slim as a stick. Of course, Suz said she envied Kari's boobs, of which she had none, so that probably made them even. "It was an unusually skillful bit of writing for the *Daily Slur*. I wonder if they hired a new reporter."

"Suz!" Kari pulled her plate back. "You're supposed to be on my side!"

"Oh, I am, babe," Suz said. "But you have to admit, it is a little bit funny. In one article, they made you out to be the luckiest woman in town, a fool for buying a money pit of a shelter, and possibly a cold-blooded murderer. Who also happened to be a victim of vandalism. Who knew you were so multifaceted? I feel honored to be your friend."

"You know, I can still write you out of my will," Kari said. "I could leave my millions to that politician's goat. Or Queenie."

Suz snorted. "Dude, by the time you get done fixing up that rescue, you won't have enough to pay for this breakfast. Besides, Queenie would just blow it all on catnip. You might as well keep me in the will. It's not as though you want to give the money to your family."

Kari shuddered at the thought. "Oh, heck no. I'd rather leave it to the darned goat."

After breakfast, Suz went off to groom a hyperactive labradoodle and Kari returned to the shelter to help out with the cleaning. The cat cages, the larger shared cat room, and the dog kennels had all been attended to already, and the animals given fresh food and water, but there were always dishes to be done and piles of laundry.

Daisy had told her that when the place was full, they had gone through six or seven loads of laundry a day, since every cage got a new blanket or towel laid down when it was cleaned, and all the cat and dog beds had to be washed every couple of days. Daily, if an animal was sick. One look at the ancient donated washer and dryer had Kari adding *Buy new industrial machines* to her list.

That list now rivaled the length of the collected works of Shakespeare.

When she got there, Sara was sitting at the newly built front desk, a polished oak L-shaped unit that had an area for greeting people when they came in, as well as a functional area on the other end that included a phone, computer, and printer. There were two ergonomically designed stools with lumbar supports and padded seats. Sara had taken on the project of creating new intake, adoption, and fostering forms, as well as weeding through all the old paperwork and tossing out anything that was no longer relevant.

There was a large box full of files on the floor next to her and a smudge of dirt on her nose, but she was clearly enjoying herself. She'd told Kari once that since they'd both retired, she and her husband found they got along best if they both spent large chunks of their days doing something besides getting in each other's faces. Dave played golf in the warm weather and skied in the colder months. For Sara, the sanctuary was the thing that kept her sane and out of his hair. What was left of it.

"Good morning, Kari," she said, looking up from her labors.

"That's a matter of opinion," Kari said glumly. She tucked her purse into the cubby underneath the desk that was labeled with her name. Sara was very big on organization.

"Ah," the older woman said. "You've seen the newspaper."

"Suz called me down to the diner and showed it to me," Kari said, sliding her butt onto the second stool. "It's a disaster."

"Nonsense," Sara said in a firm tone, tossing another file onto the top of the pile. "Hurricanes and forest fires are disasters. This is merely a minor bump in the road. Annoying, but hardly worth wasting energy worrying about." She waved her hand in the general direction of the rear of the shelter. "If you want something to worry about, you can focus on the fact that we can't open again until the sheriff allows us access to that back area so we can replace the fencing. Something he shows no sign of doing, I might add.

"Or there's this," she said, handing Kari an official-looking envelope. "Apparently the new dog warden wants to come check on Buster."

A large lump formed in Kari's throat as she read the letter. While not threatening, it wasn't particularly reassuring either. "He says he is following up on all of Myers's open cases. Especially the ones involving possible issues with public safety. He wants to come see the dog before he reschedules another court hearing. Darn it." She sighed. "I have to admit, I was kind of hoping that without Myers, the whole thing would just go away."

Sara pursed her lips. "That was never going to happen, I'm afraid. What is the name of the new dog warden? Maybe it is someone I know."

"Um," Kari looked at the bottom of the letter. "Jack Falco. I've never heard of him. Have you?"

"Not that I recall," Sara said, leafing through another folder and releasing a wave of musty-smelling aromas into the air. "Perhaps he's new in town."

"Drat," Kari said. "I guess we'll have to wait and see what he's like. He has to be an improvement over Bill Myers, right?" But she didn't feel any less anxious about it.

As she was getting ready to get up and get to work,

Bryn came out of the back, slamming the door behind her. The other two women looked up, startled.

"I can't wait until we get that soundproofing," Bryn said. "Those dogs are going to make me crazy with their barking. It's like bedlam in there today." She scowled at Kari. "They're all going stir-crazy, not being able to get out into the yard. Two fifteen-minute walks a day aren't enough for active dogs. We need that new fence."

Kari and Sara glanced at each other. Bryn was normally pretty even-tempered, and she had more patience with the animals than anyone else there.

"I'm sorry," Kari said. "You know I can't get the fence put up until the crime scene is cleared.

"A lot of help that is now," Bryn said. "I spend so much time walking the dogs, I don't have time to tend to anything else." She grabbed two leashes down off the holder on the wall.

"Jim and Emma are happy to walk the dogs during their shifts," Sara said in a mild tone. "As am I, although I try not to take the very large ones, since they tend to yank me off my feet."

"Well, Jim and Emma aren't here on Saturdays, are they?" Bryn said. "It's just us, the early cleaning volunteers, and *her*." She glared in Kari's direction. "Daisy was a lot more help, that's for sure."

Kari was taken aback by Bryn's vehemence. Daisy still came in some days for a few hours, mostly to help them figure out the paperwork mess and help with the dogs, but she was trying to hand the reins over to Kari as much as possible. Kari had thought she'd been doing a pretty good job stepping into Daisy's shoes, but maybe she wasn't doing as well as she'd assumed.

"That's hardly fair," Sara said, abandoning the files

and standing up. "Daisy was here for a lot longer, and she built the whole place up from nothing, starting it out of her apartment before there was even an official space. Kari has only been around for a couple of weeks and she's still getting up to speed. I think she has done remarkably well, all things considered."

"You know what's not fair?" Bryn said, twisting the leashes in her hands. "They're going to arrest my aunt for murdering Bill Myers. *That's* not fair." And she burst into tears.

Eight

Wait, what? They're going to arrest Izzy?" Kari's jaw dropped open. No wonder the poor girl was so upset. If Izzy was arrested, it would be a disaster for Bryn in more ways than one, since she lived at Izzy's house rent-free, although Kari was pretty sure that wasn't the girl's major concern right now.

Izzy was older than Kari by about twenty years and had started working at the library when Kari was in her teens. The library had always been a refuge for Kari, a place to escape from the family drama that stemmed from her father's drinking, constant criticism, and bad temper, but when Izzy arrived, it became even more of one. The other woman had gone out of her way to recommend books she thought Kari would enjoy, let her sit in a back corner for hours doing her homework, and listened without judgment on the rare occasions when Kari was willing to admit that there was something wrong at home.

Izzy was one of Kari's favorite people in town. The

thought that she might somehow be caught up in this murder unpleasantness made Kari's stomach clench.

Apparently Sara had been right—the newspaper article was the least of their worries.

Ever practical, Sara guided Bryn to a chair, handed her a tissue, and sat down next to her. "Why don't you start from the beginning," she suggested. "That might be more helpful than picking a fight with Kari, who clearly isn't part of the problem."

"She found the body," Bryn muttered, sounding for a moment like someone ten years younger.

Sara snorted. "Well, you can hardly blame her for that. It's not as though she murdered him and left his corpse there on purpose."

"Are we sure about that?" Bryn blew her nose noisily and sighed. "Sorry, Kari. Of course you didn't. I'm just really upset about my aunt."

"Why didn't you mention this when you got here?" Sara asked.

Bryn bit her lip. "I kept hoping it was just a bad dream. And really, how do you start that conversation? 'By the way, they hauled my aunt off to jail this morning. How is your day going?'"

Kari thought about sitting in the diner looking at the newspaper. "Not great, actually. But you know, if they arrested your aunt, I would have thought everyone in the diner would have been talking about it."

Bryn glared at her briefly before sighing again. "They didn't exactly arrest her," she admitted. "But they did insist on her going to the station with them, and they asked her all kinds of questions. I'm not really mad at you. I'm mad at myself. It's all my fault."

"The beginning is starting to look better and better,"

Sara murmured. "Why don't I make you a cup of tea, and you can tell us why the police suspect your aunt of having something to do with Bill Myers's death."

She was heard threatening him," Bryn admitted a couple of minutes later. "I love my aunt, but she's not exactly subtle. It amazes me, because at the library, she is always the heart and soul of politeness, but outside of work, if you get in her face, she's not going to hold back."

"And Bill Myers got in her face?" Kari asked. She knew Izzy, even considered her a friend although they didn't see as much of each other these days, but she'd never seen the woman lose her temper. She found it hard to imagine.

"Not exactly," Bryn said. "He got in mine."

Ah, Kari thought. *That makes a lot more sense.* Izzy adored her only niece, and Kari could definitely imagine the otherwise well-mannered librarian jumping to Bryn's defense. "What did he do?"

Bryn stared at the floor.

"Honey? No one is judging you," Sara said. "Just tell us. We can't help if we don't know what was going on."

"He was kind of harassing me," Bryn said. "At first, it was small stuff. He'd stop by to check on a dog, or to let us know that someone's animal had gone missing, so we'd know to alert him if it turned up. And while he was here, he'd ask me out. You know, just for coffee, or a movie.

"Nothing big. I always turned him down. I mean, not only was he kind of nasty, he was a lot older than me, and not exactly my type." She blushed, glancing up from underneath long dark lashes at Kari. "Your friend Suz is more my type, just for the record."

Kari smiled at her across her cup of tea, not terribly

surprised. "Which just goes to show you have good taste. I'm guessing that Myers didn't take no for an answer?"

Bryn shook her head. "Not hardly. At first he was nice about it. Brought gifts like a box of candy, which I just shared with the rest of the volunteers. Then, after he'd started coming down hard on Daisy, he said he'd give the shelter a break if I'd go out with him." She bit her lip, blinking back tears. "And by 'go out with him,' he obviously meant sleep with him. When I still turned him down, he threatened to go to the administrators at the college and tell them I'd been practicing veterinary medicine without the proper certification."

"That bastard," Sara said. "Kind of makes me wish I'd killed him myself."

"Me too," Kari said with feeling. "I'm so sorry you had to deal with that." She suddenly understood why Bryn had been so defensive about whether she treated the animals that first day they'd met.

Bryn wiped her eyes again and looked away. "I sometimes feel guilty about not just giving in," she said in a voice barely louder than a whisper. "It might have made things easier on Daisy. Easier on the animals. Maybe Buster wouldn't be facing a death sentence if I had just gone along with what he wanted."

"No," Kari said, in a tone that didn't allow for argument. "You can never make things better by giving in to bullies and abusers. This I can assure you on."

Sara raised an eyebrow in her direction but didn't comment other than to add, "Plus there is no reason to believe that a man like Myers would have kept his promises. He would undoubtedly have taken advantage of you and then done whatever he was going to do anyway."

"Oh," Bryn said. "I hadn't thought of that."

"That's the way they work," Kari said, patting the girl on the hand. "They keep you so off balance, you just react instead of thinking. I'm really impressed with you for not caving. Good for you."

Bryn sat up a little straighter. "Thanks. I just . . . couldn't. But now my aunt is in trouble, and it is all my fault."

"It's that jerkwad Myers's fault," Sara said acerbically. "Not yours."

"Jerkwad?" Kari repeated, biting her lip to hold back a smile.

"Hush up, you." Sara turned back to Bryn. "So your aunt found out that Myers had been giving you a difficult time, and she got into an argument with him? Is that what happened?"

"It wasn't exactly an argument," Bryn said. "From what the police said, she accosted him in the grocery store and told him that if he didn't leave me alone, she'd cut off all his favorite body parts and feed them to her cockatoo."

Sara choked on her tea and Kari had to pound her on the back for a minute until she could catch her breath.

"Oh, bless her heart, I do love that woman," Sara said. "Although that seems like it might be unnecessarily cruel to the bird."

"Oh, I don't know," Kari said. "I've met that bird. He's not a very picky eater."

Bryn stared from one woman to the other as if she thought they'd both lost their minds. "How can you make jokes about this?" she asked. "They dragged my aunt down to the sheriff's office and questioned her for two hours. And she doesn't have an alibi. I was staying at a friend's house, not that they would have taken my word for anything anyway. She told them she was up late reading, but it's not like she could prove it."

She blinked back more tears. "I could never live with myself if my aunt went to jail because of me."

"Do you think she did it?" Sara asked.

"No! Of course not."

"Well, then," Sara said, "the solution is obvious. We just have to keep working on finding the real killer, so Izzy won't go to prison for something she didn't do."

"Or me, or Daisy," Kari added. "Also not guilty."

"Exactly. So we just need to find out who is." Sara stood decisively. "Now, who's up for walking some dogs?"

They managed to get all the dogs out for some fresh air and exercise before Bryn had to head out for the day. She wanted to cook something nice for her aunt, to make up for how crappy the morning had started out. Apparently her grandmother's meatloaf recipe was the cure for most of life's misfortunes, especially when paired with mashed potatoes and gravy.

Sara and Kari were just getting ready to attack the old files again when Sara got a call from her friend Rachel at the town offices.

"What are you doing at work on a Saturday?" Sara asked, putting her phone on speaker so Kari could hear.

"I just came in to pick up that information you wanted," Rachel said. "I was going to bring it to you yesterday, but things got hectic, and I forgot it on my desk." She paused for a minute. "Look, I'm happy to give you what I've put together so far, but I'd just as soon not be involved anymore after that. I'm sorry."

Kari and Sara exchanged silent glances.

"May I ask why not?" Sara said in what was clearly an intentionally neutral tone.

"You're going to think I'm being overly sensitive," Rachel said. "But Marge Farrow came by when I was printing everything out and she acted kind of weird about it. Accused me of wasting the taxpayers' time and sullying the name of a dead man and a bunch of other stuff that didn't even make any sense. I've never seen her so worked up. I didn't even think she liked Bill Myers."

"How odd," Sara said. She tapped a pen against the desk in a thoughtful kind of way.

"It was," Rachel said. "But you know, I've got to work with the woman every day, and I'd just as soon not get on her wrong side. Besides, I think I've got pretty much all the info there is. I hope it helps you with whatever you're trying to figure out."

"I'm sure it will be fine," Sara said. "We certainly don't want to make things uncomfortable for you. There's probably nothing to find in all those records anyway."

"Well," Rachel said slowly, "I'm not so sure about that. While I was pulling everything, I noticed a few strange patterns. Maybe it's nothing. Maybe it's not. Either way, I'll be glad to drop the folder by your house tonight, if you're going to be home. Then it will be your problem instead of mine."

"Okay," Sara said. "Thank you so much for doing this. I do hope we didn't get you into trouble."

"It should be fine," Rachel said. But she didn't sound convinced.

"Well, that was odd," Sara said when she ended the call. "It isn't like Rachel to get so easily spooked."

"Why would a court clerk care if someone was looking into the public records of a dead dog warden?" Kari asked. "Heck, why would anyone?"

Sara shrugged. She was wearing an old, faded, pink

tee shirt that would have looked shabby on anyone else, but on her it still managed to appear neat and dignified. "I suspect it is a control issue, more than any real interest in what Rachel was doing. Some of the folks who work for the town get kind of territorial after a while. It's like they think the public is a nuisance that gets in the way of their jobs, rather than the ones who pay their salaries."

She rolled her eyes. "We had a secretary at the school who had been there so long, she used to boss the principal around like he worked for her instead of the other way around."

"And she got away with that?" Kari said, amazed.

"Oh goodness, yes," Sara said. "Never argue with the person who knows where everything is filed." She glanced at her watch. "I know I said I'd stay until five and it is only four, but I'd like to get home and wait for Rachel, if you don't mind."

"No problem," Kari said. "The only thing left to do is give the animals their evening meal. It won't take long, with the limited number that are still here." She was a lot more comfortable with the dogs than she had been when she first arrived, although she still found the noise a little overwhelming. Most of the cats got fed together in the big feline room, except two sickly three-month-old kittens that were kept in a cage in the front room away from all the others.

"Great," Sara said, looking relieved. "And you've got things covered for tomorrow?"

"You bet," Kari said. She still couldn't believe that both Sara and Bryn came in six days a week, for at least a few hours a day. Thankfully she could pay Bryn for her time now, although Sara still insisted it was practically a vacation after teaching ninth graders for over forty years.

"One of the volunteers is coming to help with the cleaning in the morning," Kari said, picking up the box of discarded files as she walked Sara to the front door. She staggered a little under the unexpected weight of all that paper, but managed to heave it into the recycling bin beside the dumpster that was located next to the building. "And Jim is working from eight until noon, so he can deal with the feeding and help me walk the dogs."

"I'll see you on Monday, then," Sara said as she got into her shiny silver Prius. "I'll let you know if I find anything interesting in the files Rachel pulled for us. My guess is it is probably a wild-goose chase."

As long as I don't have to feed any of those, Kari thought. *I've got enough on my plate without adding waterfowl to it.*

She had just finishing measuring food into the last of the cat bowls under Queenie's careful supervision when she heard a car pull into the drive, its wheels crunching on the fresh gravel. The kitchenette, a small room off the main area that held a double sink, a row of cabinets filled with empty stainless steel and porcelain pet bowls, a drying rack full of newly washed ones, stacks of canned and dry food, and two refrigerators—one for animal food and medicines, and one for the use of the people who worked there—hadn't been updated much. It was too tiny for everything in it and tended to be stuffy, which was why she'd opened the narrow window through which she detected the arrival of a visitor. The limp beige curtains had seen better days, but they were still on the Want list.

She wasn't expecting any of the volunteers, but Dr. McCoy had mentioned he might stop by to check on the sick kittens, so she figured it was him. The thought made her unexpectedly cheerful, so she went out to greet him with a smile on her face, still holding a somewhat stinky can of cat food in one hand and a bowl in the other. Queenie traipsed after her, trotting along with her tail held high in the air.

But her smile died away when she saw Deputy Carter standing by the front desk. He was rifling through the papers Sara had left lying there, squinting at them in a way that made her think he probably needed glasses and was too vain to wear them.

She cleared her throat loudly and the police officer jumped.

"Hello, Deputy. Is there something I can help you with?" She gestured with her full hands. "As you can see, I'm just getting ready to feed the animals." At her feet, Queenie let out a low growl, and Kari nudged her with one foot to get her to stop. Not without a certain sympathy for the sentiment, however.

Carter thrust his chin out, thick mustache bristling. The smell of his musky aftershave almost knocked her over, easily overwhelming the strong fishy odor rising from the can of cat food she held. "You want to help me, Miz Stuart? How about you start by sticking to your job, and leaving mine to me."

Kari almost took an involuntary step back at his vehement tone. "Excuse me?"

Carter tossed the papers he'd been holding down on the desk, not even pretending he hadn't been looking at them. "I hear you've been poking your nose where it doesn't belong. Asking a bunch of questions that are none of your business. Like I told you that first night, the last thing we need is civilians who watch too many cop shows getting in the way of a real investigation."

Well, this is interesting, in an unpleasant kind of way. Kari wondered how he knew she and the others had been asking questions. Diner gossip? Or had one of the people they'd talked to complained? Either way, she didn't see how they'd done any harm, but she wasn't about to tell him that.

"I don't know what you're talking about," she said instead. After all, she didn't know the *specific* thing he was referencing. "But I hardly see how it is going to help your real investigation to come by here and harass me."

The deputy's face turned scarlet, and for a minute she was worried he was going to have a heart attack in the middle of their newly refinished floor.

"You think this is harassment, missy?" he sputtered. "Wait until you get a ticket any time you drive two miles an hour over the limit. Or the building inspectors make a surprise visit to check out your permits."

"I'll have you know that all my permits are completely in order," Kari said, holding on to her temper by a thread. She knew—logically—that it was unwise to provoke any cop, especially one who was probably in charge of the murder investigation in which she was the prime suspect, but men who tried to intimidate or bully her just put her back up. "As you can see from the paperwork you were rooting around in."

She took a deep breath and tried a more conciliatory tone. "I'm sorry if my talking to people about Bill Myers has caused you any problems, but I'm just trying to get a better idea of what he might have been doing up here the night I found him."

"You mean, the night you found his *dead body*," Carter said, his voice full of meaning. "It looks darned suspicious that you are going around asking questions about a case you are the main suspect in. You are going to make things worse for yourself and for this shelter you say is so important to you. I strongly suggest that you would be better off feeding the bunch of mangy cats and dogs you've got here, and leaving the detecting to the professionals."

My animals are not mangy! Kari bit back about three rude responses in as many seconds.

"Was there something you needed here?" she said instead. "Because if not, I'd really like to get back to what I was doing."

"I'm here to tell you to mind your own business," Carter said, walking over to her and thrusting his sizable gut into her personal space. "For your own good."

"The man died on my property and you seem determined to blame me. That makes it my business," she said, refusing to back away, although her skin crawled to have him so close.

A loud cough made them both swivel in the direction of the door. Angus McCoy stood there, his medical kit in one hand and a bag of prescription cat food in the other. One eyebrow was raised quizzically as he gazed at Deputy Carter's clearly aggressive stance.

"Do you need some help, Kari?" he asked.

"I'm fine," she said through gritted teeth. "I've got the situation under control." That might have been a small exaggeration, but she was determined to take care of herself without help from any man, no matter how well-intentioned. Or cute. Queenie let out a plaintive yowl, as if to protest. "Shhh," Kari muttered. "Do *not* take his side."

"You just mind what I said, Miz Stuart," the deputy said. "Stay out of this investigation and out of my way." He turned to leave and tripped over his shoelaces, which had somehow mysteriously come untied. "What the heck? How did that happen?" He bent down and hurriedly retied them, then stalked out with as much of his dignity intact as possible.

Kari had to put her hand over her mouth to keep from laughing out loud, nearly dropping the bowl she held in the process. Angus gazed at Queenie with amazement.

"Did that kitten just undo his laces on purpose?" He set the sack of food down on the desk and pulled a treat out of his pocket. The little black kitten jumped up adroitly and plucked it from his fingers, purring loudly.

She hadn't, had she? Surely that was giving even the clever Queenie too much credit. Or was it? "I'm sure it was just an accident," Kari said. "She's a kitten. She plays with everything."

"Uh-huh." Angus looked out the window at the sound of squealing tires as the deputy peeled out of the parking lot. "It looked like that officer was giving you a hard time. Is everything okay?"

"*Okay* is sort of a sliding scale around here at the moment, but yes, more or less," Kari said. "Although I have to admit your timing was pretty good."

She deliberately changed the subject. "Did you come to look at the kittens? Their eyes are still awfully goopy, even though I've been putting the ointment in them twice a day as directed." She waved the bowl and the can of food in the direction of the kitchenette. "If you can wait a couple of minutes for me to feed everyone, I will be right with you."

"No hurry," Angus said, his attention already on his

patients, who were peering at him through the bars of their cage across the room from the front desk. The poor kittens, a brother and sister that a Good Samaritan had rescued from a local trailer park, had been battling some kind of upper respiratory illness for over a month, which was why they hadn't been adopted or moved to one of the other shelters. The little girl gave a snuffly meow, her stuffed-up nose giving her a plaintive sound.

"I've got a new antibiotic to try on them, now that they're a little bit older," the vet said. "We don't like to give it to younger kittens, because it can affect the development of their teeth later in life, but they're old enough that I'm willing to risk it now, and this has hung on too long already. I'm also going to give them each a B-12 shot. Sometimes that helps to boost their systems." He cooed at the kittens, an endearing sight that made Kari smile despite everything.

"Okay," she said. "I'll be right back if you want me to hold them while you give them the shots." She took a deep breath. "And thank you for being willing to step in, even though I didn't need it." Taking on a belligerent cop wasn't something everyone would do.

"You're very welcome," he said with a grin. "Even though you didn't need it."

Smarty pants.

Nine

Kari awoke to the sound of barking dogs and some other noise that her subconscious said meant trouble. She had been up late working on paperwork and had barely fallen asleep when the noise started, so she hadn't even needed the kitten to alert her.

"Darn it, not again," she muttered as she threw on her jeans and tee shirt. As she ran out the door, she could hear the phone begin to ring behind her. "On it, Mr. Lee. I'm on it."

The sandals she'd shoved her feet into flapped on the rough path as she hurried toward the shelter. The moon was nearly full overhead, shining so brightly that she hardly needed the flashlight. This was starting to feel like one of those nightmares that repeated itself over and over.

"Not the new paint job," she said to herself, or maybe the universe. "Please let it just be a bear." At her feet, the black kitten kept pace easily, having somehow made it out the door while Kari was distracted.

"If it's a bear, save yourself," Kari said, panting as she

drew up in front of the building. She really needed to get a gym membership, now that she could afford one. Not that she had the time to use it, but still.

The moonlight glinted off something clear and glittery lying on the ground. "CRAP," Kari said with feeling, scooping up the kitten so she wouldn't cut her paws on the broken glass. "No bear did that, Queenie."

All the windows at the front of the shelter were broken. Not just broken, but smashed to smithereens, even the wooden framing hanging crooked in places. The sound of the breaking glass must have been what woke her up. Inside the shelter, the dogs were howling, and faint frantic meows could be heard from the direction of the feline room.

The animals! Kari had a sudden panicked vision of the cats being sprayed by sharp-edged glass. The dog kennels didn't have windows, but the big feline space did. If the vandal had broken those . . .

She ran around the left side of the building, trying to hold on to the kitten and use her cell phone at the same time. Despite the late hour, it only rang a couple of times on the other end before the person she was calling picked up.

"What's wrong?" Suz said, sounding ridiculously calm and alert.

"Someone broke a bunch of windows at the shelter," Kari said, coming to a screeching halt as she faced the rest of the disaster. "Maybe all the windows, darn it. There's broken glass in the cat room. Can you come help?"

"On my way," Suz said. "What about the cops?"

"That's my next call, but I don't expect a lot of sympathy," Kari said. "Deputy Carter was here today, well yesterday now, reading me the riot act for interfering in the investigation."

"Call them anyway," Suz said. In the background, Kari could hear noises that were presumably her friend getting dressed in as big a hurry as she had.

"Wear boots," Kari warned. "There's glass everywhere. I'm going to have to go back to the house to change out of my sandals and lock up the kitten. And I guess I'd better call Mr. Lee to explain what's going on before he calls the police."

"Well, that's one approach to getting them out there," Suz said, practical as usual. "I'm on my way. Ten minutes, tops."

It was actually more like eight, but felt like forever. By the time Suz got there, Kari had called the police; her part-time worker Jim, who she knew only lived a few miles away; and after some hesitation, Bryn. She had a feeling the girl would never have forgiven Kari if she hadn't. The sheriff's department said they'd send someone, but they hadn't sounded as though they felt any sense of urgency about it, since she told them there was no sign of the intruder still being in the area.

Luckily, Jim and Bryn took the situation more seriously and drove into the lot soon after Suz did. Their tires grinding on the gravel were like music to her ears.

Kari had already unlocked the side door and gone into the back to try to calm the agitated dogs, but when the others got there, she returned to see them pulling various objects out of their vehicles. Jim had some large pieces of plywood and a tool box in the bed of his pickup truck, Suz had the small emergency kit she used if a dog she was grooming got nicked, and Bryn had brought extra brooms and dustpans.

"Did you take pictures?" Suz said in lieu of hello, nodding at everyone else and going over to give Kari a rare hug.

Kari shook her head. "I was mostly just thinking about the animals. We need to get into the feline room to make sure no one is hurt."

"I'll take the photos," Bryn said, pulling out her phone. "And then I'll start sweeping up the glass by the door, so we can at least get in and out without dragging more of it into the shelter and ruining the new floor."

Kari shot her a grateful glance. "Thanks. I went in through the side door, which doesn't have a window right next to it, so there is a clearer path. Suz and Jim, do you want to come with me to check on the cats?"

"Do you have any idea who did this?" Jim asked, grabbing one of the brooms as he followed her inside.

"Somebody who *really* doesn't like me or the shelter?" Kari guessed. "Other than that, I have no idea. I mean, presumably whoever vandalized the place the last time, unless we have two people who hate us."

"*Hate* is a pretty strong word," Jim said as they went in the side door. Lights blazed into the night, highlighting the extent of the damage. Luckily the window smasher hadn't made it inside—probably didn't want to stick around that long—but there was glass sprayed everywhere there had been a window. Glass crunched under their feet, even when Jim tried to sweep a clear path in front of them.

"Well, this isn't exactly a love letter. We clearly touched a nerve somewhere with our poking around," Kari said.

"The question is where," Suz said. "But for now let's figure out the best way to deal with this. We don't want to let the cats out, since there is as much glass out here as there is in there. Are they likely to make a run at the door when we open it?"

They were standing in front of an interior door newly painted a cheerful turquoise and neatly lettered with *Feline Shared Space* in cursive script. Unfortunately, the door was one solid piece, so there was no way to look inside.

"I doubt it," Kari said. "If they're really freaked out"—and from the sound of the yowling cries inside, they certainly were—"they're probably trying to hide. But why don't you and I go in first, and Jim can stand by the door until we're inside and catch anyone who bolts."

"Good idea," Suz said. "Hang on." She ran back to the main room and grabbed a couple of large cat carriers. The shelter had plenty of the hard-sided plastic carriers in various sizes, since any resident who was in the cages in the main room had to be put in one while their cage was being cleaned, and animals were often transported to the vet, spay/neuter clinics, or foster homes in them. "We can put the cats in these until we can get the room cleaned up and safe."

"Hopefully no one has escaped through the broken windows," Jim said. "We'll have a heck of a time rounding them up if they have."

Kari groaned. She hadn't even though about that possibility.

She and Suz hurried into the room, wincing at the sight of broken glass at the base of the two windows. Fortunately, the vandal seemed to have expended most of his energy on the front of the shelter, or else he was rushing by the time he made it this far, so while the windows were cracked and splintered, they weren't as badly smashed as the ones out front.

Tripod meowed at them from his favorite bed near the door, clearly unhurt, and Kari passed him back out to Jim to put into another carrier.

One by one they plucked terrified cats from the tops of the cat trees, underneath the tables, and in Tabitha's case, out of the litter box she used more as a safe space than as a bathroom. Kari did a quick head count and breathed a sigh of relief—everyone was present and accounted for.

It appeared they'd gotten lucky with injuries too. Only two of the cats seemed to have gotten cut, probably because the first strike against the window would have scared them enough to make them move as far away as possible from the noisy threat to their usually tranquil sanctuary.

Felix, a large black-and-white male cat who was missing half of one ear and a piece of his tail from his days running wild, had a couple of minor cuts on his paws. Fortunately, he was much mellower than his battered appearance would lead one to believe, and he allowed Suz to take him into the small room that doubled as a surgery and exam room so she could clean the wounds and make sure there was no glass still in them.

Tinkerbell, unfortunately, hadn't been so lucky. A tiny once-feral cat who had been turned over to the shelter along with her newborn kittens, the calico had never mellowed enough to be adopted. She spat at Bryn when the girl tried to get close enough to figure out where the blood in Tinkerbell's fur was coming from.

Bryn talked to the cat in a soothing tone all the while speaking in an aside to Kari. "We're going to need Dr. McCoy, if you think he'll come out at this time of night. I think she needs stitches." The petite calico hissed at Bryn from where she was backed into a corner. "And probably a sedative, frankly."

Kari felt like she could use a sedative herself, but that would have to wait until the crisis was over. "I'll try calling him. Do you think you can catch her and get her into the treatment room without getting scratched?"

"Grab me a big towel," Bryn said. "This girl and I go way back. We'll be fine. If I can get a towel wrapped around her, she'll calm down some. I think it makes her feel less vulnerable."

Kari ran to get a clean towel from the long shelf that lined the hallway between the rooms and handed it to Bryn. She watched long enough to see that the girl was okay and able to grab poor Tinkerbell, then walked back into the main room, where Jim had stacked all the cat carriers against the wall as far from the mess as possible and was sweeping the broken glass into one corner.

"Bryn and Suz got the last of the cats out of the feline room," she told him. "If you could put plywood over those windows, we can clean up the glass in there first. We'll have to sweep up the big pieces, then damp mop, and vacuum all the cat trees and rugs. At least we can just toss new clean bedding in there, so we'll know that's okay."

She could have wept at the thought of all the work it would take to make sure the place was completely free of even the tiniest sliver. But she told herself it could have been worse—at least it happened when they weren't up and running at full capacity.

Leaning against the wall, feeling half-crushed by exhaustion and anger, she called and woke up Angus, who promised to drive right over. She felt like she could have stayed propped up there forever, or at least for five minutes to catch her breath, but flashing red lights warned her of the belated arrival of the law.

She was pretty sure that if Deputy Carter walked through that door with his bristling mustache and snarky attitude, she was going to burst into tears.

Thankfully, however, it was the sheriff himself, with a very nervous Overton trailing behind him.

"Quite the mess you have here," Sheriff Richardson said. "Somebody *really* doesn't like you."

"I kind of got that message," Kari said wearily. "And I'm such a sweet and charming person, too."

The sheriff surprised her by laughing at her lame joke. "You're not bad, as murder suspects go. Believe me, I've met worse." He turned to the young deputy, who was still hovering in the doorway. "What the heck is wrong with you, Overton? Just because it is Carter's night off and he isn't here to hold your hand doesn't mean you don't have to do your darned job."

"It's okay, Deputy," Kari said. "The dogs are all locked up. And there are no windows in their kennels, so you won't have to go anywhere near them. As long as you don't mind cats, you should be fine."

The man's overly broad shoulders stopped hunching up by his ears and he relaxed enough to come inside. "Oh, good. I like cats. My mom has one."

"Jeez, Overton," Richardson said, rolling his eyes. "I don't care if your mother has a pet boa constrictor. Go get the camera and take pictures of the crime scene, will you?" He glanced around. "I see you've already started cleaning up. You really should have left things the way you found them, Ms. Stuart."

Kari grimaced. "There were broken windows in the feline room, Sheriff. We have two cats that were injured as it is. If we'd waited, there might have been more."

"Hmmm," he said. But he didn't disagree. Kari remembered Sara telling her he was a dog lover, so maybe he cared about the animals after all. It was just her he didn't like. Ironically, that actually made her feel better.

He pulled out a notebook and had her run through everything that had happened from the time the noise had woken her up. At one point, Angus came in, medical bag in hand, and nodded at her as he walked through on his way back to the treatment area.

"Well, there isn't much we can do here," Richardson finally said, flipping his notebook shut with a sigh. It occurred to her that he was probably almost as tired as she was.

"What about taking fingerprints or something?" she asked.

"Of what?" Richardson gestured at the piles of glass on the floor. "Those? Besides, you've had volunteers, employees, and workmen coming through here for days. There's no way to eliminate all those people. Not to mention that the culprit probably used something like a baseball bat and then took it away with him."

"Or her," Suz said cheerfully from where she was taping heavy plastic over the empty frame of a window. They'd run out of plywood already. "Never underestimate the power of a pissed-off woman."

The sheriff gazed at her, taking in her height and the muscles that came from wrangling hundred-pound dogs, and nodded.

"Okay, or her. But either way, the odds are against our finding out who did this, unless someone saw or heard something suspicious and comes forward to report it." He rubbed one hand through the stubble just starting to come out on his chin. "My recommendation, Ms. Stuart, is that you get an alarm system and some security cameras. That way if your unwanted visitor comes back, you might end up with something we can work with. Or scare him"—he glanced at Suz—"or *her* off before they can do any more damage."

"Security systems are pretty expensive, aren't they?" Kari asked.

The sheriff waved one hand around the room. "Cheaper than having to replace all your windows and repaint the place on a regular basis, I'd say."

He had a point. Besides, Mr. Lee would *love* the sound of an alarm going off in the middle of the night. Nothing like making friends with your neighbors.

Kari sat at the front desk, one hand propping up her aching head as she gazed blearily at pictures of alarm systems on the Internet. They'd finally gotten things as under control as possible by around three in the morning. Tinkerbell's cut was stitched up and she was settled into one of the cages in the main room until it healed enough and Angus decided it was safe for her to go back in with the others. As far as Kari was concerned, the vet was her knight in shining armor. He hadn't even let her pay him, although she'd vowed to herself that she'd find some way to show her appreciation when things had calmed down.

The windows in the feline room were secured with plywood, although a local company was due to come this afternoon and replace all the glass. This time she was going to spend the extra money for the more expensive safety glass that would break into tiny harmless pieces, although just for that space. The rest of the shelter would get regular glass, which would be costly enough. She didn't know if the person who broke the windows was trying to scare her or punish her, but mostly they were really starting to piss her off.

In the meanwhile, the other cats had also been placed in the largest of the individual cages, some of them together, if they got along. Once the windows were repaired and the volunteers had come in and finished the cleanup, they could go back into their room.

She'd sent Suz and Bryn home to get some rest, but Jim had insisted on sleeping at the shelter, just in case their intruder came back. He'd hauled a sleeping bag out of the back of his truck and spread it out in the middle of the floor, and there had been no budging him. Jim was what Daisy referred to as a diamond in the rough—his manners weren't very polished and he wasn't well educated, but his dedication to the animals made those things seem incidental and unimportant. Initially, his head-to-toe tattoos and lack of conversation had made Kari doubt him, but after tonight she'd never do that again.

He'd finally left around eight when everyone else showed up to do the morning feed and clean. Once the other volunteers and part-time employee Emma had been brought up to speed, and Sara had finished complaining that no one had woken her up to come help, he'd finally agreed to go get some breakfast.

Now it was a little after eleven and things were almost back to normal. All the glass had been swept up and placed in the dumpster, the floors had been mopped and vacuumed twice, and the dogs had been walked as far away from the areas of destruction as possible. Other than the occasional vocal complaint about being locked into cages instead of roaming free in their room, the cats seemed to have recovered from the trauma of the night before.

Kari wished she could say the same.

It wasn't that she was having doubts, exactly. She still believed that buying the shelter had been the right thing to do, and despite the fact that her lottery winnings were

disappearing at a slightly faster rate than she'd antici-
pated, there was still plenty left for the long-term work of
saving as many animals as possible.

It was just that, well, she hadn't been expecting all the
rest of this. The dead body—that was *really* unexpected,
but in a way, it wasn't the worst of it. (Although the nightmares of those ghastly staring eyes could stop any time
now.)

But the vandalism, and the clear malice behind it, that
was starting to wear on her, along with the late nights and
the constant frustrations. Part of her wanted to give up
on trying to figure out who had killed Bill Myers in the
hope that whoever was targeting the shelter would lay off
if they did. But as Suz had said last night when Kari had
voiced that thought aloud, as long as the real killer was
unidentified, Kari and Daisy and Bryn's aunt Izzy were
all in danger of being arrested. And then there was poor
Buster.

As if her thinking about the issue had conjured up one
more problem, a dark green SUV with magnetic *County
Dog Warden* signs on the sides pulled into the parking lot.

Kari stared at her empty coffee cup. She had really
hoped to get more sleep before she had to deal with the
new dog warden, but apparently neither the sleep gods nor
the coffee gods were on her side today. If there were run-
down-rescue gods, they had been conspicuously absent
since she made her first appearance, although Sara kept
insisting they'd sent Kari in the first place.

A compact but muscular man wearing a simple uniform of khakis and a tan work shirt pushed open the front
door and looked around. He had short dark hair and green
eyes that were surprisingly vivid in his tanned face, which
made it clear he spent more time outside than sitting be-

hind a desk in an office. Kari thought he was probably about her age, although it was hard to tell for sure.

"Hello," he said, pleasantly enough. "I'm looking for Kari Stuart or Daisy Parker."

Kari came forward to greet him, trying to remind herself that just because the last dog warden had turned out to be an evil man who didn't care about animals, that didn't mean his replacement was the enemy. She hoped her doubt and nerves didn't show. Queenie, who had been sleeping in a box of papers on the desk, lifted her head in interest but didn't bother to get up.

"Hi," she said. "I'm Kari. What can I do for you?"

"I'm Jack Falco, the new dog warden," he said, holding out one callused hand for a firm handshake. "I'm here to follow up on a report about a dog named Buster."

Kari took a step backward. "Oh," she said flatly. "I see."

"I'm trying to get up to speed on all the pending cases listed in my predecessor's files," he explained. "There seem to be a lot of them."

"Yes," Kari said in a dry tone. "From what I can tell, he was very enthusiastic about his job."

"That's one way of putting it," Falco said. "I just moved to the area, but I was the dog warden in the city I lived in back in Ohio, and I didn't have half the cases he did." He gazed at the wide swaths of plastic covering the holes in the walls. "Are you renovating? Most people don't remove the old windows until they have new windows to put in. This really isn't safe for the animals."

Kari hadn't had either enough sleep or enough coffee for this conversation. "You don't say. That never would have occurred to me." She moved toward the coffeemaker, which had thankfully been in the glass-free zone. "Can I make you a cup of coffee, Mr. Falco?"

"No, thank you." He made a few notes on the clipboard he was carrying. "Can you tell me when you intend to have new windows put in?"

She poured cream into her coffee, put the container back into the mini fridge that had been added to the main room during the renovations, and added a spoonful of sugar. After a moment's hesitation, she put in a second one. Kari had a feeling her morning was going to need all the sweetening it could get.

Taking a deep breath, she turned back around to face the new dog warden, trying to plaster a convincing smile on her face. From his expression, she wasn't sure she'd completely succeeded.

"I'm sorry, Mr. Falco. It was a long night. Someone vandalized the place last night and broke all the windows, as you can see. We were up late taking care of the cats who were in a room with broken glass, and trying to clean up the mess." She took a long swig of coffee. "I'm afraid you're not catching me at my best."

His eyes widened. "Someone did this on purpose? Why?"

Kari shrugged. "Your guess is as good as mine," she said. "Apparently whoever did it wasn't an animal lover." For a split second she wondered if the Lees had come over from next door and trashed the place in an effort to get them to leave, so their nights would be quieter. But she dismissed the thought as crazy, even for her.

"Were any of the cats hurt?" the dog warden asked, the lines around those remarkable eyes deepening with concern. "What about the dogs?" He glanced at his clipboard again. "You still have some of both here, correct?"

"Yes, that's right," Kari said, trying not to overreact to his official tone. He was just doing his job, after all. "Eight dogs and twelve cats. Usually the older cats are in the feline room, but we don't want to put them back in there until the windows are replaced. The glaziers are coming later this afternoon," she said, only a little defensively. "I'm paying them extra to fit us in right away.

"Anyway, in answer to your questions, only two of the cats were hurt, and the vet has already been out to take care of them. The dogs are all fine. The kennels don't have windows in them."

"They really should," Falco said. "All animal areas are required to have adequate ventilation."

Kari thought he sounded as though he had memorized the rule book. Luckily, so had she. "'For natural ventilation to be effective, it must function well in all types of weather. Since favorable external winds and weather conditions cannot always be relied upon, vents should be installed to increase air circulation.'"

She walked back to the desk and held up the big blue binder they kept there with copies of all the forms the shelter used, rules for cleaning and feeding the animals, volunteer duties, and the section she had just quoted from, the entire mandated state code for shelters. "We have vents. We will also be installing air-conditioning, but it's on the Need list, not the Do Yesterday list."

Kari was pretty sure she was babbling. But hey, she'd only had three hours of sleep, and it had been a stressful night.

Falcon held up one hand. "I'm sorry, we seem to have gotten off on the wrong foot. I wasn't criticizing. You clearly are well aware of the regulations. It had been my understanding that the shelter was in violation of a number of the codes, but perhaps my predecessor was mistaken."

She slumped against the desk, letting the book fall

onto the surface with a thud. "There were a few issues, all of them due to lack of money. Daisy, the former owner, was trying to stem a flood with a teacup, but she did the best she could, and helped a lot of animals that wouldn't have been helped otherwise. Now that I own the place, I'm getting everything up to speed as fast as I can."

"Ah, I see." Falco nodded, giving her a sympathetic look. "Bit off a little more than you can chew, eh?"

Kari rolled her eyes, irrationally peeved at him despite that fact that he was only saying what she'd been thinking right before he walked in. "It would be a lot easier if I weren't having to deal with vandalism on top of everything else."

Falco stared at her. "This wasn't the first incident?"

"Second," she said. "The first time someone painted *murderer* and *whore* in bright red paint all over the newly redone exterior. Well, *hore*." She spelled it out for him.

"Ouch," he said, wincing. "Maybe you should get a security system."

She pointed at the computer screen. "I was working on just that when you interrupted me."

He winced again. "Sorry. I'm just doing my job. I'll try to get out of your hair as soon as possible. What can you tell me about this dog Buster?"

"No, I'm sorry," Kari said, wiping one hand over her face. "I don't mean to be rude. I'm just tired and frustrated."

"We seem to be apologizing to each other a lot," Falco said with a crooked smile. "Shall we try again? Hello, I'm Jack Falco, and I am the new dog warden. I promise, I'm one of the good guys."

That remained to be seen, depending on how things went with Buster, she thought. But at least she could give him the benefit of the doubt for now.

"Why don't you come back and meet Buster?" she suggested, waving him toward the door that led to the dog kennels. "He's really a sweetheart. No one who works here believes that he bit anyone." She turned to the desk. "Queenie, we're going to go visit Buster. Do you want to come?"

Queenie jumped off the desk and sauntered toward them, her tail straight up in the air and her small face eager as she walked to the door.

Falco raised an eyebrow. "You let that kitten go in the dog area?"

"It's less a matter of 'letting' and more a matter of her going wherever she wants," Kari explained. "She's my personal cat, not one of the shelter's. In fact, she's the reason I ended up owning the place. I found her as a stray not too long ago and she's been bossing me around ever since."

To Kari's surprise, the dog warden laughed. "I have one of those. Her name is Sugarsnap and she's a rescue too. She's a tortoiseshell and she's got 'torti-tude' in spades. I named her Sugarsnap because you never know if she's going to curl up with you sweetly or go for your throat. Mostly I find it easier to just do what she wants."

Kari laughed back at him. "Queenie never seems to get nasty, but she can definitely give attitude with the best of them." She opened the door. "Come on in. I apologize in advance for the noise. The place could use sound baffles but they're pretty low on the list right now."

The dogs started barking as soon as they entered the kennels, and a few of the more exuberant ones jumped up and down at the front of their cages. They stopped in front of the pit bull, and Queenie immediately squeezed through the space underneath the kennel door and went inside to leap on her buddy's back. They could hear her purring from where they were standing. Buster reached his massive head around and gave her a lick that almost sent her tumbling to the floor.

"Well," Falco said. "Isn't that something. You're sure she's safe with him?"

Kari didn't bother to say anything, since the answer was clear. Instead, she just pulled a couple of treats out of her pocket and put her hand through the bars to allow Buster to snuffle them out of her fingers. He sat down on his haunches, giving them the typical lolling-tongue pittie grin and a friendly woof. Queenie slid down onto the floor and looked up at him reproachfully but stayed right by his side.

"Buster, this is Jack. Can you say hi?" Daisy had been spending extra time with the dog, just in case, and had taught him a couple of tricks. Now he put one paw out and barked. Kari thought it was the cutest thing she'd ever seen.

Apparently Falco wasn't immune either. "I have to say, he sure doesn't act like any vicious dog I've ever met. Although sometimes aggressive behavior is situational. Ms. Parker's statement says that he gets along with other dogs, even the smaller ones?"

"He does." Kari nodded. "Dogs, cats, people. Like I said, he's a sweetheart. There's no way he bit that man, not even if he was provoked. I know pit bulls look fierce, but Buster doesn't have a mean bone in his body."

"How do you explain the report, then?" Falco asked, holding out his clipboard.

"I'll tell you how I explain it," Kari said. "Myers lied."

Falco's jaw dropped. "Are you accusing him of falsifying a report that would label a dog as dangerous and lead to him being euthanized? No dog warden would do that!"

"You didn't meet this one," Kari said, bitterly. She reached through the bars and scratched Buster on the head, then snapped her fingers at Queenie to signal that they were leaving.

"I'm sorry, but I can't believe any dog warden would do such a thing," Falco said. "I'm still trying to track down the man who was bitten, but when I do, I'm afraid this will have to go back to court."

Their brief détente seemed to have vanished, and Kari walked back out front with him without either one of them saying another word.

♟ Ten

That night, after all the work was done at the shelter and everything was quiet (at least for the moment), Suz, Sara, and Kari gathered together at Kari's house over pizza and wine to look at the records Rachel had given them. Bryn was at her other part-time job and couldn't join them, although they'd promised to report to her if they came up with anything useful.

After a brief argument about which kind of pizza to get—Suz insisted that putting pineapple on pizza was an abomination and Sara hated pepperoni, so they ended up with sausage and mushroom on one half and extra cheese on the other half—and whether you should have red wine or white with pizza (they eventually opened a bottle of each), they finally sat down to eat.

Kari's house was still not really set up for visitors, although it was better than her apartment had been. At least she had an actual living room, a kitchen, and a dining area downstairs, with two reasonably sized bedrooms upstairs. And a bathroom on each floor, which she considered the height of luxury (even if they were both out-of-date and decorated in the height of 1960s style).

She still hadn't gotten around to buying a new couch, although her ratty old sofa had at least been dressed up by a pretty garnet-colored cover that Suz had given her as a housewarming present, and her battered recliner had been so uncomfortable, Kari hadn't even bothered to move it. So for this meeting, she had pulled one of the folding chairs she used at the kitchen table over to where Sara and Suz sat on the couch, and they spread both food and folders out on the low wooden coffee table that lived in front of the sofa.

For a while there was silence as they ate and passed the paperwork around the table. Queenie snitched a couple of tiny pieces of cheese and then retreated to the top of the cat tree to supervise.

"Huh," Suz said finally, pouring a little more Chablis into her glass. "She wasn't wrong. Rachel, I mean. There's something not quite right here. It would help if we had other records to compare these to—previous dog wardens, or some kind of general statistics—but it looks to me like there are an awful lot of cases for one dog warden."

"That's what Jack Falco, the new warden, said," Kari admitted, reluctant to give him any credit at all. She had already told them about the rest of his visit.

"Not just a lot of cases, but especially those that involve loose dogs, dogs without tags, and dogs that are off their owners' property," Sara added. "All of which are circumstances when a dog warden can seize a dog and write a ticket. Some of those tickets end up being pretty expensive, especially for repeat offenders."

She tapped her fingers on the table. "Not that I'm advocating allowing dogs to run around willy-nilly. There's a guy in my neighborhood who never ties up his beagle, and the thing is always wandering into my yard and digging up my flowers."

Kari held up a couple of pieces of paper. "There's definitely something not kosher going on here, although I can't for the life of me figure out how he benefits. I mean, the dog warden position is salaried, right? The money for the fines goes to the town, as I understand it."

Suz nodded. "It does. But you're right about something being off with these records." She grabbed a brownie off a plate in the middle of the table that Sara had brought with her. "Mmmm. You make the best brownies, Sara."

"I add three different kinds of chocolate chips," Sara said with a smile. "It's hard to mess that up." She reached for one herself.

"There's something else odd here," Kari said after jotting down some notes. "Did either of you notice that Deputy Carter's name seems to crop up in these reports a lot?"

Sara chewed the piece of brownie in her mouth and swallowed before answering. "I did, but I thought maybe it was just a coincidence."

"I don't see how it can be a coincidence that he seems to come across a large number of loose or dangerous dogs while he's out on patrol," Kari said. "I mean, maybe he just happens to patrol neighborhoods with an unusual amount of irresponsible owners, but it doesn't seem likely."

"No, it doesn't," Suz said, her brow wrinkled. "But it doesn't make a lot of sense. A deputy wouldn't benefit from large numbers of dogs being ticketed any more than the dog warden would. I can't imagine the sheriff giving him a merit raise for harassing dog owners."

Sara shook her head. "We can't ask Myers about it because he's dead."

"I'm sure as heck not going to ask Deputy Carter," Kari said. "Somehow I don't see that going over well."

"I'll tell you what," Suz said. "I recognize some of the names on these lists of folks who got repeated tickets. I groom their dogs. Maybe I can try talking to a few of them and see if they have explanations that aren't obvious to us."

They kicked around a few more ideas, but didn't really accomplish anything other than putting a noticeable dent in the plate of brownies. Suz and Sara finally left around nine, promising to keep thinking about the information. They all had the nagging feeling they were missing something, but they couldn't figure out what.

I n the morning, things didn't exactly improve.

"You have *got* to be kidding," Kari said when she opened the door at seven to find her brother standing there, a big grin on his handsome face.

"Hi, sis!" Michael Stuart Jr., known as Mickey, was three years younger than her and they couldn't have been more different. The long-awaited son had been spoiled rotten as a child and had already been running wild by the time their mother died of cancer when he was sixteen. Without her influence to restrain him, and with Michael Sr. as an example, he'd taken up drinking, drugs, smoking, and motorcycles. Not necessarily in that order.

Like his father, he was absurdly attractive and charming to women of all ages, many of whom he lived off until he got tired of them or they got tired of his complete lack of responsibility. He blew into Kari's life every once in a while, usually when he wanted something. She loved her little brother, but she had given up any illusions she had about him long ago.

His curly brown hair was neatly trimmed and his large brown eyes with their ridiculously long eyelashes seemed clear, albeit filled with dancing laughter. A fancy bright red Honda motorcycle sat next to her beat-up Toyota, which she still hadn't gotten around to replacing.

"Hello, Mickey," she said, more resigned than upset. "You might as well come in."

Her brother jerked his head toward the field. "Are those chickens?"

The birds in question were wandering slowly in the direction of where he'd parked his bike, probably attracted by all that shiny metal. The chickens, which had belonged to Daisy and which Kari had apparently inherited along with everything else at the sanctuary, were brown and tan, and free range in the most extreme example of the word. She never had any idea where she was going to find them, although at night they usually made their way back to their coop without too much encouragement.

Periodically she found pale green or brown eggs that some hen had laid and then wandered off and forgotten about. Kari wondered if she was a bad person if she kind of hoped one would find its way onto her brother's flashy motorcycle.

"Yes, they are," Kari said. "And no, I'm not going to give you any money, if that's why you came."

Mickey just chuckled. "How about some breakfast, then? I've been driving for hours."

He grabbed a piece of toast as he sat down, the one she'd been just about to eat when he knocked on the door.

Kari put a cup of coffee in front of him and got one for herself before joining him. She might as well get this over as soon as possible so she could get back on with her life.

"This is charming, sis," Mickey said, waving the piece of toast at Kari, splattering marmalade onto the floor. Fred, who was sitting in his usual spot under the table, cleaned it up right away, his tail wagging. Unlike Queenie, who looked as though she was reserving judgment, Fred was fairly indiscriminating in his affection for people.

"Hi, Fred," Mickey said, having met the dog on previous visits. "Cute kitten. Is she new?" He went on without waiting for Kari to answer. "You know, sis, I could never understand why you chose to come back to this hick town after your divorce. And now you've actually moved even farther away from the little bit of civilization available in town to live in this shack miles away from anything. What on earth were you thinking?"

I was thinking you'd never come looking for me here, for one thing. "I like it out here," she said in an even tone. "And the house comes with the shelter next door, which is really why I bought the property."

Her brother stared at her. "You *bought* this shack? And a *shelter*? Why on earth would anyone buy a shelter?"

"So I could do something good with my life. Something that helps both animals and people. I realize that's not anything you would ever consider doing with a lottery win, but it makes me happy." Kari sipped her coffee calmly. *Wait for it . . .*

"Ah, well, if it makes you happy, sis," Mickey said, shaking his head. "You know I've never wanted anything but the best for you. I couldn't believe it when an old friend from town sent me a copy of the newspaper article with your picture on the front page. Congrats."

"Thank you," Kari said. "You are so kind. I'm still not giving you any money. You'd just blow it on women and booze and goodness knows what else. Besides, I'm spending pretty much all of it fixing up the shelter." She looked around at the house, which was in truth, kind of a wreck, although a reasonably cozy one. "And the house, eventually."

"I'm not drinking anymore, Kari," Mickey said. "No drugs either. Clean and sober for months now." He looked earnest, but with her brother it was always hard to tell.

"If that's true, I'm really pleased," Kari said. "But it doesn't change anything. You weren't around when I was poor or in the middle of a terrible divorce or grieving for Mom. So don't expect me to believe you suddenly find me fascinating just because I won a little money."

"Five million dollars isn't exactly 'a little money,' now, Kari," Mickey said. "Surely even with your pet project, there's enough to share with your family."

"Pet project, hah. Not one penny," Kari said. "And now that you've had breakfast, I'm going to have to ask you to leave. It has been great to see you, but I have work to get to, and this discussion is over. Scoot now."

Mickey shrugged. "What kind of work? I've got nothing planned and no place I have to be. Maybe I can help."

There was a first time for everything. "Oh, really? How do you feel about cleaning litter boxes and dog cages?" Kari crossed her arms, waiting for him to find some excuse to leave after all.

"I've done worse, I suppose," he said with a grin. "Come on, why don't you show me this money pit you've bought with the windfall you could have shared with me." Queenie got up and strolled to the door behind him and Kari gave up.

"Sure," she said. "Why not?" She gave a grin of her own at the thought of him trying to charm Sara, who'd (barely) put up with his antics in school. "And you're never going to believe who volunteers at the shelter. Boy, have I got a surprise for you."

Eleven

"Mickey Stuart," Sara said. "I should have known you'd turn up like a bad penny."

"Aw, Mrs. Hanover, you know I was always your favorite," Kari's brother said with a twinkle in his eye.

"I didn't have favorites," Sara said, shaking her head. "And if I did, you certainly wouldn't have been one of them." But a tiny smile played around the corner of her lips. The truth was, Mickey had charmed all the teachers too.

Around them the work of the morning was under way. All the windows had been replaced the previous day, so the cats were back in their room with the exception of the two sick kittens and Tinkerbell, who was still in a cage up front nursing a bandaged foot and a serious grudge. One of the volunteers was cleaning the litter and putting out new food and water for the cats in the feline room, while Jim was out back cleaning the dog kennels.

Sara and Bryn had been in the main room when Kari came in with her brother. Sara was working on the last of the paperwork and Bryn had the kittens and Tinkerbell in carriers so she could clean out their cages.

"Bryn, this is my brother, Mickey," Kari said. "Don't believe a word he says about anything."

"What kind of introduction is that?" Mickey said, an exaggerated hurt look on his face. "Especially to such a beautiful lady."

Bryn was wearing her faded work jeans and a worn tee shirt that said *I'm a vet tech. What's your superpower?* It already had several stains on it that were better left unidentified. "You're kidding me, right?" she said to Kari.

"I wish," Kari said. "He says he's willing to clean up poop. Feel free to put him to work."

"Oh, let me," Sara said with an evil grin. "The antibiotics Tinkerbell are on are giving her diarrhea."

"Don't worry," Bryn added. "I've got her on probiotics. She should be fine in a couple of days." With a deceptively benign smile, she handed Mickey a garbage bag, some paper towels, and the spray bottle of pet-safe cleaner. "But we wouldn't mind the help cleaning up in the meanwhile."

Mickey put on a brave face. "The things I do for love of my sister," he said.

"Or her lottery winnings," Kari muttered. But honestly, it was worth it to watch him try to win over Bryn while scrubbing out cages.

I've got *Stardust* and *When Harry Met Sally*," Suz said when she came over that evening for their weekly pizza and movie night. Neither of them cared that they'd already had pizza once that week. "And the latest Avengers movie in case you're in the mood for things blowing up."

"You have no idea," Kari said. "And there better be double cheese on that pizza."

"What am I, an amateur?" Suz said, putting the pizza box down on the kitchen table. "Of course there's double cheese. Tough day?" She gently removed Queenie from the table, where the kitten was continuing to ignore the "no cats on kitchen surfaces" rule.

"I've had better," Kari said. "But I've had worse. At least I didn't find any dead bodies."

"Always a plus," Suz said, grabbing plates down out of the cupboard. The kitchen was an improvement on the one in Kari's old apartment, in that it at least had adequate storage and counter space, even if what was there was all careworn and needed updating. The space opened to the living room area, which was convenient, and Kari thought that when she finally got around to redoing it, she'd install a nice eat-at central island between the two rooms. For now, though, she made do with the card table and four folding chairs.

"But my brother arrived this morning. It was that darned newspaper article. Someone sent him a copy."

Suz plopped the pizza and plates down next to the wine and put her hands on her hips, straightening up to her full imposing height. "I can't believe you didn't call me as soon as he got here. Please tell me you didn't give him any money."

"What am I, an amateur?" Kari responded, trying to figure out which of the three remotes she needed to start the movie. Once they'd grabbed their food, she and Suz would sit on the couch in front of the television, no doubt with the supervision of two cats, a kitten, and a dog.

"Mickey came over to the shelter for a while and tried

to pretend to be helpful, but he mostly got in the way and annoyed Sara and Bryn by trying to charm them." She snorted. "You should have seen his face when Tripod hobbled up and starting drooling on his designer sneakers."

Besides having only three legs, Tripod was missing most of his teeth, so he had an unfortunate tendency to dribble on innocent bystanders. It was one of the reasons he hadn't been taken in by any of the other shelters, since he was considered unadoptable. Daisy just shrugged and said every shelter needed a mascot, and Kari tended to agree with her.

"Ha," Suz said, a string of cheese hanging from her own mouth, making her look remarkably like the cat in question. "Speaking of money, and people trying to get it by nefarious means, I wanted to take another look at that paperwork Sara's friend Rachel put together for us."

"Sure," Kari said, getting up. She didn't bother to pause the movie, since they'd both seen it multiple times. "Guard my pizza, will you?" Three sets of feline eyes and one very sad canine pair gazed longingly at her plate until she returned with the folder and set it down in front of Suz. "Did something new occur to you?"

"Not new, exactly, just putting together a couple of the pieces we had already looked at separately." Suz wiped her hands on a napkin and pulled out some of the papers. "I wanted to compare some things side by side. Give me a minute."

Intrigued, Kari went back to watching the movie and gnawed on a crust until Suz was ready to share her idea. It didn't take long.

"Aha!" Suz said. She'd been jotting down some notes in the notebook Sara had brought over for them to keep track of clues, if they were lucky enough to come across any, or barring that, stray thoughts and theories.

"Aha?" Queenie had wormed her way onto Kari's lap, so she was using one hand to eat and the other to keep the kitten away from the food. At Suz's exclamation, Queenie suddenly focused her attention on the lavender-haired woman, as if she wanted to know what "aha" meant too.

"I noticed an interesting pattern the other night, but it didn't really sink in until I had some more time to think about it," Suz said.

Kari was a little confused. "You mean the pattern in the kind of tickets Myers gave out, and how often Deputy Carter's name showed up in his reports? We talked about that already."

"We did," Suz said. "But we didn't track it. Here, look." She tilted the notebook so Kari could see. "I broke down the bigger tickets—loose dogs, untagged dogs, dogs off their own properties, and so on—by date. About five years ago, Myers's records start showing a slow increase in these kind of tickets. Then, about a year later, Carter suddenly starts finding loose dogs when he is out on patrol, or calling in reports of dangerous animals."

"So Myers got more assertive about his job, and for some reason Carter decided to follow suit?" Kari pondered this possibility for a minute. "That doesn't really seem to fit what little we know of the two men. They hardly seem like the dedicated public servant types."

Suz shook her head, one lock of lavender hair falling into her eyes. "No, that's not my point at all. I think Myers figured out some way to make money off writing more tickets, and then somehow convinced Carter to help him. If you look at my timeline, the number of tickets has gone up gradually every year ever since, along with the number of dangerous dogs taken into custody."

"But how would they make money off the tickets? Don't the fines go to the town?" Kari took a sip of wine. "And wouldn't someone notice that they were both issuing more tickets?"

"Oh, people noticed, all right," Suz said, sounding grim. "Remember I said I was going to talk to my customers? I spent some time earlier today making phone calls, and heard the same story over and over again. Mrs. Swenson swears her Pekingese Peekaboo never left the backyard. There's a doggy door in the kitchen and a fenced yard, so the dog could go out during the day when Mrs. Swenson was at work. A couple of years ago, she got a call that Peekaboo had been picked up by the dog warden. Supposedly the dog had dug under the fence, but Mrs. Swenson never did find a hole."

"Well, dogs do dig," Kari said, playing devil's advocate.

"Uh-huh," Suz said. "So she paid the fine for a loose dog, and then the additional fee to collect the dog from the shelter where Myers had taken her. The impoundment fee is twenty dollars, plus a twenty-dollar-a-night charge payable to the shelter. On top of that, there is the cost of the ticket itself, which is twenty dollars for the first occurrence, forty for the second, and sixty for the third. Peekaboo supposedly got out three times, although Mrs. Swenson swears she checked the fence line every time. She finally ended up having to keep the dog inside when she was gone."

Kari did some quick math in her head. "Wow," she said. "So with three offenses, that's one hundred twenty dollars in fines, plus a minimum of sixty to the shelter, more if the dog ended up staying overnight." She whistled. "That's a lot of money."

"No kidding," Suz said. "Then multiply it by all these animals." She tapped her list of tickets issued over the last few years. "And of the customers I talked to, I had more than one who told me essentially the same story. Dogs that got out of previously secure yards. Dogs whose tags mysteriously disappeared between the time they got out and when they arrived at the shelter." She shook her head. "That's a whole separate fine, by the way. And if they're not wearing their rabies tags, you have to bring paperwork to the shelter to prove they've been vaccinated. Which is a good thing, theoretically."

"But not if someone is abusing the system," Kari said. "So your theory is that Myers was not just being more aggressive about writing tickets, but actually *purposely* creating the circumstances somehow by letting dogs out or removing their collars? That sounds crazy."

"Does it?" Suz asked, folding another piece of pizza in half and biting off the end, as if taking out her anger at the dog warden on the innocent dough and cheese. She washed it down with a hefty slug of wine and added, "You found the guy dead in the act of digging a hole under the shelter fence. Almost certainly so he could go after Buster. Face it, the man was crooked and lower than pond scum."

"Darn," Kari said. "And if Deputy Carter was in on it with him . . ." She drank some wine too. "No wonder he is being such a pain to me. He is probably worried I'm going to figure out what Myers was up to."

"You're going to have to talk to the sheriff," Suz said. "He needs to know what was going on, and that one of his officers was probably involved."

Kari dropped her head into her hands, and Queenie reached up and licked her chin. "That's going to go over well," she said, her words muffled. "I already alienated the new dog warden by suggesting that Myers made up the story about Buster biting someone. I'm sure the sheriff will be even less enthusiastic about our theories."

She sat up and gazed at Suz. "Are you sure you don't want to go talk to him instead? At least you're not a suspect in a murder investigation. And you're way more persuasive than I am."

"Sorry, no," Suz said. "It's your shelter, and your shelter dog that's being accused. I just helped you put together a few facts. I'm afraid you're the one who is going to have to go talk to him."

"Great," Kari said. "If he throws me in jail, will you feed the cats and Fred?"

🐈 Twelve

Sheriff Richardson listened to Kari without saying a word, and then looked through the paperwork and Suz's notes, still not commenting in any way other than an occasional grunt. His silence made her twitchy, which she suspected was its desired effect.

Finally he lifted his head and stared across his desk at Kari, gray eyes piercing and his expression neutral.

"So," he said, placing the papers on the tidy surface of the desk and straightening them until they sat in a neat, square pile. "Your theory is that the town dog warden, who held his position for ten years after a career in the military, and my deputy, who has been on this police force for over two decades and is barely more than a year away from retirement, colluded together to write unwarranted tickets to dog owners. And that they did this for profit, although you have not as yet come up with a theory as to how, in fact, they made money off this supposed scheme. Is that about it, Ms. Stuart, or am I leaving anything out?"

Kari sat up as straight as she could on the uncomfortable wooden chair that faced his desk. "That's about it for that part of what I came to tell you about, yes. Sir," she added hastily. "But I also wanted to tell you about a couple of possible suspects I found out about in talking to other people about Myers this last week. He made a lot of enemies during his time as dog warden, but there were two people who *really* hated him."

Richardson cocked one eyebrow and made a "go on" gesture with his hand. Kari had the sinking feeling he was just giving her the chance to dig herself into a deeper hole, but she owed it to Buster, and to Daisy and Izzy, to make sure he knew about everyone who had it in for Myers.

"As you know, Myers was trying to get one of the shelter's dogs, Buster, declared a dangerous dog. He apparently did this at an unusually high rate, leaving the dog owners furious and heartbroken." She cleared her throat, trying not to wiggle in her chair. The sheriff's undivided attention was a little nerve-racking.

"One of those owners is a college professor named Steve Clark, whose valuable purebred Irish wolfhound was accused of ravaging sheep. Myers seized the dog and had him euthanized, and Clark swears that not only did the dog not chase sheep, but there was no way he could have kept getting out without human intervention. I talked to the professor, and he is still really angry about the whole incident."

"I see," the sheriff said. "And your other suspect, Miss Marple?"

Oh, funny. Now he's comparing me to an Agatha Christie old-lady snoop. Of course, that snoop had solved a lot of crimes. Kari just wanted to solve one.

"Georgia Travis. She's a former state trooper, so she is

probably pretty tough. Myers seized her retired police dog, supposedly for uncontrolled aggressive tendencies stemming from neglect and abuse."

Richardson's eyebrow went up higher. "Is that so?"

"It doesn't seem likely that she would fight so hard to be allowed to adopt the dog and then abuse it, and according to the court papers, she denied it vehemently and accused Myers of making the whole thing up."

Kari swallowed hard, thinking about their own situation.

"He had all the necessary documentation, so the judge had no choice but to rule in his favor and allow him to take the dog." If she couldn't fix things, it seemed all too likely that the same fate awaited poor Buster. "So Georgia had motive too, plus, presumably, experience with violence."

"It might surprise you, Ms. Stuart," Richardson said in an even tone, "but I was already well aware of both Steve Clark and Georgia Travis. I didn't get this job because of my charm and good looks, you know."

Heat rose in Kari's face. "I, uh, no, sir. I mean, yes, sir." *Aw, crap.* "I wasn't trying to suggest the police weren't on top of things. I was just afraid—"

"You were just afraid that I'd already decided that either you or one of your friends was guilty, and had stopped looking for other suspects," he finished for her. "You may be at the top of my list, Ms. Stuart, but that doesn't mean the case is closed. You'll know when that happens because someone will be arrested for the murder of Bill Myers." He gave her a look that made her think he was envisioning her in handcuffs.

"As it happens, both Steve Clark and Georgia Travis were already known to us, since they had both lodged official complaints against the dog warden, although nothing ever came of them. Steve Clark's only alibi is his wife, who not only admits that she sleeps like a rock but freely told us that she was glad Myers was dead. So he's still on our radar, although I'm not convinced that revenge is a good enough motive in this case. If the dog was still alive and he could have saved it, maybe." He looked pointedly at her, reminding her that this was a potential motive for either her or Daisy.

He tapped his fingers on the file. "Georgia Travis, on the other hand, while absolutely livid about the loss of her dog, couldn't have committed the crime. You see, she had to leave the force because she was shot in the shoulder. She was deemed too disabled to be able to work because of a permanent weakness in that arm. So while she might have wanted to kill Bill Myers, she didn't have the upper body strength to have wielded that snare pole."

Kari could have sworn she saw the hint of a smile as he added, "I know Georgia, and if she'd decided to kill Myers, she would just have taken out her old service revolver and shot him between the eyes."

"Oh," Kari said. "Well, I'm sorry to have wasted your time, Sheriff."

He sighed, flipping open the folder again. "I wouldn't say that, Ms. Stuart. You're still a good suspect, and I sure as heck hope you didn't dig up this dirt just to try to throw me off your trail. Or that of any of your friends. If so, I assure you it isn't going to work. However"—he grimaced—"I think there is enough evidence here for me to look into what dealings Mr. Myers and my deputy had together, if any. What you've given me doesn't prove anything, but it definitely stinks to high heaven."

The sheriff didn't look happy as he escorted her to the door of his office. Kari could only hope that his ire was aimed at Deputy Carter and not at her. It was distinctly possible she'd made things worse instead of better.

On her way back to the shelter, Kari stopped at the bakery and bought a dozen donuts for the staff and volunteers. Okay, maybe there was a chocolate with chocolate frosting that had her name on it. It had been a rough morning. The smell of yeast and sugar that permeated the small shop had lifted her spirits as soon as she walked in. It had about a dozen tables, most with two scrollback chairs with paisley padded seats, although there were a few that could seat four instead.

A glass case filled with pastries took up most of the space at the far end of the room, along with a counter with thermal jugs filled with various types of coffee, all labeled in beautiful script. According to the blackboard propped on a standing easel by the door, today's specials were maple baklava (made with local maple syrup), Black Forest muffins, and Sumatran coffee. The owners, two sisters named Pansy and Petunia, were nothing if not eclectic. Luckily for Kari and everyone else who frequented the place, everything they sold was delicious.

Between the scents of the coffee brewing behind the counter and the attractive lineup of treats inside the glass case, Kari considered it nothing short of a miracle that she managed to make herself leave at all. As it was, she arrived back at the shelter with an extra bag full of muffins that smelled like chocolate heaven, and a to-go cup of Sumatran with extra cream, just because.

"How did it go?" Daisy asked as soon as Kari walked in the door. She was clearly asking about the visit to the sheriff, not the bakery.

The former owner still came by a few times a week, although Kari could tell she had purposely been trying to stay out of the way so Kari could make the place her own. And maybe so it wouldn't be quite as tough for Daisy to leave town once she'd been cleared of murder and the issue with Buster had been resolved.

Even when Daisy wasn't around, though, they'd been trying to keep her up to speed on everything that was going on. She'd really read Kari the riot act for not calling the night the windows got broken, although she admitted that Kari had handled it well.

Sara came out from behind the desk. "I'm glad you're back," she said. "I was starting to worry that the sheriff had gotten annoyed and thrown you into jail. Oh, donuts! Excellent."

"I can definitely see how worried you were," Kari said dryly, putting the bakery box down on the table next to the coffee maker. "I got maple glazed for you and jelly-filled for Bryn. Also, there are Black Forest muffins."

"Did someone say jelly-filled?" Bryn asked, coming through the door from the dog area. "Don't anyone eat mine while I wash my hands." She disappeared into the bathroom but popped back out quickly. "So what did the sheriff say?"

Kari pulled the folder out of her large shoulder bag and placed it on the desk. Queenie, who had been sleeping on top of the cat tree in the main room, raced over to greet Kari, purring as if they hadn't seen each other for days instead of just a couple of hours. Once Kari had poured her coffee into a real mug, grabbed her donut, and sat down behind the desk, Queenie leapt up to her usual post on Kari's shoulder.

Patting the kitten absently with the hand not holding the donut, Kari told the others about the interview with Sheriff Richardson.

"So I guess he believed me when I said that Myers and Carter were up to something funky, although the rest of the information we'd gathered was apparently old news," she said when she was done with her story. "But I'm not sure what good that does us."

She nodded at Daisy. "I think you and I are still at the top of the suspect list. You because of Buster and your long-standing feud with Myers, and me because I was found standing over the body with gloves in my back pocket after we'd been seen arguing in public after the hearing."

"What about my aunt?" Bryn asked. "Does he still think she might have killed Myers because he was hassling me?"

"I think so," Kari said. "But he wasn't exactly sharing his thoughts with me, beyond making it clear that he thought it was possible I was bringing him the information in an effort to distract him from my guilt or the guilt of one of my friends."

"And he was such a nice boy in school," Sara said, clucking her tongue. "Who knew he would grow up to be so suspicious?"

Kari laughed. "Well, you might say that's part of his job description. Queenie, what are you doing?" The kitten had hopped down off Kari's shoulder and was up to her usual tricks, shoving at the folder and moving it around. Before Kari could set the remains of her donut onto her napkin, Queenie had shoved the folder over the side of the desk. Paper rained down and spread out over the floor like confetti.

"Queenie, really," Kari said, getting down on her hands and knees to try to find all the contents. Bryn joined her, saying, "At least the new floor is cleaner than the old one." They both picked up handfuls of paperwork, now completely out of order, and handed it up to Sara, who tried to organize it.

"Hey," she said. "What's this?"

Kari stood up. "What's what?"

"I don't remember seeing this before," Sara said, a thoughtful tone in her voice. "I wonder if it was stuck between two other pieces of paper. Or maybe it was toward the back and we just didn't get that far the other night."

She held out what looked like an official form of some kind for the other three to look at. Kari narrowed her eyes at the kitten, who was seriously involved with washing her face and ignoring the rest of them completely.

"What is it?" Daisy asked.

"Answers to one of our questions, I think," Sara said in a grim voice. "It's an application to turn this building into a shelter that could be used to house animals picked up by the dog warden. It is signed by Bill Myers."

"That son of a gun," Daisy said, clenching her fists. "No wonder he was trying to drive me out. He wanted the sanctuary for himself."

"And if he could make things really difficult for you, he could get it at a cheap price," Kari said. "That explains a lot. Including why he went after Buster. You know, now I'm kind of sorry I wasn't the one who killed him."

"Me too," Daisy said through gritted teeth. "Heck, I'd like to steal his body from the morgue, bury him, dig him back up, and kill him all over again."

"As long as you're not holding a grudge," Sara said, nibbling daintily on the edge of a muffin and somehow miraculously not getting any crumbs on herself.

"Do you think that's why he was harassing Daisy so badly?" Bryn asked. "And then digging under the fence in a last-ditch attempt to cause trouble and make Kari change her mind about the shelter so she'd sell it to him?"

Daisy nodded. "The sad thing is, it probably would have worked. If he had succeeded in getting Buster loose again and persuaded the judge we couldn't be trusted to keep the animals safely contained, and Kari hadn't come along with her offer to buy the place, I'm not sure I would have been able to carry on." She pulled a tissue out of her pocket and blew her nose. "I was just so tired and worn down."

Sara patted her on the shoulder. "You did more with less for longer than most people would have, Daisy. You have nothing to feel guilty about."

"Unlike some dead dog wardens," Kari said, more grateful than ever that the fates had blessed her with that lottery win and a little black kitten to steer her in the right direction.

"You know, he was actually quite clever," Bryn said in a thoughtful tone.

"What?" a chorus of voices protested.

"I'm not saying he was a nice guy," the girl said. "Just that he came up with a heck of a scheme for making extra money from his job. Which I happen to know doesn't pay very well." When the others looked at her, she added, "I thought about applying for the position in Perryville when it opened up, but then I saw what it paid and realized I could make more working part-time as a desk clerk at the Lakeview Motel."

"So first he figures out a way to make more money from writing extra tickets, and gets the deputy involved in his plan somehow," Kari said, sipping at her coffee and definitely not thinking about getting another donut. Definitely not. "Although we still haven't discovered how he was making more money that way, since in theory all fines are paid to the town. But there has to have been some way, or he never would have gone to all this trouble."

"Right," Daisy said. "And if he could buy the shelter from me for way under market value, then he could also have charged the boarding and impoundment fees when owners reclaimed their dogs."

"Suz and I talked about those. They can add up to a *lot* of money," Kari said.

"Especially if he was skimping on the costs of taking care of the animals," Daisy said. "Which I'm guessing he would have." She scowled at her coffee cup, probably imagining dogs being fed the cheapest food possible and kept in underheated kennels.

"Huh," Sara said. "This is interesting." She had been examining the application more closely.

"What is?" Kari asked. She gave up and fetched the other donut, moving the kitten off her seat when she got back.

"There's a letter of recommendation attached to this," Sara said. "Saying how much money having a dedicated shelter would save the town, since at the moment they pay part of the cost toward maintaining a contract with the one they use. And suggesting that Myers would be the perfect person to run it, if they granted him the permits to buy this place for that use, since he would charge the town less."

"That's convenient," Bryn said. "Who is the letter of recommendation from, Deputy Carter?"

Sara narrowed her eyes at the paper, as if she could see through the sheets to some hidden meaning underneath. "No, that wouldn't have made much sense. But I'm not sure this does either. It's signed by Marge Farrow, the court clerk."

"Well, I guess she would know how much the fines add up to, since the penalties are usually read out in court, and she is in charge of collecting the money," Daisy said. "I had to write out a couple of checks to her, unfortunately, which is how I know." She tilted her head, thinking. "I don't think things like the impoundment fines go through her. They get paid directly to the shelter. But since she works at the town hall, it wouldn't be surprising if she is aware of what the town spends on that kind of thing."

"But why would she write a letter to support Bill Myers?" Kari said. "Were they friends?"

"Not that I know of," Sara said, fine wrinkles appearing on her forehead. "But I can think of one reason why she might do it."

"What's that?" Daisy asked.

"If she was in on the scheme, whatever it was," Sara replied. "In which case maybe Bill was going to give her a kickback if he got the shelter. They could have been in on it together."

"Wait, you mean that Bill Myers and Deputy Carter *and* Marge Farrow were all in on this together?" Bryn looked doubtful. "That is a heck of a conspiracy theory."

"I don't know," Daisy said slowly. "Think about it. We couldn't figure out how Myers and Carter would have been making money from writing more and more high-priced tickets, since the fines didn't have anything to do with them."

"But Marge Farrow is the court clerk, and handles the money from every ticket that is paid in court or for any court-related fees," Kari said, sitting up straighter and almost dislodging Queenie, who was perched on her shoulder again.

"Huh." Daisy petted Tripod, who tended to follow her around like a dog. "That would explain a lot. But you've met Marge. She hardly seems like the criminal type."

Sara gave a distinctly unladylike snort. "The most successful criminals don't exactly walk around advertising. And who better to get away with something than a middle-aged woman. Once you hit a certain age, you are nearly invisible."

"You're not invisible, Sara!" Bryn protested.

"You'd be amazed," Sara said, a rare hint of bitterness in her normally even tone. "But I also make an effort to stand out." She pointed at the turquoise streak in her hair. "Would you even recognize Marge if you met her outside the courtroom?"

Kari thought about it. "Maybe? Maybe not." She pondered for a moment. "Perhaps I should make up some kind of excuse to go talk to her, and see if I can get a better sense of the woman. I'm sure as heck not going back to Sheriff Richardson to accuse anyone else—much less the court clerk—of being involved in Bill Myers's nefarious activities until I have a lot more than just our suspicions."

"I still don't see the three of them working together. Myers and Carter are two of the worst misogynists I've ever met," Bryn said, fiddling idly with one of her braids. "They both seem to despise women out of general principles. Even when he was chasing after me, Bill Myers always treated me like I was some kind of lower life form, barely capable of making my own decisions. I can't see either of them being willing to work with a woman or trust one with anything important."

Daisy shrugged. "You're not wrong there. But maybe Marge was just a minor player who did what she was told? She doesn't seem very assertive."

"Don't mistake drab for stupid," Sara warned them. "I don't know if Marge is wrapped up in any of this or not, but Kari, I want you to be careful if you go talk to her. Remember—somebody killed Bill Myers. It might have been an angry dog owner, or it might have been something to do with this racket we think he was running. Until we find out for sure, you need to treat every suspect as a possible murderer. Even Marge Farrow."

ξ Thirteen

Sara's words were still ringing in Kari's ears as she walked into the court clerk's office, but looking at the woman sitting behind the desk, it was hard to imagine Marge Farrow hurting anyone.

Up close, Sara revised her estimate of the woman's age downward by about ten years. The neat but frumpy pantsuit and graying blond hair had given the impression of someone in her late fifties, but Marge had the relatively unlined face of someone in her midforties, with the exception of a few wrinkles around her faded cornflower blue eyes and the edges of her lips. A pale pink lipstick and slightly too-peachy blush did nothing for her pallid complexion, and a conservative pair of pearl earrings added to the impression of staid middle age.

Kari was no fashion plate herself in plain jeans and a tee shirt, but she still itched to take the court clerk for an urgent makeover. Instead, she forced herself to focus on the task at hand.

"Hello," she said in what she hoped was a cheerful but

not too perky tone. "I'm not sure if you remember me from court the other night. I'm Kari Stuart, the new owner of the Serenity Sanctuary."

Marge looked up from examining a complicated form that appeared to have been filled out in bright purple ink. "Oh, yes, of course," she said, putting the form aside with what sounded to Kari's ears like a grateful sigh. "What can I do for you?"

"I hate to bother you," Kari said. "But I have a few questions if you have a moment. I'm afraid this is all very new to me, and I'm still trying to figure out how everything works. I don't want to mess up something important because I didn't know the rules."

"Very sensible," Marge said, gesturing toward the chair in front of her desk. "Although of course there are quite a few guidelines for shelters." She got up and pulled open one of the three large gray metal file cabinets behind her and plucked out a thick sheaf of papers stapled together at one corner. "This ought to get you started."

"Oh, thank you," Kari said, although Daisy had already given her a copy of both the state and town rule booklets. "I was actually hoping to get more insight into the court side of things. That's why I came to you. For instance, I was wondering how I would know when the next court date was, since the original one had to be postponed. You know, because of, uh, the dog warden's unfortunate demise."

"Unfortunate. Indeed." Marge rolled her eyes. "Such a loss."

Kari hoped the court clerk wasn't trying to be convincing, because she'd never seen anyone less grief-stricken. "I'm sorry, I was being insensitive. The two of you must have worked closely together for years."

"I wouldn't say 'closely,'" Marge said. "We crossed paths professionally, of course, since Mr. Myers was a frequent visitor to court in his official capacity, but that was the only time we saw each other." She sniffed. "He was hardly a personal friend."

Methinks the lady doth protest too much? Kari thought. Or maybe it was just a statement of fact. She really couldn't tell. The court clerk was extremely hard to read.

"Oh," Kari said. "Okay."

"You will get a letter notifying you of the next court date," Marge said. "The judge is only waiting for a report from the new dog warden, so it should be sometime within the next week or two. Did you have any other questions?" She glanced back down at her paperwork, as if it was starting to look less annoying than the current conversation.

"I was wondering about fines," Kari blurted out, thinking she should have prepared for this better. She would never make it as a private investigator. It was a good thing that had never been one of her career goals. "Like, how much the fine would be if one of the dogs got out before we could get the fence fixed. The police still won't let us have any contractors come work on it, you know, because it is still considered a crime scene."

"How frustrating for you," Marge said. She still seemed perfectly innocuous and friendly, and Kari was beginning to feel foolish. They'd clearly jumped to the wrong conclusion somehow. There was no way this woman was a criminal, especially not a violent one.

"It kind of is," Kari said.

"Well, the fines start at twenty dollars for a loose dog, for the first occurrence," the clerk said. "That's doubled if the animal isn't wearing his or her tags. It can mount up surprisingly fast." She rose again and went to a different cabinet (*F* for fines instead of *S* for shelter regulations, from what Kari could tell). While she was up, Kari happened to notice a grouping of photos on the corner of the desk. They were angled so they could be seen from either side, with deceptively simple frames that looked like they could have been some kind of antique brass or even dull gold.

It took her a moment to recognize the central figure in the pictures as the woman in front of her, since the settings were more exotic than anywhere one would have expected to find the drab civil servant. There was one photo in front of the pyramids of Egypt, and another on a pristine white beach at what looked like a high-end resort. Another showed her with her arm around a pleasant-looking man with short blond hair, standing in front of an expensive sports car.

None of them looked like the kinds of things anyone could afford on a court clerk's salary. Maybe the man was her husband and he made most of the money?

"Those are great pictures," Kari said when Marge sat back down again and handed her the list of dog-related fines. "I've always wanted to travel, but somehow I've never managed it."

"You really should do it," Marge said with the closest thing to a smile Kari had seen. "I love going places I've never been." She pointed at the picture of the car. "Would you believe that was taken after the winning race at Monte Carlo? That was the driver of the car that won." A dreamy look brightened her face. "He was very sweet."

"Oh," Kari said. "That sounds like quite an adventure. I thought maybe he was your husband."

"Ha, I wish," Marge said. "I live with my elderly mother

and a Siamese cat named King Tut." She pointed at the picture of the pyramids. "As you can see, I have kind of a thing for Egypt. I've been three times."

Kari's eyebrows rose involuntarily. "Wow," she said. "That must get expensive."

"I'm very careful with my money," Marge said, pressing her lips together and giving Kari a suspicious look. "You know, now that you've won the lottery, you might want to consider taking a couple of trips yourself. Long ones."

"Uh, well, that sounds like fun, but I've got the sanctuary to deal with now," Kari said.

"If you keep it," Marge said in an offhand tone. "I heard there might be some questions about the permits for the work being done out at the shelter. Plus there are all those noise complaints from your neighbor. Not to mention being the number one suspect in a murder investigation."

She gave Kari a sympathetic look that didn't quite reach her eyes. "No one would blame you if after your name is cleared, you decided to give up the whole thing as a bad idea and leave town altogether. You might want to think about it."

Picking up a pen, she put slashes through three sections of the form in front of her in rapid succession and then whacked a large *DENIED* stamp down on the top so hard it made Kari jump.

"Was there anything else?" Marge asked in a cool tone. "Because if not, I have work to do."

"Right, sorry." Kari pushed her chair back with an unfortunate scraping noise. "Thank you for all your help."

"Just doing my job," Marge said. "Do yourself a favor and think about what I said about traveling. You might find it to be a much better alternative than staying here."

*   *   *

A little rattled by her interview with the court clerk, Kari decided to stop by the town library. Libraries had been one of her happy places since she had been a child. She had spent many an afternoon there when she hadn't wanted to go home after school, immersing herself in the life of Laura Ingalls Wilder and taking imaginary journeys through *A Wrinkle in Time*. Even today, her idea of heaven was a cup of hot chocolate and a good book. (And a cat or two, of course.)

Lakeview was small enough that the library was only open four days a week. It was housed in an old Victorian that had been donated by a wealthy patron with no family and a love for books, and was painted a light gray with blue-gray shutters and accents. The first floor was taken up by the main room, which held the checkout and information desk, two computers for public use, magazines, and the new books shelves, as well as an adult fiction room and the children's space, where story hour was held every Saturday morning at ten.

Upstairs, there were two smaller rooms of nonfiction, a meeting room used by the book club as well as other shared-interest groups, and a couple of offices, including Izzy's. After checking the new books to make sure there wasn't anything that she had to have right this very minute, Kari made her way to Izzy's office and rapped on the doorframe.

"Hey," Izzy said, looking up from her computer. "I wasn't expecting to see you. Come on in. I have good news." She gestured at Kari to shut the door behind her.

Kari could see the resemblance between aunt and niece in the shape of their faces and their matching high cheekbones. But Izzy's skin was a darker hue and her hair was clipped into a short Afro that hugged her head instead of Bryn's many tiny braids. The librarian tended to dress in brightly patterned skirts and tops, a look not everyone could have pulled off, but on her it just looked fun and cheerful. The children loved her and called her Miss Izzy.

Speaking of cheerful, Izzy's attitude had improved a lot since the last time Kari had seen her.

"I could use some good news," Kari said. "Come on, don't keep me in suspense."

"The police have cleared me of suspicion in Bill Myers's murder," her friend said gleefully. "And I owe it all to an elderly prostate."

Kari blinked, slightly taken aback. "That's great news. And *what*?"

Izzy chuckled. "I told the sheriff that I was up late reading in my living room on the night of the murder, but of course, with Bryn staying at a friend's house, there was no one to corroborate my story. Astonishingly, they didn't find the word of my three cockatoos to be at all helpful."

"So what changed their minds?"

"My neighbor, Mr. Selkirk, is in his eighties. Apparently, he has to get up several times in the middle of the night to pee, and he happened to glance out his window around the time of the murder and notice me sitting in my chair. He told the cops he made a note of the time because he'd wondered if it was earlier than he'd thought, since I was still awake." She grinned at Kari. "So it was a case of aging prostate for the win."

Kari shook her head. "Not a phrase you expect to hear, but I'm glad you're off the hook. I'm sure Bryn is very relieved. As am I, of course."

"Any progress clearing your own name?" Izzy asked. "Or Daisy's?"

"Nope," Kari said, trying not to sound discouraged. "We're still suspects number one and two, as far as I can tell. I talked to the sheriff about a couple of people who I'd found out had grudges against Myers, but he knew about them both already. I don't think he was all that impressed with my poking my nose in." She gave a half-hearted laugh. "He actually called me Miss Marple."

Izzy snickered. "I love those books, although you're not exactly what I envision when I think of her. Still, she always did figure out whodunit in the end."

"I'm not sure I'm getting any closer to having answers," Kari said. "It seems like everything I turn up just raises more questions. I should probably just leave the crime solving to the police . . . but I'm afraid that might end up with either me or Daisy in jail, or that by the time they realize we're right about Myers being crooked, poor Buster will already have been put to sleep."

"Myers was crooked?" Izzy said. "Are you sure? I know Bryn always said he had the morals of an alley cat, but I thought she was just talking about the way he treated her." She looked surprisingly fierce for a moment, and Kari got a glimpse of why the police had suspected Izzy might have been capable of murder. Thank goodness that wasn't an issue anymore.

"Yeah, it's starting to look as though he was inventing charges and fining people for things their dogs didn't do, probably even letting some animals loose so he could claim he'd found them wandering and then give the owners tickets they didn't deserve."

"The rat fink!" Izzy said with feeling.

"Worse yet, we've found evidence that he was working with Deputy Carter, who would do the same thing," Kari said. "Although we're pretty sure Myers started it and then persuaded Carter to help him out."

"I never liked that deputy," Izzy said, frowning. "He bends down the corners of the pages in books." She made a tutting sound. "I don't trust anyone who mutilates books."

Kari suppressed a smile. "Definitely an indication of criminal leanings," she said.

"You know," Izzy said in a thoughtful voice. "I don't like to repeat gossip, but in this case I might have to make an exception. I heard a rumor that Deputy Carter was seen having a yelling match with Myers on the town square the day before he was killed. According to the patron who told me, no one was close enough to hear what they were arguing about, but it was apparently quite heated. Maybe you should mention it to the sheriff."

Kari winced. "Uh, I don't think so. For one thing, someone has probably told him already, the way news spreads in this town. For another, I don't think he is all that eager to hear any more of my theories. But I'll keep it in mind, thanks."

Izzy got up from her chair and came around the desk to give Kari a hug. "Well, you keep digging, Miss Marple. I'm sure you'll come up with something that will help solve the case."

"Hopefully before I'm arrested for a crime I didn't commit," Kari said.

"That would probably be best," Izzy agreed. "Too bad you don't have a neighbor who can vouch for you."

"I think Mr. Lee would be more likely to say he saw me standing over the dead body with an axe, a smoking gun, and garrote, especially if he thought that would get the shelter closed down," Kari said with a laugh. "But thanks for the good thought."

Kari was finishing cleaning the cat cages around five o'clock when the phone rang. She checked the caller ID and it said *Last Stop*. Her stomach clenched and acid rose into her throat. There was only one reason she could think of why anyone would be calling her from there, and it wasn't to congratulate her on her lottery win or ask to adopt a cat.

"Serenity Sanctuary, Kari Stuart speaking," she said when she picked up the phone. It wouldn't hurt to sound professional just in case she was wrong.

"It's Curtis Fry," a gruff voice said. "I own the Last Stop. You know where it is?"

"Sure," Kari said. Everyone in town knew where it was, either so they could go there or so they could avoid it. "Is there something I can do for you?"

"Yes, there damned well is," Fry said, speaking loudly over a combination of country music and yelling. "You can come get your brother, that's what you can do. He's been here all day, and he's drunk as a skunk. Which I don't mind none, except he's causin' trouble and I ain't gonna be responsible if somebody hits him over the head with a chair to shut him up."

She took a deep breath. "Why don't you just toss him out?" she said in as calm a tone as she could manage.

"Darned fool won't leave," Curtis said shortly.

"Well, why don't you just call the cops, then?" She had enough on her plate without getting sucked back into her family drama. A night in jail might do him some good.

Curtis made a choking sound that Kari eventually realized was supposed to be laughter. "Call the cops?" He choked some more. "Are you kidding me? I don't want cops out here. I'm sure as heck not going to call them myself. Jeez. Call the cops." He laughed so hard he started wheezing. "Just come out here and get him, will ya?" There was a click on the other end and she was listening to dead air.

Darn it. Kari hung up the phone, popped the kittens back into their newly cleaned cage, and washed her hands.

Reluctantly, she shut the place down for the night, turning off the lights and turning the new alarm system on before she stepped out the door. Queenie leapt onto her shoulder and hitched a ride down to the house, probably picking up on Kari's need for comforting.

"Sorry, sweetie," Kari said, putting out food for the cats and Fred as quickly as she could before grabbing her purse from the table by the door. "You are definitely too young and innocent to go with me to this place." She scooped the kitten up and kissed her on the nose. "I'll see you when I get home."

Luckily the bar wasn't far from the shelter. In fact, you had to pass it on the way out of town to get to Goose Hollow Road. The Last Stop was located right past the boundary that separated the town's domain from the county's.

It definitely looked better at night, when the lights were low and the neon sign of a devil descending into the flames of hell distracted from the sagging roofline and peeling white paint. In the daytime, it looked seedy and run-down, and it was easy to see the weeds growing up through the cracked asphalt in the parking lot. She avoided one pothole that looked big enough to swallow up a VW Bug, swerving so wildly that she probably looked as drunk as most of the patrons.

Even this early in the evening, the place was doing a booming business. A line of Harleys edged the right side of the unevenly shaped lot, grouped together like a herd of metal horses in front of an old hitching post that dated back to the days when the original building had been a roadside tavern. On the opposite end, separated by an invisible and entirely informal division of society, a ragged row of pickup trucks represented the antisocial farmer contingent, the kind who despised the "hoity-toity" bars in town that catered to the tourists and dared to serve drinks with fancy names.

A few random Toyotas and Hondas probably indicated the presence of students from Perryville looking for a walk on the wild side, although they might have been pulled in by the large sign in the smudged window that said *Fifty-Cent Wings*.

Curtis's grandfather had been famous for having a still hidden somewhere in the woods outside of town, and the booze at the Last Stop was so bad, the locals joked that Fry was still using it. Kari had driven by the place plenty of times, but she had never been inside. She would have been perfectly happy to keep it that way.

It was easy to spot her brother once she got through the door. He was sitting on the last barstool closest to the door, slumped over the scuffed and graffiti-scarred surface of the wooden bar, arguing with a stocky, middle-aged bald man wearing a half apron covered with red stains. Kari hoped they were wing sauce and not blood.

The odor of stale beer and desperation hung in the air like ghosts of patrons past, and the faint scent of cigarettes seemed to linger, even though smoking in bars had been outlawed in New York State many years before.

"Kari, my favorite sister!" Mickey said when he spotted her, almost sliding off his stool. "You're just in time. This guy is refusing to pour me another drink. I told him my sister was rich and I could afford it, but he still refuses to serve me. Tell him who you are."

Kari rolled her eyes. "I'm a woman who was up to her elbows in cat litter ten minutes ago and still has to go back to the shelter and walk three more dogs. That's who I am. Whose wife or girlfriend did you hit on?"

She turned to the bald man, who was glowering at them both so hard she was worried his bushy eyebrows might fall off. "Sorry about this. Next time just don't serve him at all. It'll save us both a lot of trouble."

Curtis snarled at her. "I'm a businessman. How am I supposed to make money if I don't sell people booze?" He held out one meaty hand. "Unless maybe you'd rather pay me not to let him drink, if you're as rich as your brother says."

"Forget it," Kari said. "But don't expect me to come get him again. This is definitely a one-off." She half led, half dragged her brother toward the door, her feet sticking unpleasantly to the floor, which clearly hadn't been cleaned any time in the recent past. The whole place— and its owner—kind of gave her the creeps. No wonder he had such a bad reputation around town. Kari would be happy if she never met up with him again.

As she was trying to get Mickey into her car, she wondered if—no matter what she'd said to Suz—it might be worth it to give Mickey a chunk of money, just to get rid of him. The problem with that, of course, was he'd just be back for more as soon as whatever she gave him ran out. It was a no-win situation.

"I thought you quit drinking," she said.

"I did," her brother replied. "But I had to celebrate your good fortune, didn't I?"

A muddy dark green SUV pulled into the parking lot and drove up next to her. Jack Falco peered out the driver's-side window. "Hello," he said. "Do you need a hand?"

He'd obviously been out doing his job, since there was a cute but very dirty midsized dog in a cage in the back seat, its tongue lolling as it gave a few halfhearted barks. "Hush you," Falco said. "You've caused enough trouble for one day." Then he looked back at Kari. "Seems like maybe you know the feeling."

She could feel her face flush. "Yeah. My darling brother is back in town for a brief visit. Getting briefer by the minute. Sorry." She was so embarrassed. This was definitely not the impression she wanted to make on a man who was going to be dealing with her in a professional capacity for what could be years. Her brother gave a perky grin.

"Hi there!" he said. "I'm her brother."

"Nothing to apologize for," Falco said, getting out of his car and walking over to her. He lifted Mickey up effortlessly and then slid him into the passenger seat after Kari opened the door. "I had an uncle growing up who had a drinking problem, so I get it. You're not responsible for someone else's bad choices. Even if they're related to you." He gave her a quick smile that was even more startling compared to his usual stern expression.

"Are you going to need help getting him out of the car when you get him home?" Falco asked. He tilted his head toward the dog. "Corky there isn't going to mind another few minutes before he gets taken back to his owners. He apparently gets loose around once a month. Personally, I think he just likes being driven around in a crate. I might suggest to his people that they buy one for their own car."

Kari almost liked it better when he wasn't being nice

to her. She didn't quite know how to cope with this. "I'll be fine. He can sleep it off while I go back to the shelter. But thanks for your help. I really appreciate it."

"No problem," Falco said, and drove off, Corky panting happily in the back.

After walking the couple of dogs she hadn't gotten to before the call from Curtis Fry, Kari reset the alarm and walked back down to her house. She was getting quite fond of the place, even if none of the walls were straight and the floors slanted so much that all the cat toys ended up rolling into the same corner. Old farmhouses had character, even if they weren't perfect.

Kind of like her brother, who had made himself at home and was sitting at her kitchen table, eating the leftovers she'd been planning to have for her own dinner. He seemed to have sobered up remarkably fast.

"Hey, sis," Mickey said cheerfully. He had a lipstick smudge on one corner of his jaw and his curly hair looked like someone had been running their fingers through it. "Sorry about the fuss. I promise, it won't happen again."

Kari sighed. She loved her younger brother, who had actually stood between her and their father as soon as he'd gotten old enough and big enough to do so. She often thought his charming nature was a defense mechanism he'd developed as a way of getting around their father's perpetual anger. But she didn't have any delusions about Mickey's somewhat flexible morals or inability to take on responsibility. She kept hoping he would grow up, but she wasn't going to hold her breath waiting for it to happen.

"Just so you know, I'm still not giving you any money.

You'd just blow it anyway," she said, grabbing a fork and spearing a piece of chicken salad off the plate in front of him. "Everything is going toward the shelter."

Mickey shrugged, as unconcerned about the practicalities of life as usual. "Whatever," he said. "Maybe I'll stick around anyway. That Bryn is quite the looker."

Kari pointed her fork at him. "Don't even think about it," she said. "That girl is way out of your league."

Her brother laughed. "You may be right. And I'm already tired of cleaning the dog yard. I mean, I like dogs as much as the next guy, but man, they generate a *lot* of poop."

Kari snickered, remembering Bryn's warning about that on the first day Kari had walked through the door. There really was an incredible amount of poop involved in running a shelter.

She and Mickey finished off the food and retired to the living room to watch something mindless on TV. Kari was exhausted from both work and dealing with the drama, and she was happy to sip at a glass of iced tea and pet Queenie, who had crawled into her lap as soon as Kari made one. She never could stay mad at Mickey, and he was surprisingly good company when he wasn't getting into trouble she had to get him out of. She knew he'd be on his way again soon enough, so she was content to just enjoy this quiet moment of sibling camaraderie while she had the chance.

Suddenly, Queenie sat up straight and nudged Kari's arm so hard that the movement almost sent the tea flying. The kitten meowed loudly, green eyes wide.

"Hey," Kari said. "What is your problem?" She set the glass down on the table next to her just as a piercing noise shattered the night. "What the heck?" Kari put the kitten down on the floor. "Crap. That's the security alarm!"

She and Mickey exchanged glances and got up at the same time, running toward the door. As soon as she opened it, she could hear the dogs barking and howling, their sensitive ears no doubt even more upset by the loud siren than she was. Her ringtone rang out, adding to the noise.

Kari grabbed the phone just in time to hear Mr. Lee ranting.

"First the barking and now this terrible noise! You are the worst neighbor ever!"

Kari didn't hear the rest, since she hung up and tossed the phone back toward her brother. "Call 911 and tell them there is a problem out at the Serenity Sanctuary," she shouted, and took off toward the shelter with Queenie and Fred racing ahead of her and Mickey on her heels. This time she was going to catch whoever it was before they got away.

Fourteen

Kari bolted toward the shelter, feeling a terrible sense of déjà vu. She was torn between hoping that the alarm had scared off whoever it was and praying that they were still around so she could beat them senseless with her bare hands. Although, really, she'd be better off siccing her brother on them. He might be undependable in practical matters, but he was great to have by your side in a fight. She'd known that since they were kids, when he had defended her from the bullies at school.

When they came to a halt in front of the shelter, the security lights were blazing and the alarm was even more deafening. There was one broken window, but it looked like that was as far as the vandals had gotten this time before the new system had kicked in.

It was hard to think with all that noise and the dogs barking. Which might have explained why the two men trying to pry the cover off the rectangular metal alarm box on the outside of the building didn't hear Kari and her brother come up. The controls to the alarm were inside, so Kari could only assume they were just trying to find some way to smash it into silence.

"Do you recognize them?" Mickey asked. He looked almost happy to be about to jump into trouble. He always had loved a challenge.

"Oh, yeah," Kari said, barely able to believe her eyes. "We've met."

Still unaware they had company, Deputy Carter and his partner had given up on trying to pull open the panel and were pounding on it with rocks. Luckily, neither of them was in uniform, or Kari suspected they would have been trying to shoot it open.

Overton was sweating and cursing. "Man, those dogs are going to get loose any minute now. Somebody is going to hear this darned alarm. We've got to get out of here! I can't believe you talked me into this."

"Shut up," Carter growled. He wore a baseball cap pulled down low over his eyes, but his silhouette and voice were unmistakable. Both men were dressed head to toe in black jeans and sweatshirts, like rural ninjas. "That girl is never going to be brave enough to come down on her own. She's going to call the department and wait for them to get here, and we'll be long gone before that happens. Just help me get this open so we can turn the freaking thing off. I swear, it feels like my ears are bleeding."

Fred, apparently unimpressed by the noise, demonstrated yet again his complete uselessness as a guard dog by running up to Overton and jumping up on him and trying to lick his face. Kari thought the poor deputy was going to pass out, he shrieked so loud.

"Don't worry," she shouted over the alarm. "He's just being friendly. Hello, deputies. Fancy meeting you here."

Carter jumped almost as high as Overton had when he

realized she was there. "What are you doing here?" he asked, staring over her shoulder at Mickey. He'd clearly had no idea there was anyone else around besides Kari.

"I live here," she yelled. "I might ask you the same question."

"We were passing by and heard the alarm," he said loudly, trying to sound innocent and failing miserably. "We came to investigate. You should get back to your house and leave this to the professionals."

"Professional whats?" Mickey muttered, just loud enough for her to hear. "Idiots?"

"They're the cops," she told him.

"You've got to be kidding me." Mickey gazed at Overton, who was still cringing away from Fred's affectionate advances, and Carter, standing with his gut thrusting out from underneath a shirt that looked like it had been borrowed from a smaller man.

Just then, a police car pulled into the driveway. Carter stared in dismay as the sheriff and another deputy, a youngish man in a neatly pressed uniform that showed off his broad shoulders, got out and came around the corner to gape at the scene.

"What the heck is going on here?" the sheriff asked, looking around in disbelief. "Ms. Stuart, go turn off that darned alarm! Your neighbor is having a fit. He sent me out here to arrest you for disturbing the peace, violating the noise ordinance, and being a general nuisance."

She ran to do as he'd ordered, fumbling her key in the lock and then entering the code on the alarm box located right inside the door. Blessed silence descended on the night. She ran back outside in time to hear the sheriff ask Carter and Overton the same question she had.

"What on earth are you two doing here?" Richardson

wanted to know. "You're not even on duty tonight. And why are you wearing those ridiculous getups?"

Overton turned so pale, he almost blended in with the white walls of the shelter, but Carter kept his cool. "We were just passing by, Sheriff, and heard the alarms going off. We knew the place had had issues so we figured we'd better check it out."

"I see," the sheriff said. Kari couldn't tell if he was buying Carter's story or not.

"He's lying, Sheriff," she said. "My brother and I came running up here as soon as the alarms were tripped, and caught these two trying to smash open the box from the outside. There's already one broken window up front. That must have been what set the system off."

"She probably did it herself," Carter blustered. "For all we know, she is responsible for the other vandalism too. Probably trying to look like a victim so we don't blame her for Bill Myers's death."

"That's ridiculous," Kari said. "For one thing, I didn't have anything to do with Myers's death, and I certainly wouldn't vandalize my own building and create a giant mess I'd then have to clean up. For another thing, I actually know how to spell *whore*."

Her brother snickered, and the other deputy had to lift his hand to cover a smile.

"What?" Carter said.

Kari rolled her eyes. "You know, in the time you spent trying to silence the alarm, you could have broken all the other windows and gotten away. But it wouldn't have mattered."

"What the heck are you talking about?" Carter glared at her and then caught himself and added, "Not that we were trying to do that. We were checking to see if some-one had damaged the alarm, that's all. Right, Overton?"

Overton nodded up and down like a deranged bobble-head doll.

Kari raised one finger and pointed overhead. "There's something you might be interested to know, Deputy Carter." She looked the sheriff in the eyes. "I got the top-of-the-line system. It has cameras. Lots and lots of cam-eras." Not having to worry about getting the cheapest model for once had actually paid off.

"Crap," Overton said, turning to Carter. "You didn't tell me there were cameras." He was clearly so terrified of his boss, he'd forgotten all about the dogs and was absent-mindedly petting Fred, who was leaning against the young man's shaking legs. "I didn't want to do it, Sheriff. Carter made me. Aw, jeez, I'm gonna get fired, aren't I?"

"You think?" Richardson said. He turned to Carter, anger and sorrow warring on his face, and formally read him his rights. He clearly didn't intend the bit about the right to keep silent, though. "Tell me, Deputy, does this mean you killed Bill Myers too?"

"What? No! I, no!" Carter sputtered. "I never! I was at a poker game with my buddies until right before I went on duty. You ask them, they'll tell you. And Overton was with me when we got the call about the body."

"As if I'd take his word for anything involving you," the sheriff said, shaking his head. "I just don't believe this. What the heck is going on in my department?" He glared at Carter. "If you didn't kill Myers, why on earth are you out here vandalizing the shelter?"

"I *swear*, Sheriff. It wasn't me. I had nothing to do with his death. It had to have been Marge Farrow."

"Marge Farrow? The court clerk? That Marge Farrow? Mousy middle-aged woman who never raises her voice?" The sheriff's jaw dropped. "Why in the name of heaven would Marge Farrow kill the dog warden? Have you lost your mind?"

"Because of the money, sir," Overton put in helpfully.

"What. Money?" Richardson said through gritted teeth. The deputy he'd brought with him was standing there with his head turning from person to person, as if he was watching the best live performance he'd ever seen. Kari was pretty sure he was trying to memorize the entire thing so he could recite it word for word down at the diner in the morning.

As for her, she just couldn't believe the two cops were still talking. But then, they'd already proven they weren't exactly criminal masterminds. And maybe Carter thought if he came clean now, the sheriff would go easier on him. Either that, or the deputy was just an idiot who didn't think what he'd done was all that bad. Or the alarms had rattled his brains.

"The embezzling," Carter explained. "Marge has been embezzling from the town for years, and Myers found out. He tried to blackmail her, and she must have killed him to shut him up."

The sheriff looked like his head was going to explode. Kari couldn't blame him.

"And how, exactly, did you know about this supposed embezzling, Deputy?" Richardson asked. "Since I never heard a word about it."

Carter had the grace to stare at his boots for a minute before answering. "We were kind of working with her," he admitted. "Not on the embezzling! I had nothing to do with that. Myers only found out right before he died, and we got into a big fight because I wanted a cut of whatever he got from Marge. But he said he was on to something else big and he'd changed his mind about blackmailing her, since she'd earned us so much money over the years."

Aha, Kari thought. Now they were getting to it. She gave her brother a subtle nudge with her hip and he raised one eyebrow in question. She just nodded in the direction of the drama playing out in front of them.

"Earned you money how?" the sheriff asked. He turned to the deputy next to him. "Don't just stand there gawping, Nelson. Take out your darned notebook and write this all down." He muttered a few profanities under his breath before turning back to Carter. "You were saying?"

"Me and Myers, well, we had this scheme going. It was his idea, not mine," Carter added quickly, as though he thought that would somehow make a difference. "Anyway, we'd cook up all these bogus tickets. Myers would go around letting people's dogs out—he always said that if they didn't want their dogs getting loose, they should be more careful anyway."

"Be more careful," Kari said indignantly. "Some of those dogs were in fenced-in yards *on chains*."

"Yeah, well, Myers was kind of a jerk sometimes," Carter admitted.

"Ya think?" Mickey murmured into her ear.

"So where does Marge Farrow come into this?" Richardson asked, crossing his arms over his chest. Kari had a feeling he was making an effort not to reach out and strangle his deputy. "Are you trying to tell me she ran around town letting dogs loose too?"

Deputy Nelson guffawed, probably at the image of the prim and proper court clerk climbing over fences, earning him a glare from his boss. He bent his head and scribbled in his notebook, but Kari could see the grin on his face in the lights from the security system. She'd only disabled the alarm, and left all the outside lights on.

"Of course not," Carter said. "She'd skim money off the fines from the animals' owners and split it with us. Sometimes she didn't register the fines at all, or she'd put down that it was a first offense instead of a third, and take the difference. I mean, nobody ever looks at that boring paperwork."

"Nelson, make a note to have my secretary schedule me an appointment with the mayor and the town council," Richardson said in a grim tone. "Apparently I have to speak to them about ordering an audit of the town's books."

Nelson gulped and wrote it down.

"I'm confused, Carter," the sheriff went on. "If the three of you—" He glanced over at Overton, who was still trying to be as invisible as possible, and the young deputy shook his head in frantic denial. "If the three of you were working together all this time, why would Marge Farrow suddenly decide to kill Myers?"

"Well, you see, Sheriff, we knew she was embezzling money from our cases. But then Myers found out she had been doing it to all of them, all the court cases she worked on, and he wanted a bigger cut to keep his mouth shut. He told her that what we were doing was small potatoes compared to her, and that we'd get a slap on the wrist if anyone discovered it, but she'd go to jail for years and lose all that money she had squirreled away."

"Oh, you're going to get more than a slap," the sheriff said, clenching his fists. "So you think she killed him to shut him up?"

Carter nodded eagerly, happy to point the sheriff at

anyone who wasn't him. "She denied it when I asked her, but right after that, she sent me to harass Miz Stuart here, so she and her friends would stop looking into the murder. Why would Marge do that if she wasn't guilty?"

"Why indeed?" Richardson said, sounding thoughtful.

Kari had a moment's hope that maybe she and Daisy were off the hook. After all, this was why they had all been looking into things in the first place, to clear their names and find the real killer. Now they'd found out who vandalized the shelter—although frankly, the two deputies were the last people she would have suspected—and probably Myers's killer too. Maybe this whole nightmare was finally over and she could get on with reopening the shelter and Daisy could go and live with her sister and get on with her life.

"Are you done with us, Sheriff?" she asked. "I need to take care of that broken window and call the glaziers. Again." She glared at Carter.

"The sheriff's department will take care of the window," Richardson said, adding his icy stare to hers. "I'll need you and this gentleman"—he nodded at Mickey—"who is—?"

"This is my brother, Mickey. Michael Stuart Junior," she said. "He's in town for a few days. He happened to be at my house when the alarm went off."

"Fine," Richardson said. "I'll need you and your brother to come down tomorrow and file a formal complaint against my *former* officers. You can bring me the video surveillance recording at the same time. We have plenty to hold them on in the meanwhile."

"Does this mean I can call the workmen and get the fence started finally?" she asked.

"Let's not get ahead of ourselves, Ms. Stuart," he said.

"Just because Deputy Carter has made some accusations doesn't mean we've proven anything. I still have to look into this matter further."

Darn.

"Yes, sir," she said. After all, she wouldn't have taken Carter's word for anything either.

Squealing tires and screeching brakes alerted them all to a new arrival. A car door slammed and a diminutive Korean man in striped pajamas and loafers came stomping around the corner of the building. He came to an abrupt halt at the sight of the four lawmen, Kari, and her brother.

"Sheriff Richardson, it's about time someone with authority showed up," Kari's neighbor said. "I demand to know what is going on out here."

The sheriff sighed. "I don't blame you, Mr. Lee. I'd like to know that too."

Kari went in to the sheriff's department first thing in the morning, bearing coffee from the local coffee shop and three different kinds of muffins she'd made herself. She was something of a stress baker, and she hadn't been able to get to sleep after the police had left and her brother had returned to his bed-and-breakfast. He'd come back again this morning in time to eat three muffins and follow her over to the sheriff's department on his shiny red motorcycle, which he'd reclaimed from the parking lot of the Last Stop.

The officer at the front desk took her back to Richardson's office. They went past a locked chest-high gate and through a large room full of industrious-looking men and women in uniform, mostly sitting at metal desks and working diligently at computers. A couple of the cops had people seated by them, probably either witnesses being interviewed or criminals being questioned. Kari wished she had a better idea of which one she was. Mickey was dropped off with a cute female officer in the main room, which made him look a lot more cheerful.

The desk sergeant who escorted her through the room stopped at an open door and rapped on it briefly before poking his head through and saying, "Ms. Stuart is here, sir. She brought muffins." He gave her a pitiful look and she handed over a couple before walking into the lion's den.

"A bribe, Ms. Stuart?" Richardson asked. He looked as though he had been up all night. Dark circles ringed his eyes and an electric razor sticking out of a partially closed drawer suggested that he had just finished shaving here instead of at home.

"Only if you think that would work, Sheriff," Kari said, placing two containers of coffee and a container of muffins on the desk between them. "I wasn't sure how you took your coffee, but I didn't want to get one and drink it in front of you, so I took a chance on a latte. The muffins are blueberry, bran, and chocolate with chocolate chips, and I made them fresh this morning. Well, last night. Never mind, it doesn't matter." She realized she was babbling and shut her mouth with a snap. No wonder Carter had talked so much last night. Richardson seemed to have that effect on people.

"A latte is great," Richardson said gratefully. "The station coffee is just as bad as you hear about on television." He hovered over the bran muffins for a moment before giving in and taking one of the chocolate ones instead. "But I'm afraid that bringing me treats doesn't change anything."

"I didn't really think it would," Kari said. She handed over a thumb drive. "This is the video footage you asked for. It shows Carter and Overton quite clearly, I'm afraid."

Richardson sighed. "I didn't expect anything else. On behalf of the Lakeview Sheriff's Department, I would like to apologize for the criminal actions of my officers and all the difficulty they caused you." He paused and winced. "You can send the bills for all the previous vandalism incidents here as well as the one for last night's broken window."

"That's not necessary, Sheriff," Kari said. "I assume that if they are found guilty in court, they'll have to pay for the damages. I can wait for that."

"Overton has already pleaded guilty and spilled his guts about Carter," Richardson said, shaking his head. A few stray muffin crumbs scattered over the paperwork on his desk. "I expect Carter will do the same once we show him that we have him on film. Either way, both deputies have been fired and Overton is being charged with criminal mischief, which is a misdemeanor. Carter, as the ringleader, will face charges of vandalism, harassment, and a few other things."

"But not murder?" Kari said.

Richardson looked, if possible, even more disgusted. "No. Not murder. His original alibi didn't hold up—apparently he left the poker game earlier than he said. But when he realized he was going to be arrested for murder, he admitted he'd actually been with his mistress, who is one of the hairdressers at the Bashful Beauty Boutique. She corroborated his story. He was with her until right before he and Overton went on duty. So he's now out a job *and* a wife, but he can't have killed Myers."

"Drat," Kari said. "I'd really hoped he was the one and this would be over."

The sheriff raised an eyebrow at her over his coffee. "Carter accused you of trying to pin the crime on him because you had done it yourself or were covering for Daisy."

"Really?" Kari said. She had a muffin in front of her but she was mostly just playing with it. There was too big a lump in her throat to be able to swallow anything more than a latte. "I'd like to point out that I only met Daisy when I bought the shelter. I barely know her. Certainly not well enough to risk everything to cover it up if she had committed a murder. Which she didn't.

"Plus," she added, "the information I gave you about Carter and Myers working together turned out to be true. So I'm hardly trying to 'pin' anything on him. He really is guilty of a whole bunch of crimes."

"That doesn't mean you're not guilty of the murder itself, Ms. Stuart," the sheriff reminded her. "The two sets of crimes could be completely unrelated. Maybe when you found out about Carter and Myers, you decided to give me that info as a distraction. It doesn't change the fact that you were the one found at the murder scene and that you might have caught the victim in the act of digging under your fence. Maybe you lost your temper, seeing him go after your dogs. Or maybe you thought you were acting in self-defense."

"Oh, come on," Kari said. "You don't really believe that, do you?" She sure hoped he didn't, although when he put it that way, she almost believed it herself, and she *knew* she hadn't done it.

Richardson shrugged. "I used to see you at the diner, carrying those heavy trays full of food on your shoulder. You're plenty strong enough to have done it. I'm afraid you're not off the hook yet, even if you were right about a few things and the victim of a crime."

"What about Carter's claim that Marge Farrow murdered Myers?" Kari asked, trying not to sound desperate.

The sheriff grunted. "That man can't figure out which story he's telling from one minute to the next, and I wouldn't believe him if he said the sun was hot. But I'm looking into it. That's the best you're going to get for now."

"So still don't leave town?" Kari said, getting up from her chair.

"Still don't leave town," he said. "And try to stay out of trouble."

Like I hadn't been trying that already. Too bad she didn't seem to be very good at it.

🐈 Fifteen

Once they'd both given their official statements, Kari drove herself and Mickey back to the shelter. Her brother pitched in to help with surprising enthusiasm for someone who normally didn't get up before noon if he didn't have to. The fact that he was assisting Bryn might have had something to do with that. Kari didn't have the heart to tell him it was a lost cause. Besides, it amused her to see him cleaning the dog yard.

Other than a quick text from Suz telling her that Marge had been seen going into the sheriff's office and hadn't come out for over an hour (news courtesy of the diner grapevine at lunch), the rest of the day went pretty smoothly until around three.

Then things went downhill fast. Kari suspected this was not a coincidence.

"Uh-oh," Daisy said, looking out the window. "That new dog warden is back."

"Jack Falco?" Kari said, peering out over her shoulder. "I wonder what he wants."

"Nothing good, I'll bet," Daisy muttered darkly, flicking her long braid back out of her way.

Kari hoped the other woman was wrong, but the expression on Jack's face when he came in wasn't encouraging. Nor was the official-looking paperwork he had in his hands.

"Hi, Kari," he said, then nodded at Daisy. "You must be Daisy." He held out the papers. "I'm afraid I'm the bearer of bad tidings."

"None of the dogs have gotten loose," Kari said. "We've been really careful."

"I know," he said. "This is about Buster. Apparently Marge Farrow found Bill Myers's notes on the case and contacted the man who claims Buster bit him. This is a summons to appear in court next Thursday, a week from tomorrow. I'm very sorry."

"Marge found the notes," Kari said. "I see." Was there a connection between Marge being questioned about Myers's murder and the conveniently located witness? Somehow it felt a little too timely. Or a little bit too much like spite. The hand she held out for the summons only shook a little, she was glad to see.

Jack excused himself and quickly left, backing out the door with another apology. The faintest aroma of Old Spice lingered where he'd been standing. And to think, that used to be Kari's favorite aftershave.

As soon as he'd gone, Daisy sank onto one of the stools behind the desk and burst into tears, burying her head in her hands.

Bryn, who had come in from the kennels as soon as the dog warden's car pulled up, ran across the room and put her arms around Daisy's shaking shoulders. "This is all your fault," she said to Kari. "You just had to go stirring things up."

"Hey!" Kari said. "That's not fair." After all, they'd all agreed it was necessary to look into who might have killed Myers. She had been trying to help Daisy, not to mention Buster. But Bryn clearly wasn't in the mood to be rational.

"We should have just left it alone," the younger woman said. "Everything is worse now. Maybe it would have been better if you'd never bought the place."

Part of Kari thought Bryn was just distraught and taking it out on the person who was the easiest target. But a part of her wondered if maybe the girl was right. What if Kari had screwed everything up? Even without this latest development, half the time she felt like she had no idea what she was doing. Maybe she'd bitten off more than she could chew. Maybe the entire thing had been a mistake from the start.

Queenie jumped up on Kari's shoulder and rubbed her little furry black face against the side of Kari's jaw. "Meow?"

Kari hugged the kitten and then headed back to visit with Buster while she still could. They would think of something. They just had to.

Two days later, Sara came rushing in after taking her lunch break and pulled Kari and Bryn away from the last of the cage cleaning. Bryn had apologized to Kari for overreacting, and the two of them had returned to their previous cautious détente.

"What on earth are you so excited about?" Kari asked. Sara was usually the most rock steady of them all. Kari didn't think she'd ever seen the former teacher so worked up.

"You are *not* going to believe what I heard," Sara said, putting the to-go boxes she'd brought back for the others down on the front desk and turning around to face them. "They've arrested Marge Farrow for Myers's murder."

"What?" Kari couldn't believe it. She groped behind her for a chair to sit in and sank down into it before she fell over. "I guess the sheriff took Carter's accusations seriously after all."

"I'll say," Sara replied, leaning against the desk. "According to the diner grapevine, which is rarely wrong, he called in a forensic accountant. They specialize in looking into fraudulent activity. And apparently they found it. This accountant was able to prove that Marge had been embezzling court funds, probably for years."

"That doesn't mean she killed the dog warden, though, does it?" Bryn said, opening her container and munching on a couple of fries. The diner made the best fries in town by far, using fresh potatoes with the skin still on.

"Ha!" Sara said. "It gets better."

"Better?" Kari said. She ate a couple of her own fries, dragging them through a pile of the diner's special spicy ketchup. After all, a person had to keep her strength up.

"Well, not better for Marge," Sara admitted. "On the strength of the audit results, the sheriff was able to get a search warrant for Marge's house and car. In her house, they found large amounts of cash, and get this, plane tickets out of the country. There were differing stories about where she was supposedly going, but far away from here seemed to be the general consensus."

"That doesn't necessarily add up to murder," Kari said. She was all in favor of Marge being the guilty party, but it still wasn't sounding solid.

"Oh, I'm not done yet," Sara said, looking almost smug. She flipped the turquoise streak in her hair for emphasis. "Get this. In the trunk of her car, they found a rifle, weights, and a tarp. And when the sheriff confronted her, she admitted that she had been planning to lure Myers to the lake, shoot him, and then dump his body where it was too deep to be found. Cindy at the diner says Marge has won awards for target shooting, so she could easily have done it. Plus, there were texts on her phone arranging for them to meet up."

Kari felt as though she should applaud. That was one hell of a story. And Sara had only been gone for lunch for half an hour.

"But wait," Bryn said, munching thoughtfully on another fry. "That's not what happened. I mean, he wasn't shot. He was strangled with his snare pole. How did Marge explain that?"

Sara rolled her eyes. "According to Cindy, Marge swears that somebody else beat her to it and she didn't kill Myers. But she'd have to say that, wouldn't she? I mean, she admitted to the planned murder because they had all the evidence, but she's not stupid enough to actually confess to doing it."

"The sheriff arrested her, though, right?" Bryn said. "So he must think she did it."

"One would assume so," Sara said.

Just then the phone rang. Bryn picked it up, because she was closest, and listened to whoever was on the other end for a couple of minutes before hanging up with a strange expression on her face.

"Speak of the devil," she said. "That was the sheriff, Kari. He wants you to come down and talk to him."

* * *

So you're officially no longer under suspicion," the sheriff said, leaning back in his chair. "And we've finished gathering evidence from the crime scene, so you can go ahead and put your new fence up. The sheriff's department appreciates your patience."

Kari thought that calling her patient about the whole thing might be a bit of an exaggeration, but she definitely breathed a sigh of relief at no longer being a murder suspect. Still . . . she had to wonder if they had the right person locked up.

"I heard that Marge had a gun in her car and was planning to shoot the dog warden," she said, hesitant to even bring it up. "If she already had a plan, why kill him out at the sanctuary? I mean, doesn't that seem a little odd?"

Richardson rolled his eyes at her. "Everything about this case seems a little odd, Ms. Stuart. Including discovering that one of my deputies had been involved in illegal activities right under my nose for years without my realizing it. Believe me, I'm not happy with the entire mess. But we have enough evidence to prove that Marge Farrow had motive, means, and opportunity for the crime. That's good enough for me."

"Why would she change her approach at the last minute, though?" Kari asked. "She doesn't strike me as the kind to go off a plan once she had one set up."

"She doesn't strike me as the type to steal money or murder her accomplice either," the sheriff said, sounding a little exasperated. "People are full of surprises. We're assuming that she was following him, saw a better opportunity, and took it. Case closed." He gave her a wry look. "Do you *like* being a murder suspect, Ms. Stuart?"

Kari shuddered. "Holy crap, no. It has been awful."

"Then I suggest you just be grateful we arrested some-one other than you," he said. Then added in a slightly less acerbic tone, "I appreciate all your help on this matter, although it may not have seemed like it at the time. We might not have gotten to Marge before she left town if it hadn't been for your information about Deputy Carter. So thank you, and good luck with the sanctuary."

He stood up. The interview was clearly over.

"Always happy to be a good citizen," Kari said. "If you're ever looking for another dog, feel free to come up and see us."

The sheriff nodded, and she walked out the door. She was definitely relieved, but something about the whole situation nagged at her. The sheriff was right, though. It was time to get back to working on the shelter and mind-ing her own business.

She had almost made it to the front door of the station when the desk clerk hailed her and waved her over to his desk.

"I've got a message for you," the man said. With his squat build and prominent jowls, he reminded her a little bit of a bulldog they had at the shelter. His nametag said *Sergeant Dooley* and he had a handlebar mustache that wouldn't have looked out of place in an old western sa-loon.

"A message for me?" she said, puzzled.

"One of our prisoners left it for you," he said, a disap-proving look on his homely face. "Marge Farrow would like to talk to you. She says it is urgent."

❧ Sixteen

Somehow, Kari had thought that no one could visit an inmate at the jail except a lawyer, or maybe a member of their family. Apparently that wasn't true. At least at this point, while Marge was still in a holding cell at the back of the sheriff's department. Kari just had to sign in with an officer and show her ID. Then she waited about fifteen minutes for Marge to be brought into the visitor's room. A counter separated them, and an officer stood at the back of the otherwise empty room. The wooden chairs were stiff and uncomfortable, and the room stank of sweat and disinfectant. Not a place anyone would want to linger, which was probably the point.

Kari had no idea why Marge wanted to see her. It wasn't as though they were friends. In fact, the last Kari knew, Marge was so angry with Kari's interfering, she'd sicced the new dog warden on her and threatened Buster.

Buster was the only reason Kari had come when the court clerk asked her to. If there was any way to help him,

Kari was willing to take it, even if it meant talking to a supposed murderer.

When Marge entered the room, she was wearing the county regulation prisoner clothing, but her hair was still carefully brushed and she looked as neat and poised as if she were walking into her own courtroom. Only the fine lines around her eyes and a certain tension in her shoulders gave away the fact that she wasn't as at ease as she was trying to appear.

Once she was seated opposite Kari, with the bland gray concrete walls as a backdrop behind her, she clasped her hands together in front of her on the counter.

"Thank you for coming," Marge said. "I wasn't sure if you would."

Kari shrugged. "To be honest, I'm not quite sure why I'm here. I can't imagine why you want to talk to me, of all people."

Marge bit her lip. "Because I believe you are the only one who can help me," she said, reluctance clear in her voice. "And I really do need help."

Wow. The woman had nerve. You had to give her that.

"I'm not a lawyer," Kari said. "I'm a former waitress who now spends most of her time cleaning cat cages and trying to figure out how to run a shelter. I don't see how any of that can possibly help you."

"You're smart, tenacious, and you seem to have a gift for getting to the bottom of a mystery," Marge said. Despite the complimentary words, bitterness colored her tone. "I wouldn't be sitting here today if that weren't true. There was a beach house in the Bahamas just waiting for me to come sit on the deck and drink piña coladas. But you managed to find answers that even the police didn't. And now I need you to put that gift to work for me."

"I'm sorry," Kari said, feeling completely lost. "What are you talking about?"

"I didn't kill Bill Myers," Marge said, slapping her hand down on the counter. At a glance from the officer in the back of the room, she sat up straight and made an effort to get her emotions under control. "I want you to find out who did."

"You want *what*?" Kari said. This whole conversation was more than a little surreal.

"Look," the older woman said. "I admit that I wanted to do him in. He was a thorn in my side from day one, and when he threatened to blackmail me for my hard-earned money, I wasn't about to put up with that." Her normally mild countenance took on a surprisingly sharp and cruel edge, as if a songbird had suddenly turned into a hawk.

"You mean the money you stole?" Kari said in a deliberately mild tone.

Marge waved away the nuances. "Whatever. Either way, yes, I had planned to get rid of him. But what matters is that I didn't. Someone else beat me to it. I have no idea who, and I want you to find out."

Kari opened her mouth to protest, but Marge kept on talking.

"The sentence for embezzling is a heck of a lot less harsh than the one for murder. I serve a few years, get out, and get on with my life. If I go away for murder, that's it for me. And since the sheriff and the district attorney are convinced they have the guilty party, they aren't going to look any further to find the killer. That's why I need you."

Kari had a feeling that no matter how hard the forensic accountant looked, he wasn't going to find all the money the court clerk had stolen over the years. If Marge got out, she would no doubt vanish to her island paradise, taking a lot of other people's cash with her. On the other hand, if she really hadn't murdered Myers, should she go to prison for the crime?

"Why should I help you?" Kari asked, since that was more the question for the moment. "We're not exactly best pals. You sent Deputy Carter to vandalize the sanctuary, then told Jack Falco that you could prove Buster bit someone. You are the *last* person I feel like helping at the moment."

Marge pursed her lips. "You don't have to like me," she said. "I don't particularly care. But if you want to keep your precious Buster alive, you'll do your best to prove I didn't commit this murder."

"What are you talking about?" Kari asked, trying not to raise her voice. The woman was such a piece of work.

"I know where Myers kept his record book," Marge said, lowering her voice and looking over her shoulder at the officer seated in the corner, far enough away to give them a modicum of privacy but close enough to jump in if there was trouble.

"What record book?" Kari asked, suddenly a lot more interested.

"That arrogant man kept a notebook detailing all the things he accused dog owners of, and what happened afterward. He was a petty bully, and I know for a fact that he used to take it out and revel in it whenever he was feeling down, because it made him feel powerful and superior." Marge sneered at the memory.

"The point is, that book will clear poor Buster. But I will only tell you where it is if the murder charge against me is dropped. I'm thinking that gives you pretty good incentive to find the real killer. And fast, before it is too late for your precious dog."

* * *

You agreed to that?" Bryn said, her voice high in disbelief. "You have got to be kidding. The woman is a murderer and a thief." They were all gathered around the front desk at the shelter, where they'd started to meet up out of force of habit. A plate of Sara's homemade brownies had already been decimated as Kari had shared her story with the rest. The rich smell of chocolate almost overwhelmed the faint aroma of the special nontoxic cleaner they used on the cages.

Sara cocked her head and looked thoughtful. "She's definitely a thief, but I'm not so sure about the murderer part. I always thought there was something a little odd about the idea of her following Bill Myers here in the middle of the night when she already had a plan to meet up with him later."

"Besides," Suz added, "why would she go to the trouble of asking Kari to track down a killer she knows doesn't exist? If there is nothing else to find, what would be the point?"

"Huh," Bryn said. "That kind of makes sense. What would she have to gain?"

They were all silent for a moment.

"I can't think of anything," Suz finally said. "But that doesn't mean we should go looking for answers. Isn't that what the cops are for?"

"It is," Kari said reluctantly. "But let's face it—Marge is right about one thing. If they already think they have their man, or in this case, their woman, they're not going to be looking any further, are they?"

Daisy, who hadn't said anything up to this point, asked

in a quiet voice, "Do you really think she has evidence that can save Buster?"

Kari thought for a moment, reviewing the entire conversation with Marge in her head. "Well, on the one hand, we know the woman is a liar and a thief, so we have to take everything she says with a grain of salt. But what she said about Bill Myers having a secret book he took out and gloated over rings true. And if there is something in there that can prove he lied about Buster . . . honestly, how do we not at least try?"

"Maybe we should check out Myers's house and see if we can find this book," Bryn suggested. "I'll bet I can slip in through a back window."

"No!" the rest of the women said in unison. Suz snickered at the offended look on Bryn's face.

"Your aunt would never forgive me if you got into trouble," Kari said. She didn't even like to bring a book back to the library late. There was no way she was going to call Izzy and tell her that she'd gotten Bryn arrested.

"And let's be realistic," Sara added. "The cops have undoubtedly been over his house with a fine-toothed comb, especially after they found out about his illegal activities. If this book exists, it is either stashed somewhere else or really well hidden. Clearing Marge of the murder may be our only chance of getting our hands on it."

"Great," Kari said. "Um, anyone have any idea how to do that?"

They all looked at each other in silence for a minute. Clearly nothing brilliant had occurred to anyone.

Queenie, who had been sitting quietly on Kari's lap, suddenly meowed and jumped up on the counter, nearly knocking both the phone and the plate of brownies onto the floor.

"Stay away from those brownies," Kari scolded her. "Chocolate isn't good for kitties."

Queenie meowed again, sounding offended, and then the phone rang, startling them all. Sara, who was the closest, picked it up.

"Serenity Sanctuary," she said. "Sara speaking. How may I help you?"

She listened for a moment without saying anything, but Kari could hear the buzz of a frantic voice on the other end.

"What?" Sara said, when she could get a word in edgewise. "How is that possible? Yes, of course. Look, take him to the vet's. Kari and I will meet you there. No, of course they won't take him away from you again. Just do it, Georgia. It will be okay, I promise. We'll be right there."

She put down the phone and looked at the others in disbelief. "That was Georgia Travis. Remember I told you that Myers had seized her German shepherd, Pepper— short for Sergeant Pepperspray—and supposedly euthanized him? Apparently the dog just showed up at her back door."

"What?" Daisy and Bryn gasped together.

Kari felt her jaw drop. "Is she positive it is the same dog?" she asked.

"She swears she knows her own dog," Sara said in a grim tone. "Georgia says that Pepper is gaunt, and ate like he hadn't been fed in days, plus he had a rope around his neck that he had clearly gnawed through to escape from wherever he was. She said he's in rough shape. She's terrified that the new dog warden will take the dog away again, but Pepper obviously needs to be seen by a vet." She looked at Kari. "I told her we'd meet her there to be supportive, just in case."

"Of course," Kari said. She stared at Queenie, who was innocently licking a paw, as if she hadn't warned them that the phone was about to ring. "Besides, I have a funny feeling this has something to do with our search for who really killed Bill Myers." *A little kitten told me so.*

![cat] Seventeen

By the time Kari and Sara got to the veterinarian's office, Georgia was already in with Dr. McCoy. The receptionist led them back to the room where a serious-looking Angus was examining a gaunt German shepherd. The metal exam table had been lowered to accommodate the larger animal, who was being cooperative despite his weakened state, and was clearly a statuesque and handsome dog when he was at his best. The dog kept turning to stare at the woman next to him with big brown eyes, as if he wanted to make sure she was still there.

Georgia Travis was a tall woman with cropped dark blond hair—she and her dog probably made an impressive pair when things were normal. She was wearing cut-off denim shorts that showed off long powerful legs and a dark blue tank top. Old scar tissue could be seen underneath one wide strap, but she didn't strike Kari as the kind of woman who would be self-conscious about such a thing.

At the moment, all her focus was on her dog, although she

looked up when Kari and Sara entered the room, and smiled gratefully at the former teacher.

"Thank you for coming," Georgia said in a voice that shook a little bit. "I didn't know what to do when Pepper showed up at the back door. For a minute, I thought it was a ghost. Then I remembered you asking me about what happened, and I figured I should call you."

"He's no ghost," Angus said, shaking his head so a lock of slightly shaggy red hair fell into his eyes. He brushed it back with one hand while steadying the dog with the other. "But he's been through a very tough time of it, that much is clear." He nodded at the newcomers in greeting, then returned his focus to his patient.

"Is he going to be okay?" Kari asked. She didn't know who she wanted to hug more, the animal or his owner. Both of them looked equally rocky.

"He's going to be just fine," Angus said, smiling at her and then at Georgia. "He's got some nasty sores around his neck where the rope was, and it looks as though he hasn't eaten in days. One paw seems to be a little bruised too. But a few days of rest and food, and he should be as good as new."

Sara walked over to where a piece of rope had been cut and then tossed on the counter. One ragged end showed where the determined dog had gnawed through it.

"This is awful," she said. "Who would leave a dog tied up without food?"

Kari swallowed hard. "Someone who didn't realize he wouldn't be coming back?" she suggested.

"Bill Myers," she and Sara said in unison.

"What?" Angus's head popped up as he stared from one to the other. "Why on earth would the dog warden have Pepper?"

"That's the million-dollar question, isn't it?" Georgia said, patting the dog's head.

"Are we sure this really *is* Pepper?" Kari asked. After all, the dog was in pretty rough shape and it was possible that Georgia was just wishing her own dog had come back to her. Although the way the dog was behaving made it pretty clear he knew his person.

"Oh, yes," Angus reassured her. "He has a microchip and the numbers match. But I thought you said Myers had the dog euthanized. Why would he lie about a thing like that?"

The expression on Georgia's face made Kari think that if Bill Myers was still alive, the woman would happily reach out and strangle him with her bare hands, bad shoulder or no bad shoulder. "When I asked him for Pepper's body to be returned to me, that officious jerk had the nerve to tell me that the county had already sent him out to be cremated. And you're telling me he had my dog all along? Why?"

Sara played with the colored stripe in her hair. "That's a very good question. Here's another one. If Pepper is still alive, is it possible that some of the other dogs Myers supposedly had put to sleep are also out there somewhere?"

"Oh, lord," Kari said, putting a hand over her heart, which had suddenly started beating twice as fast. "He must have left some food for Pepper, which eventually ran out. What if there are other dogs who are in the same place, and they're starving and can't get loose?"

Georgia turned pale. "That would be horrible," she said. "But Pepper can't tell us where he was. What can we do?"

Sara got a resolute look on her face that Kari was quite familiar with. The one you never argued with, if you knew what was good for you.

"You have to go to the sheriff," she said to Georgia. "He needs to know about this."

Georgia shook her head. "Bill Myers is dead, Sara. The sheriff will be unhappy to learn that Myers was up to even more dubious activities than you've already uncovered, but it isn't as though the sheriff's department has the manpower to do a countywide search for some dogs that we don't even know for sure are missing. And if they are alive, there is no way to know if they are even in this area."

"We need to talk to Deputy Carter," Kari said. "He was in on Myers's dirty deeds as dog warden. Maybe he'll know."

"You have to go," Georgia said, putting her arms around Pepper. "I can't leave Pepper right now. After Dr. McCoy is done bandaging his neck and giving him fluids and a B-12 shot, I'm taking my dog back where he belongs. I can go in and talk to the sheriff tomorrow, but there really isn't much to tell him. I heard a noise at the back door, and Pepper was there, limping and whining."

Kari looked at Sara and the older woman nodded at her. "Okay," Kari said. "You take your baby home. I'll see if I can find us some more answers."

She wasn't looking forward to talking to the sheriff again, but at least this time she had good news. Of a sort.

So let me get this straight," Richardson said in a determinedly patient voice. "Georgia Travis's German shepherd, the one that Bill Myers said he was going to have euthanized, showed up at her back door alive and well. And you think this is a bad thing?"

Kari clenched her hands on her lap, hopefully out of

sight from where the sheriff was sitting across from her, and took a deep breath before she tried to explain the whole thing again. "Obviously, Pepper being alive is a good thing."

"Pepper?" the sheriff said.

"Pepper. Short for Sergeant Pepperspray. Georgia's dog." The sheriff nodded, so she went on. "But obviously Myers lied about having the dog put to death, so now we're worried that maybe there are other dogs out there, tied up without food or water, in who knows what kind of conditions." She held up the chewed-through rope she'd brought with her, to make her point.

Richardson held out his hand for the rope and looked at it for a minute. "I see your point, Ms. Stuart. But the dog warden is dead. There is no one to punish for this, and I can't send out officers who are needed to deal with actual crimes to search for theoretically possible dogs that may or may not be in trouble. For all we know, Myers just hadn't gotten around to having this Pepper put down yet."

Well, Georgia had called it, almost word for word. Kari guessed that the woman would know how a law officer would think, since she'd been one herself. "But, Sheriff," she said.

He shook his head. "I'm sorry, Ms. Stuart. I know your heart is in the right place, but I'm afraid it is too late for all those other dogs. Unless you can bring me some kind of evidence that Myers kept any of them alive and locked up somewhere, there is nothing I can do."

Kari bit her lip. "Actually, there is one thing you can do. I promise it doesn't involve sending anyone out looking for theoretical dogs."

"Oh?" Richardson raised one eyebrow. "And what would that be?"

"I'd like to talk to Deputy Carter," she said.

The eyebrow went up a little higher. "You know he's not exactly your biggest fan, Ms. Stuart."

Kari made a face. "The feeling is completely mutual, Sheriff. But if anyone knows what happened with Pepper and if there are any other animals still out there, it's him."

Richardson pondered her request for a moment. "Well, you could be right, although I don't know if he'll talk to you. And I want to be there if he does."

She wanted to protest but figured she'd probably pushed him about as far as she was going to get. "It's worth a try," she said. "And if it were your dog, I'm pretty sure you'd go to any lengths to find out if he was still alive."

The sheriff glanced at the picture on his desk, which featured a handsome golden retriever proudly holding a stick in his mouth.

"All right, Ms. Stuart. I'll see what I can do. But I can't make the man talk to you." He pushed back from his desk with a scrape of wooden chair legs. "I'll be right back. Stay put."

Kari waited until he left the room to cheer quietly to herself. Richardson might say he couldn't make Carter talk to her, but it would take a stronger man than the former deputy to say no to the sheriff if he was determined to make someone say yes.

Carter scowled at her across the visitor's table, his already unattractive face further marred by bloodshot eyes and uncombed hair. He looked as though he'd aged ten years since he'd been arrested, and although he was just as unpleasant as always, his belligerence seemed to lack its usual force.

Kari wasn't sure if that was due to the sheriff's presence, which seemed to loom over them even though he was leaning against the wall in the far corner, or just because Carter no longer had the power of a uniform to hide behind.

"What the heck do you want?" was the only greeting she got.

"Nice to see you too," she said. And it was. Nice to see him behind bars, anyway. "I was hoping you could answer a few questions for me."

Carter crossed his beefy arms over his chest. "What's in it for me?" he asked. "Because last I checked, I didn't exactly owe you any favors."

"Considering the damage you did to my building, I'd say you owe me plenty of favors," Kari said in an even tone. "But what did you have in mind? I'm pretty sure the sheriff would frown on me smuggling a file or a lock pick into the jail inside a cake."

"I would," Richardson said. "In fact, I don't see anything Ms. Stuart can do to help your situation. Maybe you should consider answering her questions because it is the right thing to do."

Carter snorted. "Sure. I've lost my wife, my job, my pension, and I'm sitting here in the same place I sent actual criminals to just because I bent the rules a little bit. I'm feelin' all kinds of warmth and kindness toward the both of you just at the moment."

Richardson sighed and pushed off from the wall. "I told you this was a lost cause, Ms. Stuart," he said. "Let's go."

"Hang on a minute," Carter said, holding up a meaty hand. "I didn't say I wouldn't talk to the lady. I just want something in return."

"What's that?" Kari asked.

"I want my sentence reduced," the former deputy said. "For cooperating."

The sheriff made a rude noise. "Not likely. You broke a dozen laws, not to mention the vandalism to Ms. Stuart's animal rescue. The extent of the damage makes that one a felony, which is why you're sitting here today."

Carter's bloodshot eyes narrowed. "Not if she drops the charges, it doesn't. Everyone knows she's rich now." He rubbed two fingers together to represent her wealth. "Replacing a few windows is no big deal. You want me to talk, I want those vandalism charges dropped. Everything else might get me a few months, instead of a few years. Or maybe just probation and some fines."

"Okay," Kari said.

"Now wait a minute," Richardson started to protest.

She held up a finger. "One, I will only drop the charges if the information you give us actually helps us locate other missing dogs. And two"—she held up another finger—"if you ever come near my sanctuary or bother anyone who works there ever again, I'll have you back in here so fast it will make your head spin."

Richardson raised an eyebrow, but then he shrugged. She guessed that he was figuring that with everything Carter had already lost, additional jail time was almost superfluous. "Up to you, Ms. Stuart. I can't force you to press charges."

Carter sat up straighter. "So what's this about missing dogs? If someone else is taking animals, I don't see how I can help you none."

"Why don't you start by telling us what Myers did with the animals he seized," Kari said, ignoring his comment for now. "Did he actually have them all euthanized, or was there something else going on?"

"Oh," Carter said, looking away. "Well, that was kind of his special side project," the former deputy said. "An extra earner, he called it."

Richardson stood up a little straighter, and Kari could tell he was suddenly interested, although he didn't interrupt her.

"Extra earner how?" she asked. "Did he make people pay to get their dogs back?"

Carter shook his head. "No. That wouldn't have worked, because then he'd have had too many folks knowing he was up to something shady. Sometimes, like with that professor's dog, if the animal was really valuable, after Myers was done collecting the money for the tickets he'd declare the animal dangerous and seize it. But instead of having them put to sleep like he said he would, he'd sell them to someone far from town. There's a big market for some of them purebreds, you know."

His thick eyebrows pulled together in a frown. "Mind you, that was just *his* gig. I didn't get a penny from those dogs."

"What a shame," Kari said sweetly. But inside her heart was racing. "Are you saying that Steve Clark's dog is still alive?"

"Steve Clark? Oh, the professor. Yeah, that was the Irish wolfhound, right? Dang, those things are worth a *lot* of money." He rolled his eyes. "Who the heck pays thousands of dollars for a dog? I just don't get it."

Richardson pushed himself off the wall. "So the dog really is alive? Where is it?"

"How would I know?" Carter said. "I already told you, I had nothing to do with that end of things. You'd have to look in Myers's record book to find that kind of info."

"Record book?" Richardson said.

Now it was Kari's turn to sit up straight. "Marge Farrow told me that Bill Myers had some kind of notebook where he wrote down all his activities," Kari said. "But she wouldn't tell us where it was." Kari thought it probably wasn't a good idea to tell the sheriff that Marge had promised them the book if they could clear her of the murder charge. But finding out where Ranger had been taken was just one more reason why they had to get their hands on that notebook.

"Huh," was all the sheriff said. She couldn't tell if he believed in the book's existence or not.

"What about Pepper?" Kari asked. "That's why I'm here, because Georgia Travis's dog Pepper showed up at her back door, half-starved with a rope around his neck. If he hadn't chewed himself free, he'd still be wherever Myers left him. But why take that dog? You said that Myers would pull this scam with valuable animals. Pepper is a retired police dog. He wasn't worth much money. Why take him?"

Carter flushed and squirmed in his chair. "Uh, that one might have been my fault."

Richardson took one step forward. "Explain."

"Well, you see, I heard this rumor that Curtis Fry had a pot field somewhere in the woods where his grandfather's old still had supposedly been," Carter said. He couldn't meet his former boss's eyes and looked at Kari instead. "Fry has such a bad reputation, it seemed like it could actually be true. And we figured, well, I figured, that if we found it, we could make a little extra cash by promising not to turn him in."

"Blackmailing him, you mean," the sheriff said through clenched teeth.

"Yeah, well, whatever. Or we could have taken the pot

and sold it. It's not like he could have called the cops, right?" Carter started to laugh at what had probably been an old joke between him and Myers, then caught himself when Richardson glared in his direction.

"So which one did you end up doing?" the sheriff asked.

"Neither," Carter said. "The problem is that no one knows exactly where that old still was located. It was kind of an urban legend. Or a rural legend, I guess. Nobody is even sure if the thing existed. So Myers came up with the idea of fabricating charges against Georgia and kind of, um, commandeering the dog. He thought that being a police dog, Pepper would be able to sniff out the pot if Myers could get him anywhere close."

"And did he?" Kari asked. This story was getting stranger and stranger.

"I don't know," Carter said, then cringed as the sheriff took another step closer. "Honest. I have no idea if Myers found anything or not. He died before he could tell me anything."

Richardson shook his head in disgust. "What a load of crap," he said. "I'm sorry you wasted your time, Ms. Stuart. I think it's clear that Carter here just made up this story in an effort to try to get a reduced sentence."

"Sheriff!" Carter protested. "It's all true, I swear."

"What about Pepper?" Kari asked the sheriff. "He is still alive, after all. Maybe Myers really was using him to look for drugs."

Richardson sighed. "I think it is much more likely that Myers simply hadn't disposed of the dog yet when Marge killed him. I'm glad he made it back to his owner, but that doesn't mean there are any other dogs to find. I'm afraid you're barking up the wrong tree; you should excuse the expression."

He nodded at the guard to take Carter back to his cell. He protested all the way, and the sheriff escorted Kari to the front room.

"You need to let this go, Ms. Stuart," he said. "I think we've found all the answers we're going to find in this case."

Kari wasn't dumb enough to say so out loud, but she was pretty sure he was wrong. And she had an idea of where to look next.

Eighteen

Kari stopped at the veterinary offices on her way back home to see if Georgia was still there. Angus came out of one of the exam rooms as Kari was chatting with the receptionist at the front desk.

"Hey there," he said, giving her a big smile that made her feel as though there were miniature butterflies flitting around in her stomach. "If you're looking for Georgia, Pepper, and your friend Sara, you just missed them."

"Oh," Kari said. "How is Pepper doing, if you can tell me without breaking patient-doctor confidentiality?"

He helped himself to a cup of coffee from the station set up for staff and pet owners, and added a packet of sugar. Kari thought about having a cup herself but decided she was wired enough already.

"I think it should be fine, since you and your friend were in the room while I was examining the dog, and clearly know as much about the circumstances as I do, if not more." He pushed his hair out of his eyes again and Kari fought back a giggle.

"You really need to get that trimmed," she said. "My best friend, Suz, is a dog groomer. Maybe she can fix you up." Kari didn't admit it to most people, but Suz actually trimmed Kari's hair for her. Hey, if all you wanted was an inch taken off all around, who better to do it than someone who clipped tiny dogs for a living?

"I might take you up on that," he said. "I never seem to have time to make an appointment. Maybe when our other vet gets back from vacation." He sighed, looking tired.

"Anyway, Pepper is doing really well, all things considered. He was favoring one paw because he'd torn a couple of nails. Probably trying to dig himself free or get that rope off his neck. His neck has some raw spots where the rope rubbed, and he is malnourished and dehydrated. We pulled a few ticks off him. But all of that is relatively minor and should heal up on its own with a little time and some antibiotic ointment for those sores. I think he is going to be a very spoiled dog for a while."

Kari had to blink rapidly for a minute, thinking about how she would feel if she thought one of her animals was dead and she suddenly got it back unexpectedly. "Georgia must feel like this is some kind of miracle. I know I do, and Pepper isn't even my dog."

"Did you find out what happened to him?" Angus asked. "I still find this whole thing completely bizarre. I thought I was moving to a small, sleepy town, and now there is a murder and an embezzling court clerk and a crooked dog warden who was in cahoots with a sheriff's deputy and dogs coming back from the dead."

"I assure you," Kari said, "we're not usually nearly this interesting. And I have to admit, I prefer it that way. But in answer to your question, it appears that the crooked dog warden stole him so he could use Pepper, who is a retired police dog, to try to sniff out a marijuana patch that might or might not exist."

"Good grief," Angus said, swallowing down the rest of his coffee. "This just gets more and more intriguing."

He gave her a crooked smile. "Speaking of intriguing, Dr. Burnett will be back next week and I won't have to cover so many hours here. I wondered if you might be interested in having coffee with me sometime."

Kari felt a little flicker of anticipation when she realized that he meant her when he said *intriguing*. She didn't think anyone had ever referred to her that way before. She hadn't really dated much since her divorce. In truth, the marriage had made her doubt her own judgment when it came to men. But Angus McCoy had "good guy" written all over him. She had changed a lot of things about her life recently. Maybe it was time to change this too.

"Sure," she said, trying not to look self-conscious. "I'd like that."

"Great," he said. "I'd better get to my next patient. How about I give you a call next week?"

"Great," she said. "I should get going too. I'll talk to you later." Then it suddenly hit her that if things didn't go well at the court hearing for Buster next week, she might not be in much of a mood for a first date. If that was what this was. Man, why did life have to be so complicated?

After a quick text exchange with Sara, Kari headed over to Georgia's house. The former state trooper lived a few blocks off Main Street in an area made up of smaller older homes with modest yards. Many of the neighboring houses had lawns strewn with tricycles and the other debris left behind by small children. Georgia's yard was much neater, with a large oak tree in the middle and a surprisingly whimsical collection of garden gnomes lining the front walk.

Sara opened the door and led Kari through the living room into a warm and inviting kitchen. One wall was painted a deep red that matched the pottery lining the open shelves on the walls, and copper pans hung from a rack suspended from the ceiling. Kari kind of wanted to move in, especially when she saw the window seat with its comfy cushion and bookshelf full of cookbooks.

"Hi," Georgia said from where she sat at the wooden table at the far end of the room. "Help yourself to some coffee or tea. I'd get up, but well"—she indicated Pepper, who was sitting next to her with his head firmly ensconced in her lap—"I'm kind of stuck."

"I understand completely," Kari said. "I recently went to bed an hour later than I'd planned to because my kitten was too comfortable to move." She took the cup of tea Sara handed her and took a seat. "I can't believe how much better Pepper looks already."

He did, too. There was a bandage wrapped around his neck, and he was still way too thin, but his posture was erect and his tail thumped steadily on the floor as he snuggled up to his person. Kari thought her heart would burst with joy. It had been a tough couple of weeks, but this moment alone made it all worth it.

Too bad she was going to ruin it.

"Dr. McCoy did a great job with him," Georgia said. "I'm so glad he joined the clinic. I think he's fabulous."

Kari gazed down at her mug. "Yes," she said. "He's very nice." She was pretty sure her face was turning pink. Maybe they'd think it was the steam.

"Very nice?" Sara said. "Is that why you're blushing?" Or not.

"Well, he might have asked me out for coffee. You know, nothing major," Kari said.

Sara grinned at her. "We will definitely be discussing this later. But in the meanwhile, what did you learn from Carter? Was he willing to talk to you? Did he say anything helpful?"

"He did," Kari said. "But only after I agreed to drop the vandalism charges against him."

"Kari! You didn't!" Sara gasped. She gave Kari the full force of her disapproving-teacher look.

"Don't worry," Kari said. "I told him I'd only do it if his information led to us rescuing another dog, or something else equally useful. As it is, he admitted that Myers had been selling at least some of the dogs he seized and supposedly euthanized."

"That's great," Georgia said. "Now you can return them to their owners." She leaned down and gave Pepper a big hug.

"Unfortunately, we can't," Kari said, sipping at her tea. "At least, not yet. Carter swears that Myers is the only one who knew what he did with the dogs, and short of a séance, there is no way we can get the information out of him."

"Oh." Georgia slumped in her seat. Pepper reached up and licked her cheek.

"Well, it's not a completely lost cause," Kari said. "Marge Farrow told us that Myers kept a notebook with all the info about the animals he fined unnecessarily, stole, whatever. And Carter told me that the whereabouts of Steve Clark's dog, and others, are in it. The problem is, the only person who knows where the notebook is hidden is Marge, and she won't tell us how to find it unless we can clear her of the murder."

"That's crazy," Georgia said.

"Which part?" Sara asked in a dry tone. "The part where Marge expects us to clear her of murder, or the part where we actually believe anything she says?" She took a sip of her own tea, then made a face, although whether at the tea or the situation, Kari couldn't tell.

"*Do* you believe her?" Georgia asked.

Kari sighed. "I actually do," she admitted. "Well, I believe she didn't commit the murder. The police found a gun, weights, and a tarp in the back of her car, and a series of texts on her phone that proved she'd set up a meeting with Myers. And she confessed to intending to kill him but swears that someone else beat her to it. It doesn't make any sense to me that she would plan everything out so carefully and then just act on impulse instead."

"I take it that's what the sheriff thinks?" Georgia said.

Kari nodded. "Yes, it is. So he's not even looking for someone else. Marge knew we'd been asking questions and poking around already, and knows we're motivated to save Buster. So I guess she figures we're her best chance at being proven innocent."

"Well, innocent of murder, anyway," Sara said, getting up to add hot water to her cup. "She's definitely going to jail for embezzlement."

Georgia's eyebrows shot up. "Wow. I heard she had been arrested for the murder, but I hadn't heard anything about embezzlement."

"I think they're trying to keep it quiet for now, until they find out how bad it is," Sara said. "It's kind of a black eye for the town, since it had apparently been going on for some time and no one caught on. The same with what Myers and Carter had been up to. I think there are going to be some heated words at the next town council meeting."

"Sheriff Richardson is furious about what his deputies had been doing," Kari added. "I think he takes it very personally. Maybe that's why he wants to be able to hand over the murder case all neatly tied up in a bow."

"Even if he has the wrong person?" Georgia asked, sounding doubtful.

"Well, to be fair, I think he believes he has the right person," Kari said. "But we're coming at this from a slightly different angle, and I honestly think he's wrong."

"So what are you going to do?" Georgia asked.

Kari bit her lip and glanced at Sara, who nodded back, as if she had some idea of what Kari had in mind.

"I was hoping you would be willing to help us with that," Kari said. "Well, more specifically, you and Pepper." She held her breath, sure that Georgia would protest that Pepper had just gotten home, that he had been through enough and was still recovering from his ordeal.

"I thought you'd never ask," Georgia said, a fierce light in her eyes. "We're definitely in."

"You are?" Kari said in amazement.

"You are?" Sara echoed.

"You bet I am," the other woman said. "If there is any chance that someone else's beloved dog is out there waiting to be found, there is no way I'm not going to help make that happen." She hugged Pepper again, and the German shepherd gave a soft, happy bark.

"Besides," she said. "I might be retired, but once a cop, always a cop. I like Sheriff Richardson, but I agree with you that it is possible he has the wrong person locked up for this murder. I detested Bill Myers with every bone in my body, but even he deserves to have his killer brought to justice. If Pepper and I can work with you to find the answers, we're going to do it."

"That's great," Sara said. "But are you sure Pepper is up to it?"

"Doc McCoy said he needed to rest tonight and get plenty of food and water," Georgia said. "But come morning, as long as he isn't still favoring that one paw too much, we should be good to go. What exactly did you have in mind, Kari?"

"I was thinking that we could take a page out of Bill Myers's book," Kari said. "Only in reverse, as it were. Since Pepper made his way here from wherever he was kept, I thought that perhaps he could backtrack his own trail and lead us to wherever Myers was holding him."

"You think Pepper might be able to guide us to the other dogs, if there are some," Georgia said. "That's very clever. With his training, that's definitely a possibility. Although you have to keep in mind that by the time he finally got loose, he was probably weak with hunger and thirst and fear. We can't be sure he had enough focus to be aware of his surroundings."

"He had enough focus to find his way home," Sara said in her usual firm, reassuring tone that made it nearly impossible to doubt whatever it was she said. "I'm betting he can follow his own scent back to where he came from."

Kari pulled out her phone and looked at the weather app. "Fifty percent chance of rain tonight," she said worriedly. "Will that make a difference?"

"It could," Georgia said, pressing her lips together. "But we're going to have to take the risk. I'm not taking Pepper out until tomorrow, after he's had a chance to rest."

"Of course you're not," Sara said, patting her hand. "We wouldn't even consider it. We'll just have to pray for clear weather, and that Pepper feels up to it in the morning."

And that he can actually lead us someplace useful, Kari thought. *Because Sergeant Pepperspray is our only lead.*

❡ Nineteen

Kari woke up the next morning to a purring kitten nudging her face with one velvet paw, undoubtedly a subtle hint that it was time to get up and feed everyone. Padding barefoot to the bedroom window, Kari held her breath until she looked out to see a slightly foggy morning with no sign of rain.

"I think we're okay," she said to Queenie as she exchanged her pajamas for a pair of jeans and a lightweight long-sleeved cotton tee shirt. It would be cooler up in the hills, if that was where they ended up, and she wanted to be prepared for walking through rough terrain and underbrush if necessary. She'd put on her hiking boots before she headed out the door, just in case.

After the cats and Fred had eaten, and Fred had gone outside for his morning constitutional, Kari bolted down a hasty breakfast of toast and cheese and a banana with her coffee. She was too jittery to sit still, and impatient to set off on their mission. She and Queenie had a brief argument at the door when the kitten insisted she should accompany Kari, and Kari attempted to persuade her otherwise.

"We have no idea how long we'll be out or what we'll be getting into," Kari said, feeling slightly silly to be explaining things to a cat. Which didn't stop her from doing it, of course. "I'm sure you would be very helpful, but I think this time you should stay home."

Queenie gave an indignant meow and stalked off to curl up in a spot of sunlight on the battered living room couch.

"I'll give you extra treats when I get home," Kari said as she went out the door. The kitten did not look impressed by this peace offering, although a brief flick of the tail might have signaled her acceptance. Fred, as usual, showed a distinct lack of interest in anything that didn't involve food, and did not volunteer to come along. The other two cats were already asleep on the bed.

Kari popped her head into the shelter briefly to make sure everything was under control. Sara and Bryn were already hard at work cleaning the cat cages in the front room, and Jim's off-key singing could be heard coming from the main feline room. He occasionally came in on a Saturday if they were shorthanded.

"Are you sure you don't want one of us to come with you?" Sara asked, sounding a little anxious. "You know, for backup?"

"Backup for what?" Bryn asked, not looking up from the food bowls she was refilling. "They're off on a wild-goose chase." The younger woman was clearly less than enthusiastic about Kari's plan. "Do you really think they're going to find anything?"

Kari's stomach sank. Bryn was probably right. Still,

they had to try *something*. "If this doesn't work," she said, "I'm going to see if I can talk the sheriff into letting us look around Myers's house for that book. After all, when they searched the house for evidence, they didn't know the book even existed, so maybe the cops missed it."

Bryn straightened up with a sigh, pressing her hands into the small of her back. The lower cages had to be cleaned while crawling around on your hands and knees, and the largest ones—set aside for nursing mothers and their kittens, usually—involved putting almost your entire body inside to reach into the rear corners.

"If the book even exists," she said, pulling a protesting feline out of a carrier so he could be popped back into the newly cleaned space. "After everything we've learned, I'd say Marge Farrow is a pretty dubious source of information. I think you'd be better off staying here and getting things ready for us to open as soon as the new fences are up."

Now that the sheriff had released the crime scene, Kari had been able to get a local contractor to promise to come put the fencing up and reinforce the existing dog runs. It had taken some fast talking and the promise of a hefty bonus if he came out right away, but after being on hold for so long, she thought it was worth it.

"I don't expect this to take more than a couple of hours," Kari said. "I'll be back before you know it." Sara gave her a sympathetic glance but didn't say anything. Her theory was that Bryn would come around in time, and for the most part Kari believed her. Change was hard for everyone. Heck, her whole life had turned upside down, and some days she wasn't sure if she trusted herself either.

She glanced at her watch. "Okay, I told Georgia I'd be at her house at eight thirty if she didn't call me to say Pepper wasn't feeling up to it, so I'd better get going. Wish me luck."

Sara came over and gave her a high five. "Good luck," the older woman said. "I hope you come back with good news, like a couple of healthy dogs we can reunite with their owners, or some kind of clue to the location of this mystery book."

Kari didn't want to jinx it by saying anything out loud, but she was secretly hoping that Pepper might lead them to some kind of hiding place that Myers had kept up in the hills. Maybe the book would even be there, and they could use it to track his movements *and* find a clue to the identity of the real murderer.

Of course, they might not find anything at all, but she refused to even consider that possibility. This wild mission just had to work. Too much was riding on it for it not to.

Apparently Georgia was just as eager to get going as Kari was, since the former trooper was sitting out on her front steps with Pepper when Kari pulled into the driveway. As usual, the Toyota gave a weird little rattle as it shut off, and she reminded herself that as soon as she had time, she *really* needed to find another car. Preferably one that didn't have over two hundred thousand miles on the odometer.

Georgia was dressed almost exactly the same as Kari, in worn blue jeans, a dark blue long-sleeved tee shirt, and hiking boots. She was also wearing a loose denim jacket, which seemed like it might be a bit too warm for the day. Kari wondered if maybe Georgia was worried about tree branches rubbing up against her bad shoulder. Georgia's short hair was tucked under a cheerful red bandana, and a matching one was tied around Pepper's neck, almost hiding the white bandage underneath.

The German shepherd looked much perkier than he had the day before, Kari was glad to see. He rose from the steps as Kari approached and glanced up at Georgia as if for permission. When she said, "Okay, Pepper, friend," he bounded down the steps to sniff at Kari and lick her hand.

"Good morning, Pepper," Kari said. "Good morning, Georgia. He's looking so much better."

"He is," Georgia said with a warm smile. "He doesn't seem to be limping at all and he ate breakfast like a champ. He's a tough old boy, just like his mama." She walked down to join them. "We both bounce back pretty fast from adversity."

She handed Kari a small backpack. "This has a few supplies—a couple of water bottles, some snacks for us and for the dog, and a first-aid kit, just in case we find another animal in rough shape. Do you mind carrying it so I can focus on Pepper?" She also gave her a bandana that matched the one she wore. "Put this on. That way you'll be easier to spot if we get separated."

"Oh, good idea," Kari said. She hadn't even thought of bringing anything along except her cell phone, which probably wouldn't even work once they got up into the hills. "Sure, I'll take it." She slung the bag over one shoulder and tied the cloth over her hair. "Don't you need a leash for Pepper?"

Georgia laughed. "Nope. He's trained to respond to voice commands. Besides, I don't dare put a collar around his neck until the sores heal, so it's a good thing we don't need one. Here, I'll show you." She snapped her fingers and the German shepherd immediately came to attention.

"Pepper, heel," Georgia said, and the dog trotted over and stood next to her. "Stay." Georgia walked over to where Kari was standing. "Come." The dog waited for the command and then did as she said.

"That's great," Kari said, then hesitated. "I, um, didn't exactly have a plan. Do you have any suggestions for how we should start? I hate to make Pepper walk all the way back to wherever he was."

"I've been thinking about that," Georgia said. "If what Deputy Carter said is true, and not just another lie— which is a big *if*, frankly—then Myers was probably keeping Pepper somewhere up in the hills, near where he was looking for this supposed pot field."

"That's what I figured," Kari said. "But that's a lot of territory."

"It is," Georgia agreed. "But we can drive up in that direction, at least part of the way. There are a lot of small, barely used roads that lead up even farther into the back country. It's possible that Pepper will pick up on a scent that way. If not, then we'll have to come back here and start from this end, but I'd rather not do that if we don't have to."

"Sounds good to me," Kari said. "Do you want to take my car or yours?"

Georgia glanced at the Toyota with its rusty patches and the rear bumper that was held on with wire, and smothered a laugh behind one hand. "Uh, why don't we take my Jeep," she said. "That way Pepper won't be distracted by any new smells."

"You're very polite," Kari said with a smile. "But yes, your Jeep is probably a good idea if we're going to be going up rough roads. Half of my car is held together with duct tape and prayer."

"I thought you won the lottery," Georgia said, more curiosity than criticism in her tone. They walked over to her shiny red Jeep and Pepper immediately hopped into the back seat, which had a tan quilted dog cover on it. "Don't people usually go right out and buy new cars? Especially if they actually need them?"

Kari shrugged. "Most people, probably. I was going to be more practical. I was figuring out exactly what I wanted to do with the money and how I was going to make the most of it. I didn't want to go off half-cocked without thinking things through." She got in and buckled her seat belt, putting the pack down on the floor in front of her.

Georgia slid behind the wheel. "So you bought a rundown animal rescue." She snorted. "How's that working out for you?"

"Surprisingly well, other than having the dog warden murdered in my backyard, not being able to open up because we were a crime scene, being vandalized by Deputy Carter, and having a dog still under threat with outstanding charges left over from Bill Myers's tenure."

Kari was surprised to discover it was really true. Despite all those things, she absolutely loved the shelter, and couldn't imagine her life without it. Or Queenie, for that matter. "But mostly good."

"I'm glad," Georgia said. "I'd been hoping someone would step up and take it over, but for a long time it looked like a lost cause."

"I like a good lost cause," Kari said firmly.

"So do I," Georgia said. "Let's go see if we can tackle this one."

*   *   *

They headed up Steeple Road, named for the three churches that lined the bottom two miles of the street. Eventually it merged into County Route 12, which zigzagged to the left and became County Route 12A, not that there was anything other than one crooked road sign to indicate that anything had changed. Tall evergreens lined both sides of the road as they climbed higher, with the occasional ancient oak tree arching over to cast a leafy shadow on the gravel surface. The dappled shade lent a calm, almost otherworldly aura to the journey, making Kari feel as though she was traveling through another dimension.

A doe and two spotted fawns raised their heads as they cropped the grass at the verge but didn't even bother to run away. Pepper, true to his training, never let out a peep, although his large head hung out the window, watching everything.

At a split in the road, Georgia slowed the Jeep to a crawl. "Any idea which direction we should head in?" she asked Kari.

Kari bit her lip. "Sorry, no. Your guess is as good as mine."

Georgia grinned. "Oh, I don't know, mine might be a little bit better." She pulled off to the side, not that they'd seen another vehicle in over five minutes, and opened the back door to let Pepper out.

"What do you think, boy? Smell anything interesting?" After letting him sniff at the rope that had been around his neck, she walked him first up to the left-hand fork, and then to the right. Pepper sniffed the air in one direction, then the other. For a heart-stopping few seconds, Kari thought they were going to have to turn around. But then Pepper walked back to the road to the left and gave three sharp barks.

A hunter's light glinted in Georgia's eyes. "By George, Watson," she said with a smile. "I believe the game is afoot."

♟ Twenty

Once he'd been given the command "Find," Pepper set off without hesitation. He walked slowly but methodically, periodically stopping to sniff at something only he could perceive. Kari hoped they weren't following a rabbit or, worse yet, some kind of wild animal like a coyote. Plenty of those lived up in these hills. Even from her house, you could occasionally hear them howling on a quiet night.

They hiked up that road for about a half an hour, swatting at the occasional mosquito and stopping a couple of times to give Pepper a drink of water. There was no traffic and they didn't see any other people, although there were a few rustic cabins set back a ways from the road. Georgia said they probably belonged to seasonal visitors who came up to hunt or fish, and were unoccupied more often than not.

Eventually Pepper steered them off the tiny secondary road onto an even smaller tertiary one, barely wide enough for two cars to pass each other, dusty and overgrown with weeds; it was clear from the shallow ruts that it was barely used and mostly unmaintained. Cicadas buzzed in the underbrush and once a red fox scooted across the way no more than six feet in front of them. Pepper's head shot up, but he held his position. Kari started to think that maybe he really was following a real scent.

She wasn't sure whether to be happy about that or frightened of what they might find at the other end.

Another half an hour of walking made her very glad she'd worn the hiking boots, especially when the dog stopped and sat at the entrance to a narrow trail that marked the end of the road they were on. A chain was slung across it from two poles on either side, and a faded and battered sign read: *Private. No trespassing.* Faint tire impressions could be seen in the dirt track on the other side.

Georgia and Kari exchanged glances. "What do you think?" Kari asked.

The other woman peered over the rusted chain. "Looks like someone used a four-wheeler to get up and down from whatever is at the other end of this path. No way you could fit a car up there. Without any rain for the last few days, it is hard to tell how recent those tracks are. They could have been made by Bill Myers before he died, or someone could have come up here yesterday. Impossible to say."

"Do we keep going?" Kari asked. Despite her trepidation, she didn't want to give up, but she wasn't sure how the former trooper would feel about technically breaking the law.

Georgia glanced down at Pepper, who was staring intently down the tight and shadowy confines of the trail, his focus unwavering. "Heck yeah," she said. "I didn't hike all this way to turn back now."

They ducked under the chain and continued on, a little faster now as Pepper seemed to gain confidence the closer he got to his goal. Finally, after a few minutes of brisk walking, he marched up to a strong but slender tree with peeling white bark and sat down at its base, giving his mistress a quiet woof.

"Well, will you look at that," Georgia said, squatting down to examine the base of the birch. She pushed back some tall grasses to reveal the remains of a tattered rope, one end tied around the tree and the other hanging loose, fraying where it had been chewed through.

Kari joined her. "This is it, isn't it?" she said. "The place where poor Pepper was left tied up." Her heart ached at the thought of the innocent animal, left out here on his own.

"I'd say so," Georgia said. "Although I didn't bring along the other piece of rope to compare to this one. It's still in the Jeep."

She walked around to the other side of the tree and let out an "Aha!" before resurfacing with two empty plastic bowls in her hands. One was red and looked as though it had been recycled from some kind of cut-down jug, and the other might have been a restaurant take-out container at some point in its life. "I'm guessing there was originally food and water in these, although there's nothing in them now except a couple of bugs."

"So Myers did plan to come back and get Pepper," Kari said. "Or he probably wouldn't have bothered to leave those."

Georgia scowled. "That doesn't make me feel any better about him. The no-good jerk stole my dog and left him tied up in the middle of the woods. If Myers wasn't already dead, I swear I'd kill him."

"I don't blame you," Kari said, petting Pepper. "But now what?" She glanced around at their surroundings. Nothing but trees and scrub brush and the intermittent sound of birds singing. Her heart sank. "I don't see anything that would indicate any other dogs were ever here. Definitely nothing that looks like it would be a hiding place for that book. Are we at the end of the trail?"

Georgia pursed her lips, scratching at an insect bite that had somehow made it under the collar of her shirt. Finally, she shook her head. "I don't think so," she said. "There had to be a reason why Myers left Pepper in this specific spot. Maybe there is something nearby that was of some kind of interest."

"Like that marijuana field Carter said was supposedly up here?"

"Sure," Georgia said. "Although to be honest, I never even heard rumors of such a thing." She shrugged, wincing a bit as if her bad shoulder objected to the movement. "Mind you, there are plenty of people back up in these hills who grow a small patch for their own use. Back when I was on the force, we knew about most of them and just let it go. But someone with a substantial enough operation to interest Bill Myers? I don't know about that.

"Still," she said, perking up. "Myers had to be looking for *something* up here. Something that he thought only a retired police dog could find for him. And Pepper's specialty was drug detection. So we might as well keep going, and see if he can lead us to whatever it is."

Kari looked around, suddenly feeling her skin crawl as though she was being watched.

"You don't think that whoever the pot field belongs to is up here, do you?" she said hesitantly. "I mean, if there is one."

Georgia glanced at Pepper, who was alert but at ease. "I don't think so," she said. But she put her hand behind her back, under the jacket she wore, seemingly checking on something. "If we had company in these woods, we'd hear it. And Pepper would give me some kind of indication. But if you want to turn back, I'd understand."

Kari thought about the other dogs whose whereabouts were still unknown, and the need to find out who really did kill the dog warden so they could prove Marge Farrow's innocence and get their hands on Bill Myers's notebook. "I'm in if you are," she said, setting her jaw. "As long as you think Pepper is up to it."

A tiny smile tugged at the corner of Georgia's mouth. "Are you kidding? Once he's on the track of something, I practically have to carry him away to get him to give it up." She gave Pepper a treat and said, "Find, Pepper. Find."

With that, they were off again.

This time Pepper proceeded more slowly, as if he wasn't quite sure what he was looking for. He'd wander in one direction, then in another, occasionally backtracking a few paces to sniff at the tracks in the lane or at something Kari couldn't distinguish from the debris left from previous hikers. At some point they veered off the path and onto what might have been a deer track, or simply an accidental opening through the trees.

Once she started to question Georgia, but the woman just shook her head and insisted the dog knew what he was doing. So Kari followed along silently, trying to ignore the blister starting to form on the heel of one foot. This was more of a workout than her hiking boots usually got in a year.

Just as she was about to suggest they give up and come back another day, Pepper's head went up and his whole body seemed to stiffen, like an arrow pointed at a target. Georgia straightened, holding her finger to her lips, and gestured for Kari to walk behind her as she parted some bushes to reveal a small, ancient-looking ramshackle hut.

The building was tiny. Probably no more than one room, with a sagging metal roof and a crooked chimney pipe sticking out of the top like a flag of surrender. There was a window on the side facing them with two cracked panes, but it was so covered with dirt and cobwebs, it looked as though it would be impossible to see through even if you were closer than they were.

The entire structure was so overgrown with vines and weeds to the point where it was barely possible to discern it from its surroundings. Kari wondered if this was accidental or on purpose.

The place looked completely deserted. There was no smoke coming from the chimney, although at this time of year, it wasn't likely that anyone inside would need additional heat. In fact, the small wooden hut was probably stiflingly hot, even up here in the cooler forested area. She couldn't imagine anyone living there.

"Do you suppose that is the famous still?" she asked Georgia. That would explain what it was doing out here in the middle of nowhere.

"Oh, I'd say almost certainly so," Georgia said, her eyes gleaming. "That chimney is a dead giveaway. They used to boil the spirits and had to have a way to heat the still. There's probably a fireplace or something." She cocked her head to the side, looking puzzled. "But I don't understand why Pepper led us here."

"What do you mean?" Kari asked.

Georgia bit her lip, glancing from the dog to the cabin and back again. "Pepper is a drug dog. He wasn't trained to sniff out booze, even the illegal kind. And I doubt anyone has made moonshine here in decades. No matter what the rumors say, Curtis Fry's liquor is just cheap, not homemade. There's no profit in it anymore."

Kari glanced around. "Well, I am not an expert, but I sure as heck don't see anything that looks like a field full of marijuana, do you?"

"I do not," Georgia said. "All I see are weeds, trees, a really cute chipmunk, and a nasty-looking run-down hut." She narrowed her eyes. "But I have never known Pepper to be wrong. I say we should take a closer look."

"At the chipmunk?" Kari said hopefully. The rickety little cabin kind of gave her the creeps. It reminded her of something you might see in a horror movie. The kind of horror movie in which two innocent women and their heroic dog came to a horrible end.

"Very funny," Georgia said, snapping her fingers at Pepper and starting to move forward cautiously. "You can stay here and wait for us if you want."

No way. The person who stayed behind in the movies always got killed first. "I'll stick with you and Pepper," Kari said. "If it's all the same to you."

Georgia gave her a sympathetic grin, as if she had been reading Kari's mind. "No problem," she said. "But I don't want to hear any of that girly screaming."

"Not unless there is a guy in a hockey mask," Kari promised. "Or a snake. If there's a snake, all bets are off."

"I'm not worried about snakes," Georgia said in a grim tone. "Except the kind with two legs who are up to something sneaky in deserted huts in the middle of the woods."

Twenty-One

Kari expected the door to creak loudly when they pushed it open, but instead, it was surprisingly quiet.

"Oiled," Georgia said in a thoughtful tone, reaching out one finger to touch a hinge, and then rubbing her finger on her pants. "And relatively recently, by my guess. Someone is still using this place."

"But for what?" Kari asked.

"Only one way to find out," Georgia said, and walked inside. Pepper gave one sharp bark and sat down right inside the front door, as if to say, *Well, I did my part of the job. The rest is up to you.*

"Do you smell ammonia?" Kari said. The entire inside of the small building stank, despite the fact that the two windows they hadn't been able to see from the other side were propped open with sticks and shielded only by ratty-looking screens.

Georgia looked around and whistled. "Holy crap. It's a meth lab."

"What?" Kari took an involuntary step back. "Don't they explode?"

"They can," Georgia said in a grim tone. "Although not on their own. As long as it isn't in active use right this minute, we ought to be fine. But don't touch anything. There can be toxic residue on everything in here. Not to mention that it is a crime scene. We need to get back down the hill and call the sheriff."

"I don't think so," said a gruff voice behind them. The two women swung around to face the door and Pepper growled low in his throat. But he didn't move from Georgia's side. Kari guessed that the smell from the meth lab was so strong, he hadn't been able to scent the approach of their visitor. And none of them had heard a thing.

"Come on out of there," Curtis Fry said. He looked even more disreputable than ever. His bald head was covered by a battered baseball cap advertising a type of beer that hadn't been produced in ten years, and at least three days' worth of stubble crept over his chin and cheeks. Only the scowl was the same as usual.

"You just couldn't keep your nose out of my business, could you?" he said to Kari, waving a shotgun in their general direction. "Come out, I say. I don't want to accidentally blow up my cabin when I shoot the two of you."

Georgia's hand twitched in the direction of her jacket again, but she didn't do anything but give Kari a meaningful glance. "Heel," she said to Pepper, and the three of them walked out to stand in the open space in front of the hut. "Now what?" she asked Fry. "Are you really going to shoot us? Because I'm pretty sure that if we both disappear at the same time, people are going to come looking for us."

"We told our friends we were coming up here," Kari added. "So the cops will know where to look."

"Not without that dog, they won't," Fry said, gesturing at Pepper with the end of the shotgun. "He's the reason that dratted Bill Myers found this place too." He snarled at the German shepherd, who snarled back, silently lifting the edge of one lip. "I thought Myers got rid of him after that, or I would have done it myself."

Now Kari wanted to snarl. Or bite the man, although she expected he would taste pretty bad. "You killed Myers," she said. "Not Marge Farrow. It was you."

Fry narrowed his eyes at them, then shrugged. "No point in denying it, since now I'm going to have to kill you too. That idiot showed up at my bar one night, and told me he'd been trying to find some imaginary pot field up here and discovered my little factory instead. He thought he was so clever. Told me he'd be happy to keep his mouth shut for twenty percent of the profits. Like I was going to do all the hard work, risk blowing myself up, and just hand him over a wad of money for doin' nothing."

"You couldn't afford to have him blackmailing you," Georgia said. "Eventually he would have gotten even greedier, and asked for more."

"Exactly," Fry agreed, reaching one hand up to adjust his cap without ever moving the shotgun off them. "There was no way I could let him walk around, knowing what he knew. Do you have any idea what an operation like this is worth? I can make more money here in one week than I can take in at the bar in a month."

"So you followed him to the shelter?" Kari said. She hoped Georgia had a plan, because the other woman was remarkably calm. Kari just figured that the longer they kept him talking, the better chance they had of getting out of this, although she had no idea how they were going to do it.

"Stupid man never even heard me sneak up behind him," Fry said. He gestured down at his feet, where he wore sneakers instead of hiking boots like the ones they wore. He gave a low laugh. "I can be pretty quiet when I want to be. My father taught me, like his father taught him. You didn't hear me either, did ya? Not even that dog of yours."

He went on. "Myers was so focused on digging under that fence, he didn't know I was there until the noose was over his head. And then it was too late." He flexed one biceps. "I'm pretty strong after all those years of lifting kegs."

As he was showing off, Georgia gave Kari a quick nod, a tiny twitch in the direction of the ground by Fry's feet.

Kari shrieked and pointed. "Eek! Is that a snake?"

Fry looked down and jumped back at the sight of the stick Kari was pointing to. And while his attention was distracted, Georgia pulled her service revolver out of the holster under her jacket, aimed it with both hands, and calmly shot Fry in the leg.

"Ayyyyyy!" he said, screaming a lot louder than Kari had done a second before, and fell to the dirt, the shotgun flying out of his hands to land a foot away.

"Hold," Georgia said to Pepper, who promptly went over and sat on the downed bar owner's chest, sharp canine teeth only a few inches from the man's throat. "Good boy."

"Nice job," she said to Kari. "I was afraid you wouldn't figure out what I was trying to tell you."

Kari gave a shaky laugh. "Thanks," she said. "I was hoping I was right when I thought you were hinting that I should pretend there was a snake."

Fry groaned loudly, whether because of the bullet

wound, the dog on his chest, or the mention of a snake, Kari couldn't tell. To be honest, she found it difficult to work up much sympathy either way.

"I guess we should call for the cops," she said. But, of course, when she pulled out her phone, there was no signal. "Oh. Drat. We're out of service, of course. Now what?"

Georgia walked over to Fry and peered at his leg. "Nice to see I haven't lost my touch," she said. "He's probably not going to bleed to death, but we should get him down off this mountain anyway." She crouched down. "How did you get up here, Fry? Did you drive?"

"Four-wheeler," he grunted between clenched teeth. "It's hidden behind those three tall pines over there."

"Well, this should be interesting," Georgia said. She looked up at Kari. "Can you go fetch that while I bandage up his leg?" She held one hand out for the backpack Kari still wore and pulled the first-aid kit out of it.

"What about the snake?" Fry asked, twisting his head from side to side as if looking for the one Kari had pointed at.

"What, you mean this?" Kari asked, picking up the stick and waving it in the air by his nose. She smiled. "I can't believe you've lived here all this time and you don't know that there are no venomous snakes in this area. Just harmless garter snakes. I joke about them a lot, but they're actually quite useful, eating small rodents and such." She looked down at him. "Never as useful as they were today, though."

Curtis Fry groaned and thumped his head on the ground a couple of times. "I don't believe it."

Kari and Georgia just looked at each other and burst into gales of semihysterical laughter.

* * *

Getting Fry down the hill was tricky and took a lot longer than either Georgia or Kari would have liked. They didn't ask Curtis for his opinion, but from his groaning and complaining it was clear he agreed. After much discussion, Georgia decided that the best approach was to tie Fry's hands in front of him and perch him on the seat of the four-wheeler with each of the women walking along on either side. Kari held the man steady while Georgia gripped the throttle just tightly enough for the machine to move forward at a steady pace.

It was awkward and uncomfortable, and periodically they'd have to stop to rest, or because Georgia's hand slipped. Pepper trotted alongside without hesitation. The trail the bar owner had taken up to the hut was more direct than the meandering path Georgia and Kari had used, but it was still over a half an hour before they came out below the tree line far enough to get a cell signal.

Georgia promptly called the sheriff's department, who promised to send out a car and an ambulance, which showed up in way less time than it had taken them to make their part of the journey. Curtis Fry was bundled into the ambulance, accompanied by a burly deputy, and the shotgun was handed over to his partner, who politely but decisively invited the women to accompany him back to the sheriff's department.

There they were allowed to wash up and given some water (Pepper too), after which they were seated in an interview room where they waited some more. Too tired to even chat, Kari put her head down on her folded arms on the table, while Georgia talked to Pepper in a low voice, mostly telling him what a good boy he was.

Eventually, the door opened and the sheriff himself came in, along with a youngish officer with a buzz cut so short you could see the outline of his head and a pristine uniform.

"Ladies." Sheriff Richardson nodded at them. "I'm sorry to have kept you waiting. This is Deputy Smith. He's going to take notes. Before we get started, is there anything you need? Coffee? Water?"

"Are we under arrest?" Kari asked, sitting up straight.

"What? No, of course not," Richardson said. "Did someone tell you that?"

"They didn't tell us anything," Georgia said. "Just confiscated my weapon, gave us a drink, and stuck us in this room."

Richardson glared at the young deputy, who winced. "I'm very sorry," the sheriff said. "I was just clearing up a few things before I came in to get your statements. The waiting room is full of drunken college students from an off-season frat party we broke up out on the lake. Canoeing while drunk, if you can believe it. I don't even have a code for that in my manual." He shook his head. "Sorry again. I just need to get your formal statements about what happened into the record, and then you are free to go."

He nodded at Georgia in what was clearly a gesture of professional respect. "I'm afraid we're going to have to hold on to your revolver for a few days, but you'll get it back eventually. Nice shot, by the way. I spoke to the hospital and it was a clean through and through. Mr. Fry won't suffer any permanent damage to the leg, and he will be turned over to our custody as soon as the doctors have finished treating him."

He turned to Kari. "You might be interested to know, Ms. Stuart, that Mr. Fry blames you personally for his downfall. I believe he called you a 'meddling busybody pest of a female.'"

"Should I write that down?" Smith asked, pen poised over his pad.

Richardson rolled his eyes. "I have *got* to get recording devices installed in these rooms," he muttered. "County budget or no county budget.

"No, Smith, that won't be necessary," he said in a louder voice. "Why don't we just get the official statement now. Ms. Stuart, if you could start, please. From the beginning."

"The beginning?" Kari said. "If you say so. I guess it all started when I found Bill Myers's body next to our fence."

Georgia snickered, and Kari glanced over at her, remembering the other woman's years of professional experience. "Not that beginning?" she asked.

Georgia shook her head. "Maybe start with why we were up in the woods in the first place?" she suggested.

So Kari told the story of how Deputy Carter had given them the information about Myers looking for marijuana up in the hills, and how he had stolen Pepper to help him find it. Then she continued with the rest of the events of the day, right up though the point when they had been confronted by Curtis Fry.

"You yelled *snake*?" Richardson said. "I probably would have jumped too. And I know there are no venomous snakes in those woods. Good thinking." He tilted his head to the side as he looked from her to Georgia.

"So had Ms. Travis informed you that she was carrying a weapon?" he asked.

"Not at all," Kari answered. "But I'd seen her hand straying toward her back a few times, and it was way too warm for a jacket unless you were wearing it to cover something up that you didn't want seen. If it wasn't a really ugly tattoo, I figured it was probably a gun. But I didn't know for sure until she pulled it out and shot Curtis in the leg with it." She and Georgia high-fived, grinning at each other.

"I see," Richardson said, fighting back a smile of his own. "Now, Ms. Travis, if you could go back to the point where you contacted Ms. Stuart about your dog showing up, we need to get your statement as well."

Georgia gave her rendition of the day, which mostly matched Kari's, and Richardson nodded with satisfaction. "Excellent," he said. "We'll get those typed up, and if you could stop by sometime tomorrow to sign them, that should be all we need from you."

"Won't we have to testify in court or something?" Kari asked. She had kind of been looking forward to standing up in front of a jury and going through the entire thing again. It was an interesting adventure . . . now that it was over, and they were all safe.

Richardson gave a short bark of a laugh that had Pepper lifting his head to see what was up. "You watch too much television, Ms. Stuart. Most cases never make it that far, thank goodness. About three out of four plead out. Mr. Fry has already admitted to the murder, as well as to threatening you. His fingerprints are all over that meth lab, so we've got him on the manufacturing of illegal substances, in addition to about a dozen other charges. He's going to be spending the rest of his life as a guest of the State of New York, thanks to you two."

"It was mostly Kari," Georgia said. "I was just along for the ride."

"I am well aware of Ms. Stuart's role in all this," Richardson said, aiming a frown in Kari's direction. "And it is not that I'm not grateful, because I am. But you're lucky you weren't both killed. I certainly hope that you will try to steer clear of sticking your nose into police business from now on."

"I would be blissfully happy never to come across another dead body in my backyard again," Kari said. "All I want to do is get the shelter up and running, and get back to my life."

"I'm glad we're in agreement," the sheriff said. He went to stand up, and gestured for Georgia and Kari to get up too. "By the way, once you do open the shelter again, I might be interested in looking for a dog we could train to work for the department. I know they usually start with puppies, but I was reading an article the other day where a police force out in Montana adopted and trained rescue dogs, and I thought I might look into the possibility."

Kari perked up. "We often get dogs that are only a year or two old. Plenty young enough to train. I'll ask Daisy what breeds she'd recommend." Her heart sank temporarily. "She's moving to her sister's as soon as the issue with Buster is settled."

But then she realized something. "Speaking of which, if we're finished here, would it be possible for me to talk to Marge Farrow? She's still under arrest, right?"

Richardson frowned at her. "She is," he said. "The murder charges against her have been dropped, but she still has to face the embezzlement charges. The judge deemed her a flight risk because we haven't been able to find all of the money she stole, so she's still sitting in a cell out back until her trial comes up. Why do you want to see her? I didn't get the impression your first visit went all that well."

"Hardly," Kari said, making a face. "But she owes me a favor, and I'm about to collect."

🐈 Twenty-Two

Marge walked into the visiting room, sat down in the chair opposite Kari, and folded her hands primly in front of her.

"I don't know why you're here," the former court clerk said, sounding as though she didn't much care either. "I've already told you. I'm not going to reveal where Bill Myers hid that notebook until you find out who actually killed him and get the murder charges against me dropped."

Kari waited a beat and then said, "Curtis Fry."

"I beg your pardon?" Marge said, a baffled expression on her face.

"Curtis Fry killed Bill Myers," Kari said, allowing a small smile to slip out at the sight of Marge's widening eyes. "It turns out that Fry had a meth lab in his grandfather's old hut in the woods. The dog warden found it, using a retired police dog he stole, and made the mistake of trying to blackmail Fry into giving him twenty percent of the profits. So Fry killed him."

Marge raised one neatly plucked eyebrow. "He tried to

blackmail *Curtis Fry*? Goodness. That's even stupider than I would have expected from Bill Myers." She thought about it for a moment. "But just about as greedy."

"Yup," Kari said. "Apparently that was one scam too many."

"And you are quite certain that Fry is guilty of the murder?" Marge asked. "Or rather, I should say, the sheriff is quite certain?"

"Fry confessed," Kari said with a nod. "He's at the hospital under guard right now, getting a bullet wound patched up. Once they're finished, you might well see him in a cell down the row from you."

For once, the older woman actually showed something akin to surprise. "You shot Curtis Fry?"

Kari laughed. "Me? Not hardly. I wouldn't know one end of a gun from another. That was Georgia Travis. She went with me and her dog, Pepper, to try to see if Myers had other dogs stashed in the woods, and we ended up finding the meth lab—and Curtis—instead."

"Ah," Marge said. "Georgia Travis. That makes much more sense." She stared across the table at Kari. "Although, I will admit, you rather amazed me, actually solving this crime. I didn't really expect you to succeed."

Kari laughed. "People are always underestimating the quiet women in the background." She gave Marge a meaningful look. "You should know that better than anyone."

Marge tilted her head. "You do have a point there." She tapped her fingers together thoughtfully. "I suppose you kept your half of the deal, so I might as well keep mine. Bill Myers's notebook is hidden in his house."

"The police didn't find it when they went through the place," Kari said, doubt making her stomach sour. What if there was no notebook after all? Or what if Marge wasn't really going to tell her where to find it? All of this would have been for nothing. Well, not nothing, since a murderer was in jail, but still, not the goal they'd been trying to achieve.

"Of course they didn't," Marge said in an acerbic tone. "You don't think he'd leave it lying right out in plain sight, do you? It's in a special compartment in the bottom of his desk, in the corner of the living room. If you feel around underneath, you'll be able to detect two small depressions in the wood. If you press them at the same time, the compartment will open and the book should be inside."

"Oh, okay," Kari said. She hoped the woman was telling the truth. After all, Kari was responsible for her being behind bars, so there was no reason for Marge to keep her word, other than her own—undoubtedly somewhat twisted—idea of right and wrong.

"It will be there," the woman said, obviously sensing Kari's lack of faith. "I'm not completely without honor. And I am grateful not to have a murder charge hanging over my head." She rose from her chair and headed for the door, where a guard waited to take her back to her cell. Her eyes twinkled. "See you in two to five years. Maybe less, with good behavior. I'll end up in the Bahamas yet." She was still chuckling as she left the room.

"Huh," Kari said. She knocked on the door on her side, and it opened to reveal the sheriff, leaning against the wall across the way.

"Did you get what you came for?" he asked, sounding mildly intrigued.

"I hope so," Kari said. "If you'll allow a deputy to let me into Bill Myers's house, I'll be able to find out."

"I'll take you myself," Richardson said. "This I have to see with my own eyes."

* * *

The sheriff stopped his car in front of a modest two-story house on the outskirts of town, and he and Kari (who had been happy to be seated in the front seat and not in the cage in the back) got out. Kari didn't know what she'd been expecting, exactly—maybe something gloomy and neglected, with spiky plants and a permanent gray cloud overhead.

But Bill Myers's house was painted a sunny yellow, bordered by neatly trimmed evergreen shrubs, with a gravel driveway that led up to a closed freshly painted garage. The front door had aromatic rosemary bushes on either side, and bright red geraniums filled planters in front of the two windows that faced the street.

"You have got to be kidding me," Kari said, looking at the house. "Are those *plastic flamingos* under that tree?"

Richardson gave a barking laugh. "I know. It wasn't what I was expecting either. Either Myers kept the house exactly the way it was when his wife left him five years ago, or he had a serious personality disorder. Don't worry, though. The inside isn't quite this cheerful."

"Thank goodness," Kari muttered. Trying to reconcile this pleasant home with the distinctly unpleasant man she'd met was giving her a headache.

Luckily for her peace of mind, the inside was distinctly gloomy. It was clean enough, and there was nothing obviously negative about it, but it definitely lacked the charm of the outside. The entryway was bare except for a small table with a brass bowl on it, presumably for keys and things, and a plastic mat that held two sets of shoes and a pair of winter boots.

The living room was almost as stark. A gray suede

couch faced a gigantic wall-mounted television, and matching gray curtains hung over the windows, blocking the view of the outside world. It was like being inside a cave. Shelves on the wall held rows of paperback books, mostly old westerns and a few mysteries. There was, in fact, a cactus on one windowsill, and a few rather gloomy seascapes hung on the walls.

If Myers had spent his ill-gotten gains instead of simply squirreling them away until his retirement, it certainly hadn't been on his décor. The house already smelled stale and disused, even after this brief amount of time, although the faint scent of cigar lingered from an ashtray near the couch.

But Kari's eyes were immediately drawn to the antique desk in the corner. It had a standing lamp with a green glass shade next to it, and an uncomfortable-looking wooden chair pulled up in front of it. A number of small cubbyholes on the left were filled with various pieces of paper—probably bills and other such debris from daily life. Some of the cubbies were empty, since the police had taken anything they deemed of interest, and a dust-free spot on the desktop marked where a laptop had once rested.

Sheriff Richardson cast a dubious eye in that general direction. "I don't know, Ms. Stuart. We searched that desk pretty thoroughly for anything that might have a bearing on Myers's murder. There didn't seem to be anything out of the ordinary. And my computer guys said there were no files of any interest on his laptop either. Just normal emails and business records."

"Ah," Kari said, pulling out the chair and dropping to her knees so she could feel around underneath. "But you didn't have Marge Farrow to let you in on the secret." She held her breath, hoping that Marge hadn't just been having one last laugh on the woman who put her in jail.

Her searching fingertips slid over rough wood for a minute before sinking into two slight depressions about twelve inches apart. If she hadn't known to look for them, she might not have even picked up on the difference in textures and depth. But now she mentally crossed her fingers, said a brief prayer, and pressed.

Nothing happened.

So she pressed a little harder, and the ancient mechanism gave a subtle click, followed by the tiniest of creaks as the hidden section fell open. The book inside practically slid into her waiting hands.

Heart beating fast, Kari placed the notebook carefully on the top of the desk. The sheriff came up behind her to peer over her shoulder at it.

"Huh," he said. "Well, I'll be damned."

Kari finally let out her breath. "Yeah, me too."

It didn't look like much. It was an old-fashioned-looking leather-bound book. The black covering had faded a little and was worn around the edges as if it had been handled often. It smelled ever so slightly musty, although that might have been from the compartment where it had been stored rather than the book itself.

"Doesn't look like much," Richardson said. "Hardly worth risking your life for, I'd think."

"That depends on what's inside," Kari said. She opened the notebook slowly to reveal lined pages covered with small blocky handwriting and neat columns of numbers. *Jackpot!*

The page they were looking at had a date at the top from about four months before. Underneath that there were three names, with addresses and phone numbers;

another name, presumably of an animal; and a note for each one. For instance, the first example said:

Bob McCoy, Reinbold Road, "Fang" (terrier-Chihuahua mix, 4 years old), loose dog without license or tags/first offense. $20 fine.

In pencil at the end of the line, the same hand had written, *return in a week for repeat.*

Sure enough, when Kari flipped forward to the page that was dated a week later, the same name and dog appeared, with the notation *loose dog without tags/second offense. $40 fine.*

Richardson shook his head. "I can't believe he wrote all this down. I can't decide if it was arrogance or some sort of obsessive-compulsive behavior."

"Maybe both," Kari said. "Marge told me that he used to take it out and gloat over it. I think he liked the feeling of power even more than he liked the money." She flipped through the book until she got to the date when Steve Clark's dog had been surrendered. "Aha!" she said. "Look." She pointed at a line written in red pen near the bottom of the page.

SOLD: Purebred Irish wolfhound. $2,000. ($20 to Foreman Clive for transport.)

"That's got to be Steve Clark's dog. It's still alive. But there's no record of where it ended up." Her shoulders sagged. She'd really been hoping that they'd be able to return the brokenhearted professor's beloved pet to him.

"Ah, but now I know something *you* don't know," Richardson said with a small smile. "Foreman Clive is a local petty crook. He's been in and out of jail for years, mostly for small stuff. If Myers was using him to take stolen dogs to their new owners, I shouldn't have any trouble getting the information out of him.

"With any luck, we'll be able to find all the dogs Myers stole and get them back to their proper owners. I expect that the folks who paid good money for these pooches aren't going to be too happy about that, but my guess is that most of them knew there was something shady about the transactions in the first place."

"Oh, that's great," Kari said. "I love a happy ending." She bit her lip. "Now I just need one for Buster."

She flipped through the book some more, and it took her a minute to find what she was looking for. But she finally let out a loud whoop and pointed her finger at the page in front of her. Right there in black and white, it said:

Serenity Sanctuary. Goose Hollow Road. "Buster" (pit bull), released from fenced area. Loose dog/third offense. Dangerous dog. Filed report of bite wound. Court date pending. $200 fine. ($25 to Mitch Todd for pictures of bite wounds from own dog last year.)

And next to that, in pencil, *This should make that woman sell!*

Kari wiped away a tear surreptitiously and gave a little sniff. "This should clear Buster completely, shouldn't it?"

"Absolutely," the sheriff said. "In fact, I'm going to hand this entire book over to the judge. I'm guessing she is going to have to review a number of cases and refund a ton of fines. The town isn't going to be too happy about that, but maybe we can find some way to get the money out of Myers's estate, when all is said and done. And any dog owner who has a pending court case will almost certainly have it dismissed."

Kari heaved a sigh of relief, feeling as though a huge weight had been lifted off her shoulders. "You might want to make a copy for the new dog warden too. He seems like a decent guy. I expect he'll want to know which animals are innocent of the charges he has records for."

"Good point," Richardson said. He nodded at Kari. "So I guess you achieved what you set out to do after all. You not only cleared the sanctuary's dog but a bunch of other ones, and hopefully made it possible for us to re-unite some folks with dogs they thought they'd lost for-ever. What are you planning to do for an encore?"

She gave him a big grin. "Open a shelter, of course."

Twenty-Three

The official open house for the sanctuary was a big success. Although they'd actually been open for business for a week, the party was both a celebration of the shelter and a good-bye party for Daisy, who would be leaving for her sister's place the next day. She had formally adopted Buster as soon as his name was cleared, and was planning to take him with her. Kari wasn't sure which one of them was happier. The pit bull currently sat at Daisy's feet, panting happily as he gnawed on a fancy chew toy that was his going-away present from the staff.

"The place looks great," Mickey said. "You've done a great job here, sis." He slung one arm companionably over Kari's shoulder. As usual, Queenie was perched in her spot on the other side, benignly surveying her territory as if the party had been her idea.

"Thanks, Mickey," Kari said, returning the hug. He'd actually been a big help during the last couple of weeks, pitching in to get things done around her house while she'd been working on the shelter. The farmhouse was still a work in progress, but at least the roof no longer leaked and the walls had been repainted. There were even a few new shelves so she could unpack her many boxes of books. She was surprised to discover she was going to miss him when he left. He was quite handy, and very good company most of the time.

"You could stick around, you know," she said. "I'm sure I could find something for you to do." As long as he stayed sober.

Mickey laughed. "That's what I'm afraid of," he said. "Besides, I don't want to wear out my welcome."

Kari followed his gaze across the room to where an unusually cheerful Bryn was chatting with Suz, whose hair was even more lavender than usual, with bright blue tips. "Always leave 'em wanting more," she said diplomatically. The poor guy had finally figured out that Bryn was a lost cause, thank goodness. Kari had been beginning to think she was going to have to whack him across the nose with a rolled-up newspaper until he got the point.

She waved at Suz, who had been coming in once a week to give the sanctuary dogs free haircuts so they would look more appealing to prospective adopters. Suz gave her a thumbs-up and a big grin, then went back to her conversation. The dog groomer had dressed up for the occasion in new jeans and a draped purple top that matched her hair. Funky amethyst earrings set off the ensemble and made Kari feel almost underdressed in her khaki pants, fitted black tee with *Serenity Sanctuary* on it, and simple silver hoops. So at least one thing was the same as usual.

Kari let her eyes take in the entire space, scanning around the room to make sure everything was going smoothly. Everyone there seemed to be having a good time.

Georgia Travis was in one corner with Steve Clark, who had practically been incandescent with joy to be reunited with Ranger. Even the mayor, a short broad woman with a surprising amount of charisma, had come out, given a brief speech, and then stayed to get better acquainted with a pretty calico cat they'd taken in the week before.

A huge cake, donated by the local bakery, took up most of the front desk area, although there was also a sign-up sheet for volunteers and a jar—almost overflowing, Kari was happy to see—for donations. Tripod sat next to the jar, as if surveying his territory and encouraging everyone to contribute. He had a new bed underneath the desk that was reserved just for him, and he was hardly drooling at all, now that they'd had some work done on his few remaining teeth.

Pictures of all the adoptable cats and dogs took up the wall behind one side of the desk, with brief descriptions of their age, breed, and personality. A few red stickers indicated pending adoptions, and as she watched, Sara added another one to the picture of Sacha, a five-year-old Schnauzer mix with abundant eyebrows and a slight overbite.

Kari gazed with pride at the new cat cages that lined two of the other walls. They'd had to move a couple of the more skittish cats into the isolation section of the large feline room for the duration of the party, but the rest of the animals seemed to be doing fine with all the extra attention. All the cages had a raised sleeping area with a cozy bed or blanket on it, as well as a lower section for play, eating, and a litter box.

The two biggest cages on the bottom row each contained a mama cat and a litter of kittens, and Kari was pleased to see that a couple of the kittens already had red adoption pending dots next to their names too, although the new owners would have to wait until the kittens were ten weeks old before they could be taken home.

"I can't get over the change," Daisy said, coming up to stand next to Kari. "It's like a miracle. I keep wanting to pinch myself."

"Watch out for Kari's brother," Sara said with a laugh, joining them. "He'll do it for you." She smiled at Kari. "Daisy's right, though. It really is a miracle."

"A miracle of hard work, good luck, and a lot of great people working together," Kari said. "Are you sure you don't want to stay, Daisy? We'd be happy to have you." Kari still felt a little nervous about being the sole person in charge, although she'd had to call on the former owner less and less over the last two weeks.

"Thanks but no thanks," Daisy said, shaking her head. "It's your turn now. I'm incredibly grateful to be leaving the place in such good hands. Between you, Sara, Bryn, and everyone else, I know the sanctuary is going to be a big success."

"Don't forget about me," Angus McCoy said, strolling over with a glass of wine in his hand and a tiny tiger kitten snuggled in the crook of one arm. "Never underestimate the benefits of an on-call vet." He winked at Kari, who blushed as he walked off to talk to someone who was interested in one of the dogs. Some of the volunteers had been taking turns walking the resident canines in the new fenced area out back, so visitors could see them and say hello.

"What was that all about?" Suz asked, suddenly appearing by Kari's side.

"Nothing," Kari said. "He's just being nice."

"Uh-huh," Suz said knowingly. She grinned at Kari.

"Can you believe all this came about because you bought a lottery ticket on a whim while you were picking up cat litter?"

"I really can't," Kari said, looking around at her new mission and her new friends. Yes, the whole thing came with a lot of responsibility, and a certain amount of stress, but as long as there were no more dead bodies, she thought she could handle it. "So, do you still think I'm crazy for buying this place?"

Suz laughed. "Yes," she said. "But definitely a good kind of crazy. In fact, I'd say, the very best kind."

Queenie started purring loudly, as if she agreed.

Acknowledgments

The only thing tougher than writing your first book is writing your twenty-fifth book and having it be the first book in an entirely new-to-you genre. This book owes its existence to my fabulous agent, Elaine Spencer, who suggested I might have the perfect voice for cozy mysteries, ignored me when I said she was nuts, helped me figure out which kind I should write, and then found the perfect home for the books. Thanks too to Jenn (with two *N*s), my wonderful editor, who fell in love with the animals in this series and helped me to make them shine. Someday we'll find you your own three-legged cat. Everyone at Berkley who worked to make this book even better than I expected, from the cover artist to the copy editor. Massive thanks to author Donna Andrews, who not only writes some of my favorite mysteries, but was kind enough to take the time to give me lots of pointers on how to write one, and then read the early manuscript and gave me some more. All my beta readers helped to make this book better, with special thanks to Karen Buys (we'll make it to Bouchercon yet) and Judy Levine, who both read everything I send their way, and take the time to comment. I only hope that the finished product is worthy of all the efforts of those who contributed to bringing it to fruition. Big love to all my cats, who inspire me to write by insisting on eating every day. And to Magic the cat, gone now, but reincarnated as a little black kitten between these pages. Love you, baby.

Ready to find
your next great read?

Let us help.

Visit prh.com/nextread